BUCK'S

PANTRY

BUCK'S PANTRY

A NOVEL

KHRISTIN WIERMAN

SPARKPRESS

Published by SparkPress, a BookSparks imprint,
A division of SparkPoint Studio, LLC
Phoenix, Arizona, USA, 85007
www.gosparkpress.com

Published 2022
Printed in the United States of America
Print ISBN: 978-1-68463-165-0
E-ISBN: 978-1-68463-166-7
Library of Congress Control Number: 2022903794

Formatting by Katherine Lloyd, The DESK

To Matt and Connor,
who have made my life more amazing
than I could have imagined.

To Robin and Michael because you were there.

RURAL TEXAS, AUGUST 22ND

Lianna's hands gripped the steering wheel at ten and two as she drove five miles under the speed limit down the country highway. Around her, majestic trees opened onto pastures dotted by distant farmhouses—which felt about as alien from Manhattan as if she'd landed on the fucking moon. But there had been an accident on the interstate, and Google insisted this was the fastest route. She had a sneaking suspicion that Google might be toying with her but didn't see another option. It was four thirty p.m., and she needed to find a bathroom. She accelerated but immediately felt as if the rented Altima would slip from the road. Scowling, she slowed back down. She hadn't driven in twenty years.

Clutching the wheel with one hand and unknowingly decelerating another five miles per hour, she stabbed at the little blue arrow on the temperature control button. The digital screen insisted that the temperature of the air blowing from the vents was *Low*.

"Bullshit." The ventilation flaps blew nothing more than dinky wisps of mildly chilled air. She lifted her dark wavy hair away from her neck and wondered why anyone would choose to live in this goddamn inferno.

"Liahhhna, it'll be hot out here," Aimee had said when they talked on Friday, the only trace of her accent, a slight drawing out of the *ah* in Lianna's name. "Texas in August is hot, so you'll want to wear something cool when you get off the plane."

Lianna had laughed.

But when she had stepped through the sliding doors at the Dallas/Fort Worth airport, the wall of heat that slammed into her was like nothing she'd ever experienced. Standing in the blinding sun, she had actually felt her pale skin burning and her lungs trying to adjust to the thick, stifling air. Within seconds, sweat popped from every pore of her body.

"You okay there, missy?" Lianna had blinked at the source of the booming voice, certain the heat was making her hallucinate. She blinked again, but the image remained the same. Along with his jeans and white button-down shirt, the man was still wearing a boat-like cowboy hat, a belt buckle the size of a salad plate, and gleaming cowboy boots. Furtively, her eyes scanned the crowd outside the airport, searching for this Missy person.

The man stepped toward her. "You need some help, hon?"

Lianna felt her back stiffen as she realized he was addressing her. Her face tightened into the *I-will-go-fucking-apeshit-if-you-touch-me* expression that allowed her to roam mostly unbothered in New York. She stepped sideways, searching for the rental car bus sign and preparing to shriek if he came closer.

He took a step back and smiled. "If you're new to Big D and looking for the rental cars, you'll need to take the shuttle from the lower level."

Without intending to, Lianna met his eyes.

"You sure you're okay, hon?" he asked.

She registered the sheer openness of his face, the sincerity and concern in his gaze. "Y-Yes," she managed before wobbling on one impractically high heel and walking toward the escalators.

She shook her head in bafflement at the memory.

Her phone rang.

Keeping her eyes on the road, she pressed the Bluetooth answer button. "This is Lianna."

Benjamin's soft, elegant voice greeted her. "Hello, Lianna. How's Texas?"

"Fucking hell, Benjamin. You've sent me to goddamn fucking hell."

His weary sigh filled the car. "Lianna—"

"I'm speaking literally. It's over a hundred degrees in this place."

"If you want to be taken seriously as a future candidate for CFO, you've got to run an acquisition." Benjamin's voice implied his patience was rapidly diminishing. "It's been nearly two years since we've found a viable prospect, and I have no idea when another will come along. Would you prefer that I hand this over to Robert?"

Lianna had a vision of her tiny junior one-bedroom in Chelsea—basically a loft with a nook for a bed. But still, a loft that she owned. *Sterile* was the word her mother had used the one and only time she'd visited. Sterile and unlived-in because Lianna spent nearly every waking minute in her office. The most serious relationship she'd had in the past three years had been with Netflix.

She blew out a breath. "No, I do not want you to hand this over to Robert."

"I didn't think so. Just remember, diligence is the best time to get a sense of whether there's any talent. Once they know they're losing their jobs, they'll be more difficult to assess."

"We're buying them. How can they not know their jobs are at risk?"

Benjamin sighed again. "Look at where you are."

Lianna glanced left then right. All she could see were flat yellowy-green fields, a smattering of trees, and black cows.

"I think you're wise to go down ahead of the team. Call me tomorrow with your initial impressions." Benjamin's voice had taken on the distracted quality that usually signaled something else had grabbed his attention. The line went dead.

Lianna returned her attention to the road. She screamed as her foot slammed the brakes.

◆ ◆ ◆

"Ashley, honey, can you please water the geraniums and move the sprinklers in the wildflower garden?" Gillian—"*Jill-i-an with a soft J*," she'd gently correct anyone who got it wrong—said to the Bluetooth display on her black Lincoln Navigator. She zoomed around a turn, fifteen miles over the speed limit. "And make sure the little trough we put out for the deer has water. It's been hot as blue blazes this week, and I'm sure it's low." They lived on ten acres, and Gillian loved watching wild deer graze in the backyard.

"What did you do with my leopard-print cold-shoulder top?" was her fifteen-year-old daughter's reply.

Gillian bit her lip. That blouse, which Ashley had brought home from the mall two towns over a few weeks ago, was tacky. And the orangey colors looked terrible on her. Gillian had taken it to Goodwill the next day.

"Sweetheart, I told you that top was in no way appropriate or flattering."

"Mother—"

"And I'm not gonna discuss it again. But I need—"

"This is so unfair!"

Gillian couldn't be sure when her daughter had begun shrieking her displeasure like an angry bobcat, but it was happening all the time now. There was only one way to deal with it. "As God is my witness, Ashley!" she bellowed with all her might. "If you don't water those plants before I get home, you're gonna be eating a peanut butter sandwich for supper instead of that King Ranch Chicken I fixed!"

"But—"

"Don't you 'but' me, young lady. I was up half the night making those awful gluten-free muffins for Bobbie's class. And I had to go to school drop-off twice this morning because Carly forgot her spelling homework even though I specifically asked her if she had it, and she *specifically* said that she did."

"Mother—"

"I had not been home five minutes from my second trip to the school when they called and told me Bobbie threw up. I had the planning meeting for the Cattle Baron's Ball, so I had no choice but to drop him at Mama W's and get a lecture about what I'm letting him eat."

"But, Mother, none of that has anything to do with me!"

"Ashley Lauren Wilkins! I am pulling up at the UPS store as we speak to pick up your new dance shoes because UPS has apparently decided to only make one delivery attempt before they cart packages off to some drop-off location because *apparently* people are willing to pay for shipping even if that means they have to drive somewhere to pick up their stuff." Gillian glared at the wrinkled ticket stuck to her dashboard, which she'd ripped from her front door, wadded up, and thrown into the azalea bed a few hours before. "I rarely ask for your help with the garden, but I've still got to run to Sprouts or we're gonna be out of milk and bacon by the weekend." She could have easily picked these things up when she'd swung by Albertsons—yet another unexpected errand that had been thrust on her. But ever since she'd discovered the ASPCA's Shop With Your Heart website, she tried not to buy any meat or dairy from a farm that didn't have one of the ASPCA's approved humane certifications. She could not fathom the idea of being a vegetarian or, God

Almighty, a vegan. But she could spend her money at farms that were trying to treat their animals well. The Sprouts Farmers Market in the adjacent town was the only place that carried those brands.

"Why can't—"

Gillian's voice dropped lethally. "As God is my witness, Ashley, if I come home to wilted geraniums—"

"Fine." Only her oldest daughter could end a discussion as effectively as Gillian, perfectly matching her mother's crushing tone of finality. "Daddy wants to talk to you."

Gillian rocketed into a parking space and shoved the Lincoln into park. A familiar wave of disbelief and consternation filled her as she considered her daughter's unwillingness to help with even a single household task. She heard Ashley's muffled voice, "I don't know. She's talking about God now."

Gillian narrowed her eyes at Ashley's name, glowing across the dashboard display. Then she heard her husband's muted but unmistakably irritated response, "Aw, hell." She could picture him standing there, his stomach straining against his pastel golf shirt—he didn't even play golf—his tanned legs like tree trunks under a pair of hideously plaid madras shorts.

"Honey?" he asked too brightly. They'd been aggressively polite with each other since the party, two days before.

Gillian made a tight, unhappy smile at the dashboard. "Yes?" She didn't even need to ask why her husband was home at four thirty in the afternoon. He worked at his daddy's bank, so he did pretty much whatever he wanted.

"You home soon?" he asked. "I was gonna go down to the pond and see what I can catch."

"Not until closer to five thirty," she said, trying to keep her voice even. "I've still got a couple of errands to run. Then I've got to pick up Bobbie at your mama's."

"You took him to Mama's?" Trip's voice was hopeful. "Does that mean—"

"It means," Gillian growled through gritted teeth, "that Bobbie got sick, the babysitters were all in school, and I didn't have a choice." She blew out a long yoga breath, knowing she shouldn't be so mad at him.

But she was.

She could hear him walking into another room. He lowered his voice. "So you're still, uh, thinking about—"

The yoga breath evaporated as a volcano erupted in Gillian's chest. "I don't know, Trip! Because I have not had a minute to myself to think in the last forty-eight hours!" She raised her hands and shook her head, her long blonde ponytail quivering. "I thought I was going to be able to go to yoga and think about it this afternoon. But *somebody* ate the last can of Ro-Tel tomatoes!"

Trip coughed but didn't say anything.

"Which I figured out after I'd thawed the chicken and *after* I'd put everything else together. So I had to run to Albertsons because King Ranch doesn't taste right without the Ro-Tel, and—"

"You made the King Ranch?" Trip sounded like a second grader who'd come home and smelled cookies.

Gillian punched the steering wheel. Only her husband could send her world into a tailspin not two days before and still get excited about supper. "Yes. And I didn't finish until it was time to pick up the girls. So to answer your question, no, I have not thought any more about it!"

"Okay, okay." Trip had switched to the voice he used with the kids when they were hysterical toddlers. And he still hadn't apologized for eating the Ro-Tel.

Both of which made Gillian want to plow him down with the Lincoln.

She closed her eyes, hoping her fury would pass. It didn't. She tried another yoga breath. "You know what? I am gonna think about it. Tonight. I'm gonna go to a late yoga class." She snatched her phone and googled the studio, having no idea if late classes even existed. "Then I'm gonna go have a nice dinner. *By myself.* I am taking the night off!"

"You're what?" Trip's voice actually cracked.

"You heard me. Your mama's hosting garden club tomorrow, so Bobbie can't stay over. You need to go get him."

"But Gillian—"

"Y'all will be just fine. The King Ranch is in the icebox. Just uncover it and bake it at 350 for thirty minutes, then let it stand for another ten. And, Trip, don't you dare forget to put potholders under the pan or it'll burn the marble, and—"

"Dadgummit, Gillian! Let me get a pen!"

"Ashley knows what to do. And you tell her that if I don't come home to perky geraniums and a deer trough full of water," Gillian's voice dropped ominously as her finger hovered over the disconnect button, "her phone is mine."

Gillian punched End Call so hard she chipped her rose-petal-pink nail polish.

◆ ◆ ◆

Aimee circled yet another typo on the presentation deck, which she'd spent the last hour correcting. She was thirty years old, but her soft, butter-colored hair and porcelain skin made people think she was younger. She wore a pale-blue sleeveless sheath dress that looked more expensive than it was. A black cashmere cardigan—a present from her mother—was draped over her shoulders because the thermostat at the bank was never higher than sixty-three degrees.

"You about done there, sugar?" Clayton stood, too close, at her shoulder.

Aimee scooted in the opposite direction. "Almost," she said without looking up.

"I was hoping to head out a little early." He stepped around to the other side of her desk so that he faced her.

Aimee met his eyes, understanding exactly what he wanted her to say.

He flashed what she knew to be his idea of a disarming smile.

Not that long ago, she would have volunteered to type the changes for him. She circled a patch of white space where a period should have been and ignored the faint-but-still-present impulse to please—that strange feeling like a tuning fork in her stomach that had plagued her for as long as she could remember. She said nothing.

"I'd sure 'preciate it if you could just go ahead and finish it up."

She flipped another page. "I've still got a lot to do to get the office ready for Lianna. She's coming by when she gets in."

He shrugged. "I'm sure you can get her anything she needs."

"What if Big Floyd calls?" Aimee couldn't help but enjoy the apprehension that shot from Clayton's eyes when she mentioned the bank's largest shareholder and chairman of the board, Floyd Wilkins, who marched through the office on a near daily basis, his gravelly voice hurling commands and rebukes. He was almost eighty years old but looked and moved like he was thirty years younger. There were lots of stories that floated around such a small town about Big Floyd. The one that summed him up best to Aimee was this: Years ago, Big Floyd woke in the night and saw a man's arm snaking through the bedroom window, just above his sleeping wife's head. Big Floyd, who kept a five iron next to his nightstand for exactly such a scenario even though he'd never had a break-in, grabbed the arm and tried to pull the burglar inside.

"Big Floyd's out at the deer lease today." Clayton raised his chin, but fear still laced his voice.

Aimee stared at him. The man she worked for, Jonathan, who also happened to be Big Floyd's nephew and who swore the burglar story was true, had already left to go coach his son's football team. He'd mumbled exactly the same thing as he hurried out the door. She wondered if either of them had any idea what was at stake.

Her cell buzzed. She lifted the phone just enough to see her mother's smiling face.

Aimee set the phone back down.

"I am Jonathan's assistant, not yours, and I am doing this for you as a favor," Aimee said, feeling tension creep into her shoulders. She tried to ignore it, knowing Clayton wasn't the real cause. She'd been edgy all day. August 22nd always did this to her. And selfish person that she was, she hadn't even called Andy.

Clayton gave her the wounded expression that got him free coffee at the lunch place across the street. When she didn't respond, his voice sobered. "You're doing this because you don't want us to look like a bunch of stupid bumpkins."

She turned back to the presentation. *Yep*, she thought but did not say.

"There's no way that Lianna girl's gonna give you a job in New York City, Aimee."

A burst of fear flared in Aimee's stomach. Studying his haughty smirk, she realized that Clayton was simply fishing, trying to get a rise out of her. He had no idea about her secret wish. She forced nonchalance into her voice as she swiped another page, reminding herself that what Clayton thought didn't matter because there were a thousand reasons why her living in New York would never happen. "Me in New York is about the most ridiculous thing I've ever heard." She squinted at a large boxed number. Marking her place, she shuffled back through the pages she'd already read. She circled the number, scrawling a note next to it—*Inconsistent w/ p. 13.*

"Damn straight it is." Clayton laughed unkindly as he picked up her stapler and turned it over in his hands. "Come on now. How about you help me get on outta here?"

Aimee smiled and handed the marked-up deck to him, shocked at how easily the words flowed from her mouth. "Not today, Clayton."

Her phone buzzed.

◆ ◆ ◆

Lianna gasped in short, ragged breaths as she pulled onto the shoulder of the highway and put the Altima into park with a shaky hand. "Are you fucking kidding me?" she yelled into the rearview mirror.

The cow—the cow she had nearly run into, the cow who was still standing in the middle of the road—regarded her a moment, then turned to gaze the other way.

Lianna sucked in a breath and slowly exhaled, promising her bladder she'd find a place to pee. She put her hands back at ten and two, then carefully switched the car into drive. "If you're too dumb to move out of the road, I can't help you," she muttered, searching both directions for oncoming traffic. There was none.

She inched the car forward.

She stomped on the brake. "Goddamn it."

She threw the car into park, clambered out, and marched toward the cow. "Are you fucking crazy? Someone is going to hit you!"

The cow turned her massive head.

Lianna took a step back. The cow was much bigger up close.

Gentle chocolate-colored eyes studied Lianna.

Lianna blew out a rush of air, her voice softening. "Listen, you need to move. It really isn't okay for you to stand here."

The cow blinked.

"Seriously." Lianna pointed toward the field. "You need to go back there or you're going to get hurt."

The cow blinked again.

"Please." Lianna waved her hands toward the grass, swiveling her head to make sure there were no cars coming. She took a hesitant step closer, wondering if cows bit people.

The cow's tail swished from side to side.

"Fucking hell." Lianna took another step. The cow was absolutely huge. "Go!" Lianna began to jump up and down, waving her hands and thrashing her head from side to side. "Get the fuck back into your fucking pasture!"

Slowly, the cow ambled onto the shoulder and into the weedy ditch.

◆ ◆ ◆

Aimee carried the cardboard box into the bank's boardroom, just in time to see Clayton's truck pulling away. Setting the box down on the table, she stared through the window at the near-empty parking lot and wondered if he'd made any of the changes she'd marked on the presentation deck. *Probably not.*

Her phone buzzed.

She peeked at the screen with a sinking stomach. Her mother's twinkly blue eyes and homecoming queen smile greeted her. Aimee stared at the picture until the buzzing stopped, then put the phone down on the conference table.

"What've you got there?" Mr. B stood in the doorway. He'd been cleaning and taking care of maintenance for the bank's executive offices and local branch for as long as anyone could remember. Aimee had no idea how old he was. Based on his stories about being called up in the first draft lottery for the Vietnam War, he had to be over seventy.

Her phoned buzzed again. She lifted it and read the text message.

Mom: Hi honey. I found a beautiful blue blouse
for you and put it in the mail. Call me please.

Aimee set the phone back down on the table and wiped away
the frown she could feel settling onto her forehead. She smiled at
Mr. B. "That," she nodded toward the box, "is a coffee machine
made in this century." She ripped open the flaps and pulled out
the sleek black Keurig.

Mr. B eyed it as if she'd just told him it fell spontaneously
from the sky. He glanced at the mud-colored Mr. Coffee, which
Aimee suspected had been sitting on the side table long before
she was born. "Hmph" was all he said.

"Thanks for making the special trip today, Mr. B. I really
appreciate it."

"Happy to help." He swept away the box and wrappings
before Aimee had even unwound the power cord. "You said it was
important."

Aimee nodded and tried not to let concern swallow her face.
"It is. We need this place to sparkle tomorrow. We've got a big
meeting with a lady from New York."

Mr. B's eyes widened. "You want to check and see that everything looks spic-and-span?"

Aimee shook her head. "You're maybe the only person on this
planet who's as particular about cleaning as I am." She grinned.
"If you're happy with it, I'll be." Her eyes drifted back out the
window. The temporary gardener she'd called in to trim the
azalea bushes and cut the grass—her regular one was too busy
this time of year to fit in a special visit—had not been as finicky.
She'd had to march outside at least three times this morning to
point out things he'd missed.

"Looking good out there," Mr. B said, admiring the lawn. His
eyes narrowed.

She followed his gaze. "What?"

"Nothing." His voice rose in innocence that Aimee didn't believe for a second. He headed toward the door.

She peered through the window again but couldn't see anything amiss. "Wait," she called to his back. "What are you—"

Her phone buzzed.

She stared at the screen, knowing the calls would not stop until she answered.

Closing her eyes, she picked it up. "Hi, Mom."

L ianna's bladder was on fire, and she was in the middle of fucking nowhere. Spying some trees, she wondered if she should just pull over and squat behind one. Her eyes flitted frantically around the car, but there was nothing she could possibly use as toilet paper except the stack of Excel sheets in her backpack or pages from the Altima's manual.

And fuck knew what biting creatures lived in the grass out there.

A memory—vague and hazy—began to shimmer. She felt herself go still as it unfurled in her mind: An endless ride in the back of her dad's Jeep Cherokee through emerald-colored Pennsylvania farmland. She'd felt the same desperation pushing her bladder up into her stomach. Smiling, her father had stopped on the shoulder of the highway, while her mother insisted that Lianna was perfectly capable of waiting until they found a decent bathroom.

Lianna blinked. She couldn't remember who had won the argument, whether she'd been allowed to relieve herself or not.

"Shit," she hissed to the empty car, partially because her lower abdomen was screaming but mostly because her father had been dead since she was six years old, and she didn't like to think about him.

She reached for her phone, where her progress glowed on Google Maps, and used her thumb to peck out *gas*. There was something called Buck's Pantry eleven miles ahead. Surely, even in this godforsaken place, they'd have a bathroom she could use.

She breathed deeply and willed her bladder to expand. She could make it eleven miles.

A billboard came into her vision ahead, and she studied it, desperate for any distraction. Her stomach soured as she took in the headshot of a greasy-looking man with an ugly mustache. His face was transposed over an American flag along with the words: *Dicky Worth for Congress—Making Family Values* Worth *Something Again.*

"You've got to be fucking kidding me," Lianna grumbled to the empty car.

Ten minutes later, she was fuming. Not only had the green pastures on one side of the highway been replaced by decimated tracts of strip-mined land, but she'd passed a different Dicky Worth billboard every other mile.

Dicky Worth for Congress—Making American Jobs Worth *Something Again*

Dicky Worth Knows Jobs *Are More Important Than Trees*

Dicky Worth Supports Responsible Drilling

Her heart ached as her eyes traveled over the scarred gaping earth, and she made a mental note to increase her monthly donations to the Natural Resource Defense Council. Maybe to the Environmental Defense Fund, as well.

When the next billboard loomed, she screamed out loud into the car.

Dicky Worth for Congress—Making the Second Amendment Worth *Something Again*

The only thing that incensed Lianna more than watching nature being pillaged was a fucking gun fanatic. Silently, she vowed to punch Dicky Worth in the face if she ever had the opportunity.

A rotating sign that looked older than she was appeared in the distance. A moment later, she could make out a small gas station and convenience store: Buck's Pantry.

She squealed in relief as she slowed and turned on her blinker.

❖ ❖ ❖

The tires on Gillian's Lincoln screeched as she raced out of the UPS store parking lot, Ashley's dance shoes on the passenger seat beside her. Once again, she tried to make sense of what her husband had told her at the party two days before.

How could he have believed she wouldn't want to know?

Her eye caught the sparkling ten-carat diamond tennis bracelet he'd given her when Ashley was born.

A sick feeling gurgled in her stomach as she wondered if she might have to sell it.

Her phone rang, jostling her out of her thoughts. *Home* appeared on the Bluetooth screen. She smiled, knowing that Carly, her eight-year-old daughter, was the only other person in the house besides her who used the landline.

Gillian answered, picturing Carly's dreamy blue eyes and tiny freckled nose. "Hey, sweetness."

"Mama, Daddy wants to know if he's supposed to use the . . . the . . ." Carly's voice changed to a loud whisper. "Daddy, what's it called?"

Gillian heard Trip's mumbling in the background, followed quickly by the slam of the screen door.

Carly's birdlike voice continued, "Con-vec-ton oven or the other one. Oh, and Daddy said to tell you he's outside."

For the briefest of moments, Gillian considered turning the car around and going home.

She shook her head, determined to follow through with her plan. She was going to yoga. She could shower and change at the club. Then she would go to dinner. And instead of worrying about whether Trip was impatient or there was a babysitter watching the clock, instead of spending half the meal cutting up someone else's food, she was going to relax, she was going to think, and she was going to figure out what to do.

She rolled through a stop sign. "Baby, where's Ashley?"

"She's talking on her—OWWWW, UH!" Again, Carly's voice shifted to a loud whisper. "What? Oh." Her voiced returned to normal. "Mama, she says she's out watering the plants."

Gillian heard the screen door slam again. At least now the geraniums would live another day and the deer would have water. "Carly, baby, tell Daddy it's the regular oven not the convection one, okay? And tell your sister I said to help him."

"Okay, Mama. When're you coming home?"

Gillian sighed. "I'm not gonna be back until after you're in bed, but I'll come in and kiss you good night as soon as I get there."

"You promise?"

"I promise. Now, give Mama some sugar and go tell Daddy it's the regular oven."

The sound of three squelchy smacks—Carly's phone kisses—filled Gillian's ear. "I love you, Mama."

"I love you too, baby. Bye-bye." As Gillian turned the wheel, her stomach gurgled again, and the idea that she was hungry finally dawned on her.

"Shoot," she said to the empty car, realizing she hadn't eaten anything except Bobbie's leftover Rice Krispies at breakfast and would never make it through an hour and a half of yoga.

She glanced at the clock again.

A few minutes later, she wheeled into the parking lot of Buck's.

◆ ◆ ◆

Aimee tried to ignore the thick stabs of tension curling into her shoulders as she leaned against the bank's boardroom table, her phone pressed to her ear.

"Finally!" Her mother spoke to her as if she were seven years old. "I've been calling all afternoon. Did you get my text about the blouse?"

Before Aimee could answer, her mom continued, "You would not believe the day I've had. First thing this morning before I even fixed myself a cup of coffee, the garbageman was banging on my front door . . ."

Aimee sank into a chair, wondering if her mother had really forgotten what today was.

". . . not going to take my recycling anymore because I'm not doing it right and shoved a pamphlet at me with pictures of garbage all over it. Sam always sorted out the recycling and I'm trying, but . . ."

Aimee's gaze drifted to the window as she waited for her mother to take a breath. The tension in her neck crawled deeper.

". . . was not polite and that I am *go-in'* through a divorce, and he said that's too bad, but I don't think he thought that at all and . . ."

Movement caught Aimee's eye. She stood and walked to the window. Mr. B was staring up at the porch light above the side entrance, a grim expression on his face. She watched him stomp back into the building.

". . . threw that piece of paper away as soon as I shut the door, and they can just get over it if they don't like how I recycle, and then you won't believe who bumped into my buggy at Safeway . . ."

Aimee tilted her head as she saw Mr. B return to the side porch, an ancient, metal step ladder in one hand and something small clutched in the other. A light bulb, maybe?

"Aimee!"

Aimee jumped and turned away from the window. The shrill pierce of her mother's voice lingered in her ears, then burrowed deep into her head. "Sorry, Mom," she said automatically. "I'm listening,"

"You are not." Her mother's voice was quiet and disappointed.

"Mom, I told you when we talked last night that I would be very busy today at work. And I'm not even close to finished yet. Could we please—"

"The reason I called is because just as I was coming home from the store, the engine light on my car came on." Her mother said this as if she'd been carjacked and held at gunpoint.

Aimee sighed and leaned back against the window. "Which light?"

"How would I know?"

How can you be fifty-three years old and not know? The thought alone seemed like a betrayal. Aimee forced patience into her voice. "Look in the manual. There should be a list of icons and what each one means."

"I don't know where the manual is."

"Google it."

Her mother made a put-out huffing sound. "Just a minute."

"Mom, I don't have time . . ." Through the phone, Aimee heard what sounded like a door opening then banging shut. She checked the boardroom's wall clock, her mind reeling through her to-do list. "Mom?"

She heard the sound of a car starting.

"Mom? I really can't talk right now. Can we please do this to—"

"Okay," her mother said easily. "I'm looking at it right now. It's a funny little yellow thing, shaped kind of like a genie lamp."

Aimee stared at the ceiling. "That probably means you need to take it to Milton's and get the oil changed. If it's something else, he'll figure it out." She ground her knuckle into her forehead. "Yellow means it's still okay to drive."

There was no response. Only the sound of the car engine.

Aimee's hand dropped, and she straightened. "Mom, the garage door isn't closed, is it? You can't run the car if—" She heard the groan of the automatic garage door lifting.

"It's open now." There was a long sigh. "Sweetie, you know I don't know a thing about cars. And I don't go to Milton's anymore." Her voice turned hard. "I know he still talks to Sam. I need you to drive down and take care of it."

Aimee felt a pang of sadness as she thought of soft-spoken Sam, soon to be her mother's third ex-husband. "Things are really hectic at the bank. Tomorrow is the first day of a bunch of big meetings that are most likely going to determine whether or not I get to keep my job." Her head was throbbing.

"Honey, you're so smart and talented, you'll be fine. But this thing with the car is serious. When you moved away, you promised you'd still help me." She sniffed. "Don't be selfish. I am *go-in'* through a divorce."

Aimee thought of the hundred miles that now lay between her and her mother. When she'd moved a year ago to take the job at the executive offices of the bank, the distance had felt so vast. Suddenly, the pressure in her head and chest felt like it was going to send her into thousands of tiny pieces. Words—unbelievable words—were forming in her head, rising up on her tongue like an army of soldiers preparing for battle. *Mother, if you don't like Milton's, then go to the damn Jiffy Lube. Getting your oil changed is not that hard, and I'm not coming back to do it for you.*

Aimee opened her mouth.

"Aimee, I need you."

A thunderous crash erupted outside the window. Aimee spun around.

The ladder lay overturned and shuddering on the concrete porch. Mr. B was sprinting across the lawn. She planted her free palm on the window and leaned closer. Mr. B gripped a large can in one hand, and a peppery cloud followed close behind him. *Shit,* she thought, *he's gone after the wasps again.*

Aimee's mother sniffed. "Aimee?"

As Aimee ran through the building toward the front door, hoping she could get Mr. B inside ahead of the swarm and sick at what might happen if she didn't, the words her mother expected to hear marched obediently out of her mouth. "Okay, Mom. I can probably drive down on Saturday and take care of it then, but I've really got to go."

L ianna saw the parking space she wanted as she inched through the Buck's Pantry driveway. It was the only one that wasn't next to the pickup truck with monster tires and—her mouth fell open—a rack full of guns hanging across the back window. For a moment, she stared at those guns and forgot where she was, forgot that she needed a bathroom. "Trigger-happy assholes," she muttered, feeling her heart rate rise. *Guns kill. A fucking gun was the reason—*

A piercing ring shattered the thought as the rental car's dashboard lit up with an incoming call.

"Get a grip," Lianna said to herself as she crept toward the space.

Just then an enormous black Suburban-like thing whipped in front of her and hijacked the spot.

Without hesitating, Lianna shoved her palm into the horn.

A petite woman dressed in a pink tank top, pink floral yoga capris, and pink running shoes leapt from the car. Hands planted on her hips and a murderous expression on her face, she glared at Lianna for several seconds before pivoting on one sparkly sneaker and stomping toward the store.

"Fucking Tinker Bell," Lianna spat.

The phone rang again.

Lianna punched the answer button. "This is Lianna."

Meredith's nasally voice filled the car. "Why haven't you called me back? It's nearly six o'clock here!"

Lianna scowled, picturing her assistant's mousy zoomer face puffed up in the pouty expression she wore all the fucking time. Then, she remembered ignoring Meredith's call that had rung just as Lianna approached the rental car counter at the airport. She winced and begged her bladder to be patient for a few minutes longer. "I was in a rush to get on the road, then Benjamin called, and—"

"You didn't sign the contract I left for you. For Benjamin's new chair? Delivery will be delayed if they don't have it tomorrow."

Lianna couldn't be certain, but she could have sworn Meredith was eating something.

"Where should I send it?" Meredith asked.

Lianna ground her teeth. Only something for Benjamin would keep Meredith in the office past five. "Just email it to me."

"They're antique dealers. They FedExed a hard copy."

And you didn't think to ask for an electronic one? Lianna thought but did not say. Meredith was the niece of the bank's general counsel. Agreeing to hire her had been one of the worst decisions of Lianna's career. An edge slipped into her voice. "Where did you leave it?"

Meredith's reply was indignant. "On your desk."

"When?"

"Friday afternoon."

Lianna dug her fingernails into the steering wheel. The pain in her lower abdomen was now just a dull ache, which probably meant she was incubating a fucking bladder infection. "I was on the panel Friday afternoon. I left the office right after lunch."

There was a pause.

Unbelievably, Meredith's tone remained annoyed. "Just tell

me where to FedEx it, and you can scan it and fax it to them from Texas."

Suddenly, a very large man was standing next to the truck and waving. Lianna felt a shot of fear, which quickly turned into embarrassment as she realized she was still in the middle of the parking lot and blocking him in. Her hands flew up. "Fuuuuckkkk."

"What?" Meredith asked, sounding suspicious. Both she and her uncle were wiggy about foul language.

"Nothing." Gripping the wheel, Lianna maneuvered into the space next to the one the man was trying to leave. "Just send it to my hotel."

There was an exasperated sigh. "I need you to tell me where you're staying." Meredith spoke as if she were addressing a confused child.

Lianna closed her eyes and forced herself not to fire Meredith on the spot. "What do you mean you don't know where I'm staying?" Lianna had been so focused on getting to the bank, she hadn't thought to check the travel itinerary Meredith sent for the hotel address. She glowered at Meredith's name on the dashboard display. "Where did you book me?"

Silence.

"Meredith?"

"After Saint Louis, you said you would take care of your own hotels!"

Lianna finished pulling into the space and dropped her head on the steering wheel. Memories of that trip to St. Louis still tormented her—the delayed flight, arriving at the squat hotel in the terrifying neighborhood sometime after midnight, the sticky sheets, and yellowish shower water. She'd slept in her clothes, checked out at six a.m., and begged her way into a room at The Westin. The month before, Benjamin had sent out a memo about controlling costs—*Think of it as your own money!*—and Meredith had embraced the initiative with gusto. "I specifically asked you to make all my travel arrangements for this trip," Lianna said. "We talked about it."

"I just assumed." There was another heavy sigh. "Look, I really need to leave, but if you want me to find a place for you, I will. Where are you again?"

The thought of where Meredith might put her out here in the middle of nowhere was not something to be entertained. "I'll take care of it," Lianna said, "but I need you to scan that contract and email it to me."

"It's twenty pages!"

"Meredith." Lianna's voice was as menacing as she could make it.

Silence.

"Fine." Meredith hung up.

Pleading with her bladder to just give her five more minutes, Lianna called Aimee.

◆ ◆ ◆

Aimee was appalled to find herself standing in the bank's foyer with one hand on her hip and a finger wagging in front of Mr. B's nose, but she kept talking anyway. "And if Big Floyd finds out you went after another wasp nest, he's going to . . . to . . ." She shook her head and dropped her hands. "I don't know what he'll do, but it won't be good." She whipped her finger back up. "Are you sure you didn't get stung?"

Mr. B chuckled. "I'm allergic. If I got stung, I'd be swelled up like an angry bullfrog by now."

"That's exactly why you shouldn't be out chasing wasps." Aimee wanted so badly to examine his neck and hands to see for herself, but she knew Mr. B would rather suffer a thousand stings than have her fussing over him like that.

Her phone buzzed in her pocket. The tension that gripped her stomach melted when she saw the name on the screen. "Hi, Lianna."

"Aimee, hi. Do you have a minute?"

"Of course. Let me just get back to my desk." Aimee glanced at Mr. B and was shocked to see that he'd scuttled halfway to the door without her noticing. She shook her finger at him again. "No more wasps," she hissed.

Mr. B grinned and headed toward the back of the building without giving any sign of agreement.

"What can I do for you?" Aimee said into the phone as she began to walk toward the offices.

"Kill my idiotic assistant."

Aimee felt her heart leap.

Lianna cleared her throat. "Sorry, that wasn't even remotely appropriate."

Aimee shook her head at herself. "How can I help?"

"Meredith didn't get a room for me. Do you have any idea where I can find a place to stay?"

"Won't be a problem. You only have two options, and neither are ever full. The Grand Homestead downtown or the Hampton Inn. There are a bunch of motels off the old highway, but I wouldn't put my worst enemy in one of those places."

"Which is exactly where Meredith would've booked me," Lianna muttered.

"What?"

"Nothing," Lianna said quickly.

"The Grand is considered the nicest," Aimee continued, "but it's old. A girl I used to work with had her wedding there, and that's where the out-of-town guests stayed. The pictures of the reception were beautiful, and she raved about the food. But—"

"But what?"

Aimee paused, wondering if she was wading into territory Lianna would consider unprofessional. "A few people had problems with—"

"What?"

Aimee decided that if the situation were reversed, she'd want to know. "Roaches."

"Ohmigod," Lianna squeaked. "Roaches?"

Aimee felt a whoosh of relief that she'd made the right call. "Yeah. The big ones." Her voice dropped. "The kind that fly."

"They FLY?"

"Yes. Your other choice is the Hampton Inn. I stayed there a year ago when I first moved here. It wasn't luxurious, but it was very clean. The people were sweet, I felt really safe, and—"

"The Hampton. Definitely the Hampton. Can you give me the address so I'm sure I call the right one?"

Aimee laughed. "There's only one. You worry about getting here. I'll call and make the reservation. How far away are you?"

"God you're awesome," Lianna said with conviction that made Aimee's heart leap again. "Google says another hour and a half. I'm in some place called Sweet Leaf."

"I know it well," Aimee said without thinking. She coughed. "You should be here a little before seven, then."

"You don't mind staying late?"

"Not at all." Aimee thought of all the things she still had left to do. "I was going to be here a while anyway. I'll call and sort out your reservation right now."

"You're awesome," Lianna said again.

◆ ◆ ◆

Looking over her shoulder, Gillian glared at the cheap little foreign car one last time. In her mind, a pending crash was the only situation that called for the use of a car horn and *only* if it was really going to make a difference. This person, this Honker, had to be from out of town. Having grown up in Sweet Leaf, Gillian prided herself on knowing just about everybody who lived there. A small voice from somewhere deep inside her—the one that had been chirping at her ever since the party on Saturday—reminded her that she knew everyone who belonged to the country club, had a child in private school with one of her kids, or attended the First Baptist Church.

At that moment, she saw the back of Savannah Perkins's BMW pulling out of Buck's and Savannah's hand waving out the window. Savannah's twins were in Carly's class at St. Joseph's— the only Black children at the school. They'd moved from Philadelphia the year before when Savannah's husband, a surgeon, was hired at the hospital. Gillian waved back politely, if less enthusiastically. She had heard they'd applied for membership at the club but hadn't had success getting sponsored, which was a shame. They seemed like nice people. That just wasn't a situation Gillian could get involved with.

The little voice started to say something else, but she shushed it, shoving her key into the waist pocket of her pink yoga pants. As she strode toward Buck's front door, she realized she'd left her phone in the Lincoln.

"If the Baby Jesus can survive in a manger, they can live without me for ten minutes," she mumbled to herself. Her eye caught a sign in the window—BEST VALUE COFFEE IN TOWN! 16 OZ FOR $.99!!! She tried, unsuccessfully, to think of what she usually paid for a latte at Starbucks and shuddered. *Lord, am I going to have to become a bargain shopper?*

The unnaturally frigid air sent shivers down her bare arms as she stepped inside Buck's and made a beeline for the dairy case along the back wall. "How're ya'll doing?" she asked as she breezed by the young man behind the counter and the older one paying for a pack of Marlboro Reds.

"Ah'ight." The older man gave her a nod.

The young man grinned. "I'm just great, ma'am," he almost shouted.

Gillian paused and managed a startled smile. He'd only worked at Buck's for a few months and usually kept himself fairly well hidden inside a hoodie, no matter how hot it was outside. She'd never heard him speak more than two syllables in all the times she'd darted into the store for gas, cold drinks, or snacks for the kids.

The first time she saw him, she'd squinted at his name tag. "Thanks, Drew," she'd said as she raked her change across the counter. From the depths of the hoodie, his eyes had widened in what seemed to be pure terror. Now she looked at his confident smile and struggled to reconcile the two versions of him. "Well, that's just wonderful, Drew," she said, smiling and continuing through the store.

As she scoured the refrigerated shelves for string cheese, the front door opened with a bang and a tinkle of bells. Gillian's head automatically turned toward the sounds. A woman she'd never seen before marched in and, without so much as a *hello* or *how are you*, demanded to know where the bathroom was. She'd nearly run right into the old man, who was now heading out to his truck.

Drew pointed her toward the flapping door in the far left corner of the store.

Certain this was The Honker she'd just encountered in the parking lot, Gillian studied the woman from behind a row of paper towels. She wore a gray balloon-sleeve blouse that Gillian thought she recognized from Nordstrom Online and dark, pleated trousers. *Lord, she must be melting*, Gillian thought, ducking as The Honker strode by without even thanking Drew. She was pale, thin, and pretty, if a little soggy from the heat. But unbelievably, there wasn't a lick of makeup on her face. Gillian marveled at the strangeness of seeing someone so dressed up without even a smidge of lipstick.

She watched the woman disappear through the dingy white door with the silver square window and felt another wisp of sorrow for her. That bathroom was surely disgusting, and no matter how rude The Honker was, no woman deserved that. Gillian turned her attention back to the dairy case, her stomach rumbling. "Drew, hon, are y'all completely out of cheese? There's not even any of those little Cracker Barrels."

Drew raced around the counter and came to stand beside Gillian, his intensity—and size, he was much bigger than she'd thought—startling her once again. He stared into the refrigerator for what felt like a full minute, spun around, and took off toward the swinging side door The Honker had just passed through. "We may have some in the back," he called over his shoulder.

Gillian stared into the refrigerator, her disappointment growing as her gaze traveled over the packaged bologna, Chicken Dunks Lunchables that even Bobbie wouldn't touch, and pineapple Yoplait.

The side door banged open, just as she reached for a pint of chocolate milk.

Drew rushed toward her, his voice low, his expression concerned. "Mrs. Uh?"

"Wilkins." Gillian automatically reached for his hand.

The second time she'd stopped in Buck's while Drew was on shift, Gillian had tried to find out a little more about him. She didn't consider herself a busybody, but she liked to know something about the people she saw regularly. "Did you grow up here, hon?" she'd asked him as she set down a Gatorade for Carly and a Perrier—Ashley's newest passion—on the counter.

"Yes, ma'am" came the monotone reply from underneath the hoodie.

"Your mama and daddy still here?" she asked, smiling as she swiped a surprisingly unbruised banana for Bobbie.

Before Drew had a chance to answer, Carly had come running into the store, wailing and waving her tiny forearm, which bore a red welting circle the exact size of Bobbie's mouth. "Mama, he bit me!" she shrieked as dime-sized tears rolled down her cheeks.

Gillian had hoped the incident the week before had been a one-time thing. Her eyes drifted to the barely healed mark on her own hand. *Shoot*, she thought with dismay, *my Bobbie's a dadgum biter*.

As she kneeled to examine Carly's arm, Drew was suddenly beside them with a soft, clean cloth full of crushed ice from the Coke machine. His hoodie had slipped down to reveal a closely shaved, pale head and bright, worried eyes. He laid the compress on Carly's arm so gently that she didn't even wince. Silently, he placed her other hand on top to hold it in place. Without a word, he darted back behind the counter.

Now—standing in front of the refrigerators—Gillian reached for his hand, pleased to finally introduce herself.

Drew's fingers locked around hers. "Mrs. Wilkins, it's not safe for you here. I think you'd better go into the back."

Gillian stared at his wide, panicked eyes, and it was as if his fear shot straight through the air and slithered right into her. "Hon, what are you talking about?" She tried to force a laugh, but it came out more like a hiccup.

"A biker gang," he said, his eyes darting toward the door. "There's a whole slew about to pull in. I just saw them through the back window."

Gillian pulled her hand back and raised it to her chest. "A biker gang?" Instantly, her mind filled with images of that show Trip had been obsessed with several years ago, *Sons of Anarchy*.

She'd halfway watched it with him a few times, feeling put out by all the men with their tacky leather vests, tattoos, and shaggy beards. Then, one night, she'd looked up and witnessed the most horrifying gang rape scene, which she was certain would haunt her for the rest of her days on earth. Her head snapped toward the glass-covered front of the store.

She saw nothing.

Her eyebrows were nearly touching as she turned back to Drew, her mouth frozen in a confused oval.

"They're coming." Drew appeared as if he were in physical pain.

Just then, a bone-rattling rumble filled the air. Gillian turned back to the front windows. Her stomach plummeted when she saw a massive man—riding an even more massive motorcycle—pull into the parking lot. He wore a black jacket, and even from this distance, she could see a chain draping from his pockets.

The bike whipped into the space closest to the front door.

In one swift motion, a bulky boot knocked down the kick-stand, and the man's towering frame rose.

The roaring gave way to a terrible silence.

"Please," Drew whispered. "What if something happens and I can't protect you?"

Gillian saw Drew's worried face and imagined this quiet young man trying to fight off a beefy, tattooed gang to defend her.

Feeling slightly dazed, she allowed Drew to push her through the swinging door.

◆ ◆ ◆

Lianna squatted over the toilet in the tiny windowless bathroom, trying not to touch anything. The place was as gross as she'd feared—filthy linoleum floor, every surface cloudy with dust, the whole room reeking of urine and disinfectant. She desperately feared there wouldn't be hand soap. But the relief pouring out of her bladder was exquisite. Maybe she wouldn't get an infection after all.

She was thankful when the filmy soap dispenser deposited a pink glob into her hand. It smelled like cotton candy sprayed with Lysol, but at least it was there. She glanced at herself in the smeared mirror as she washed her hands. Her silk blouse was deflated and damp. She leaned closer, wondering for the thousandth time when the gray smudges under her eyes—the same color as her shirt, she noticed irritably—had become permanent. She was forty-one years old and fairly certain she looked fifty. Without wanting to, she thought of Tinker-Bell-The-Parking-Spot-Thief, who she'd seen lurking behind a shelf and staring at her. The woman appeared to be in her midthirties and was stunningly beautiful. Besides her enviable body, she had the face of a princess in a fairy tale—flawless fair skin and surprised blue eyes framed by bouncy blonde hair. It was just so weird that she was wearing workout clothes, but her hair and makeup looked like she'd just stepped out from one of the Miss America pageants Lianna's mother had insisted they watch together when she was little.

As she turned off the faucet with her elbow, Lianna thought of the guns she'd seen in the truck outside.

Memories of her dad flooded her mind: Sunday afternoons watching the Philadelphia Eagles with him at the Vet; sitting in his lap in front of the TV and cheering when the team was away. After he died, she'd wrapped herself in his old Ron Jaworski jersey on game days until the seams began to pull apart.

"Get a grip," she commanded herself as she pumped the paper towel dispenser with her pinky finger, dismayed when nothing appeared.

It was the fucking driving that was making her crazy, she thought, shaking water from her hands. There was nothing to do except keep the car from crashing and think. When she was working, her mind didn't wander. When she was working, she didn't think about—

The door to the bathroom shuddered and the knob twisted.

Lianna coughed as loudly as she could, hoping this would signal to whomever it was that someone was *in here*. The jiggling stopped. With damp hands, she grabbed her purse from the top of the paper towel holder. Using the tips of two fingers, she twisted the lock, opened the door, and ran right into Tinker Bell. Lianna didn't try to hide her irritation. "What the fuck?"

But Tinker Bell's tiny hand was coming toward Lianna's mouth, and the rest of Tinker Bell's body—which was much stronger than her petite size implied—was shoving Lianna backward.

Too surprised to do anything except get her face away from the woman's fingers, Lianna twisted her head and shuffled back toward the sink. "WHAT THE FU—"

Tinker Bell kept coming, her hand fluttering at Lianna's mouth again. "Shhhh!"

Covering her face with her arms, Lianna stumbled sideways into the wall.

A moment later she watched, in disbelief, as Tinker Bell leapt back toward the door, closed it, and twisted the bolt into place.

◆ ◆ ◆

As Aimee dialed Lianna's number, her eyes landed on the date, August 22nd. Once again, an edginess prickled through her, followed by a sickening shame that she hadn't even picked up the phone to call her cousin, Andy. Because on this day twenty-five years ago, Andy, a smiling infant with cheeks like perfect scoops of vanilla ice cream, had come to live with her and her mother.

"He's gonna need you, Aimee," her mother had said, cradling him between them. "You're gonna save him, just like you saved me." Aimee had been five years old, and she'd liked when her mom said things like that. Because having Aimee had been the reason her mom was able to leave Aimee's grandparents' house. The grandparents Aimee had never been allowed to meet.

Lianna's voice startled her out of the memory. "You've reached Lianna Matthews. Please leave a message."

Aimee leaned back in her desk chair and closed her eyes, enjoying the silence of the bank. As soon as the clock had struck five, the remaining employees had cleared out. "Hi, Lianna, it's Aimee. I've got you booked at the Hampton in a nonsmoking king suite on the top floor, which is 119 a night. Just call me back if you'd rather have two queens or a smoking room. One other thing. The restaurant's only open in the morning, and I'm sure you'll be starving when you get here." She leaned forward, stuck the phone into the crook of her neck, and tapped on her keypad. "So I'm emailing you menus from a couple of places nearby," she sat up abruptly, "which you should not read while you're driving." She resumed typing. "But if you make a pit stop, take a look and call me back. I can either have the food waiting for you at the bank or delivered to your hotel. Or we can order when you get here if that's easier or you'd rather go out. Drive safely. Call if I can do anything else. Bye."

She turned to hang up the phone and stretched her left arm, which was cramping. Her wrist bumped her glass of iced tea and sent it flying.

Aimee felt her insides jump as her mother's voice echoed inside her head—a desperate gasp that stretched and fattened into a mini-shriek and revealed itself anytime food or drink was about to make contact with something it shouldn't.

Aimee exhaled to soothe the flip-flopping in her stomach. "It's just iced tea," she whispered to herself. A memory from her sophomore year in college slipped into her mind.

On scholarship and living off ramen noodles and peanut

butter sandwiches at Rice University, Aimee, an English major, had worked in the Accounting Department to supplement her financial aid.

"You are so good," the department head's assistant said often, when she'd return from lunch and find that Aimee had distributed the mail, typed a new syllabus, and managed to keep the phones answered. Or when Aimee, on her own initiative, had organized the supply closet while the other student employees updated their Facebook pages. Aimee was baffled by the praise. But the professors seemed impressed as well, pulling her aside for special assignments like proofreading their written communications and, once, to proof an entire textbook.

Sitting next to that professor one day and explaining the grammatical edits she'd made to a particular chapter, Aimee had turned too quickly and sent his Diet Pepsi tumbling across his desk.

To Aimee's horror, her mother's gasp-shriek erupted from her own mouth.

She scooped up the can and fled to the break room, returning seconds later with two fistfuls of paper towels—one dry and one damp.

"I'm so sorry," she said breathlessly as she dropped half the dry towels on his desk, creating a dam between the spreading pool of soda and the not-yet-harmed stacks of paper on the opposite end.

The professor—an older man who had always been fairly brusque with her—had looked at her with such compassion in his eyes, sending a wave of despair shooting through her that she didn't really understand. "It's Diet Pepsi, Aimee, not acid," he said softly, picking up his laptop, which was unscathed. "My desk will survive." With his free hand, he'd patted her awkwardly on the shoulder.

Aimee's cell buzzed with an incoming call, jostling her from the memory. Hoping it was Lianna, she sat up straighter at her desk and grabbed the phone.

Mother.

Aimee closed her eyes.

Feeling the familiar tension burrowing into her shoulders, she answered. "Hi, Mom."

"Honey, I meant to ask you earlier. Have you talked to your cousin?"

◆ ◆ ◆

Pressed against the wall of the bathroom, her purse clutched to her chest, Lianna was going to lose it if that woman touched her face again. "What the fuck is wrong with you?"

"Shhhh!" Tinker Bell, whose ear was against the door, held up a finger.

"What the fuck is wrong with you?" Lianna whisper-spat.

Tinker Bell glared over her shoulder.

Lianna glared back.

Tinker Bell sighed and tiptoed over. "I'm sorry," she said quietly. "But there's a biker gang out there, and Drew thought they might give us trouble. I'm Gillian." Somehow, her fingers found one of Lianna's hands, which she squeezed. "It's real nice to meet you."

Lianna gaped at her.

"And you are?"

Lianna snatched her hand back. "What the fuck happened out there?"

Tinker Bell wrinkled her nose. "What's your name, hon?"

Lianna blinked. "Lianna," she said because that seemed like the only way to get any pertinent information.

"It's nice to meet you, Lianna." Tinker Bell smiled as if they were being introduced over cocktails. "Like I said, there's a biker gang out there, and—"

"A biker gang?" Lianna sputtered.

Tinker Bell's finger flew up. "Shhhh!"

"A biker gang?" Lianna hissed.

Tinker Bell nodded. "I think we should call the sheriff," she said softly, "but I left my phone in the Lincoln. Do you have yours?" Lianna's brain was still trying to catch up.

There was a muddled sound on the other side of the door, followed by a kind of low humming noise. Then, silence.

Lianna glanced toward the door. Tinker Bell did the same. Silence.

"Lianna?" Tinker Bell took a step toward her. "Do you have your phone, hon?"

Lianna moved sideways. Calling the police seemed ludicrous. But Tinker Bell—*What had she said her fucking name was? Gillian?*—seemed so determined, who knew what she'd seen out there. A crew of mad bikers wielding guns certainly didn't seem impossible in this place. Deciding she'd provide the phone but refuse to do anything else, Lianna rummaged through her bag. "Shit," she said, her mind's eye picturing her phone perched inside the cupholder of the Altima, the charger plugged into the cigarette lighter. "My phone's in the car."

Gillian let out a sigh that sounded exasperated. "Why'd you leave it there?"

"I was following Google Maps. Whyyyy'd you leave yours?" Lianna stretched and elongated the vowel in an unkind mimic of Gillian's accent.

"Shhh!" Gillian's face darkened. "There is no need to be ugly," she whispered.

Lianna paced to the other side of the tiny bathroom and took a deep breath. "You saw this biker gang?" she asked, keeping her voice low.

Gillian nodded. "I know it sounds crazy, but I saw them." She hesitated then raised her chin. "Well, I saw one. But Drew said there's a whole bunch."

"Who the fuck is Drew?"

Gillian's eyes flared. "He works here. At the cash register."

"You know him."

"I come in here just about every day, so I took the trouble to learn his name." Gillian thrust a hand on her hip. "I don't know him well, but he's a good boy." She took a few steps toward Lianna.

Lianna moved in the opposite direction. "He's not exactly a boy."

Gillian folded her arms across her chest.

"Okay, so you saw one man." Lianna held up a finger.

Gillian nodded.

"And?"

"And what?"

"What did he do?"

Gillian stood up a little straighter. "Drew got me out of there before the biker saw me."

Lianna's head twitched, her voice rising. "You saw one man on a motorcycle, who did nothing to you. And that made you decide to barricade yourself in here with me?"

Gillian nodded as if this were an entirely rational response.

"You are nuts, lady," Lianna practically bellowed, slinging her purse over her shoulder. "And I am fucking leaving." She pushed past Gillian, twisted the lock, and opened the door.

At least she tried to. But the door barely moved. She leaned her body against it and pushed.

Gillian, her eyes widening, hurried over and added her own weight. She scooted Lianna aside and tried again.

Lianna watched the knob twist freely and heard the click of the latch release. But the door moved only a fraction.

Gillian's voice sounded hoarse when she spoke. "Something's blocking us in."

Aimee threw her purse—a stunning Kate Spade Bundle she'd bought 75 percent off at Nordstrom Rack in Dallas—onto the passenger seat and slid into her Mustang, which was now fourteen years old. The car had been a gift from her mother's second husband, Raymond, when Aimee turned sixteen. Raymond, with his booming voice, off-color jokes, and easy laugh. Always shoving a twenty-dollar bill into Aimee's hand before she even asked. Raymond, who had been gone by the time Aimee had graduated from high school. She ran her hands over the worn leather of the steering wheel, missing Ray just a little bit as she did.

She checked the clock. It was nearly five fifteen. In the back of her mind, an almost worry prickled as she wondered why Lianna hadn't called back. But she had no business thinking she knew Lianna that well. Turning on the ignition and scrolling through iTunes, she found Fontaines D.C.'s latest album and pressed play. The music, coming through the small speakers of her phone, had a tinny quality. But the car wasn't wired for Sirius or Bluetooth, and she just couldn't handle the local radio.

The edgy punk rhythms—coupled with melodic Irish voices—matched her mood enough to settle her down. But seconds after her shoulders had finally loosened, barbs of guilt began to poke at her. She'd hurt her mother's feelings, that was for sure.

And her mom was going through a divorce. Entirely of her own making and her third one, but still. Aimee liked Sam. A successful accountant, he had taken care of her mother for the last five years. The barbs turned to something else as Aimee considered what would happen after he was gone.

Without wanting to, she thought of her junior year in high school.

"You call him, Aimee."

Aimee, just home from class, stared at her mother, who was still in her nightgown and laid out across her mint green comforter. Used tissues were scattered about the bed, like petals from a wilting flower.

"I don't want to." Aimee had hurried home to drop off her cousin, Andy, grab a snack, and change before heading to her shift at Taco Bell. "I need you to sign my report card." She reached into her backpack and pulled out the slip of paper—as usual, all As and several A+s. Her AP English teacher had written another glowing note about her performance. She hoped her mother might read this one.

"I need a pen," her mother said, struggling to sit up.

Aimee took a pen from the nightstand and handed it to her.

Her mother signed the paper without looking at it. "He'll listen to you," she said as she passed both the paper and pen back to Aimee.

"Isn't this what the lawyers are for?" Aimee's voice came out harsher than she'd expected. She had only vague ideas about what divorce attorneys actually did. But calling her soon-to-be ex-stepdad to ask for cash seemed like something that should fall on their list, not hers.

Her mother flinched as if Aimee had slapped her.

"I'm sorry," Aimee said as she laid the pen on the nightstand and tucked the paper back into her bag.

"They say there's nothing they can do," her mother said, waving her hand, revealing the tiny scars on the inside of her forearm that always made Aimee's stomach queasy. Her mother's voice turned brittle. "They're all conspiring against me. Raymond's paying them off, I'm sure of it."

Aimee glanced at her watch. She doubted this was true. But she'd be late if she let this conversation get started again.

"Okay, Mom, but I've got to get to work now. I'll call him tonight."

Aimee was just buttoning the scratchy, chemical-smelling polyester top—*how she HATED her work uniform!*—when there was a faint knock at her bedroom door. Before she could respond, the door opened. Her mother walked in and leaned against the wall.

Aimee turned to face the other direction, fumbling with the buttons on her shirt and trying to pull up her jeans at the same time.

"Honey, I really think it'd be better if you call him now." Her mother's voice was soft. "The bills are piling up."

Aimee, who had never been introduced to the task of paying bills, had recently begun to peek into the small envelopes. The amounts glaring from the tiny boxes in the past-due columns filled her with worry. She turned around to face her mom. "I know. Which is why I shouldn't be late for work. We need the money."

Something dark passed over her mother's face. "We don't need the money. Raymond has plenty."

"Mom—"

"He cheated on me!" her mother screeched, thrusting the cordless phone at Aimee. "He is living with that woman! I was a good wife to him for ten years. I took care of him. Just like I took care of your daddy, who left me with a screaming toddler, whose mission in life was to keep me from sleeping!"

Aimee winced. She was well aware that she'd been an awful baby.

"Just like I took in Andy, which God knows—"

"Mom!" Her mom wasn't as nice to Andy as she used to be. And he was probably listening through the wall.

"Just like I take care of everybody! You kids have no idea—"

"I know." Aimee spread her hands in the air, her voice as soothing as she could make it. "I know, Mom." It was risky to interrupt, but she couldn't let the conversation swing toward her mother's parents.

"And now I am destitute!"

Aimee watched her mother—standing there in a full-length Christian Dior silk nightgown that was practically see-through, her blonde hair matted in wonky curls against her head—and struggled, for the thousandth time, to reconcile her with the mother she knew. The mother she knew never left the house without her hair in flowing waves and her makeup just right, her luminous aquamarine eyes and infectious laugh turning the heads of men young and old. *Eat beans and rice if you have to,* her mom used to say, *but save up enough to get a* good *lipstick and your hair done at a* real *salon.* The mother she knew loved movies and always wanted to stop for ice cream. The mother she knew had rushed to the hospital five minutes after receiving the news of her sister's death and returned cuddling her orphaned baby nephew, a stack of adoption forms poking from her purse. Hell would freeze, she'd told Aimee, her eyes like flint, before she let her parents—the grandparents Aimee never knew—get ahold of him.

Aimee took a step back.

Her mother took two steps forward. "I need you, Aimee."

Something sour assaulted Aimee's nose. Struggling not to make a face—obviously her mom hadn't brushed her teeth today—Aimee took the phone. She waited for her mother to leave, hoping for some privacy.

Her mother turned and settled herself on Aimee's bed. "You can be such a selfish child," she muttered, hugging a custom-made pillow covered in Laura Ashley fabric to her chest. Aimee still remembered how much fun she'd had with her mom when they'd decorated her bedroom.

Aimee dialed Raymond. There was no answer. "Hi, Ray," she said softly. "It's Aimee. When you have a minute, could you call me back?"

Her mother's mouth pinched into an angry line, and her head wiggled back and forth frantically.

Aimee coughed. "Um, it's actually important. If you could call me as soon as you can?" She looked at her mother, who nodded. "Okay. Thanks. Bye." She placed the phone on the edge of the bed and glanced again at her watch.

"Try from your cell."

Aimee turned, ready to argue. But her mother's stony expression told her it would be futile. She picked up her phone from her dresser and dialed, resigned that she was not going to have time to eat anything before work.

Ray's voice was cautious when he answered, and Aimee felt a stab of guilt. She had been six years old when Ray married her mother. They must have dated for a while, but to Aimee, it simply seemed that one day she was being introduced to him at the Baskin-Robbins—this tall and jolly man who her mother somehow knew and who just happened to be getting a cone of Jamoca Almond Fudge at the exact moment she and her mom and Andy stopped in for sundaes—and shortly after that, he was moving them into a new and much bigger house.

Aimee glanced at her mother and, for the first time, noticed the red rings around her eyes and how much weight she had lost, seemingly overnight. Her mother rubbed her nose and looked at Aimee pitifully, once again revealing the cigarette butt–shaped scars on the underside of her forearm—punishment from a grandfather who Aimee had been kept safely away from.

Aimee pressed the phone to her ear and forced herself to push away all the happy memories Ray's rich voice summoned— of the way Ray would spend a half hour gently untangling the hair ties embedded in her pigtails after a day spent swimming at the lake; the way he was the only one who could remove a splinter from her finger without making it sting; the afternoons spent patiently teaching Aimee how to drive when all her mother could do was scream from the passenger seat that Aimee would surely kill them all.

"Hi," she said, trying and failing to make her voice cold.

Ray's voice relaxed. "How're you doing there, kiddo? You okay?"

In that moment, Aimee just wanted to crawl into his lap and put her head on his shoulder.

Movement caught her eye, and she noticed her mother motioning to move the conversation along.

"Do you think you could put some more money in Mom's account? She's, um, not sure how she's going to pay for everything this month."

"Aimee, honey." Ray sounded very tired. "I told you the last time that that had to be the last time. My business is not doing well. I've got Sh—" He coughed. "I've got other commitments, and I've done all for your mama that I can. The divorce is over. She got the house, her car, and your car, but this's Texas and I don't owe her anything more. And, honey, the fact is there's not much more left. Now it's high time she got a job and started acting like an adult."

Shelly, Aimee thought as her mind filled with a picture of Ray's no-longer-secret girlfriend. *You've got to take care of Shelly.*

Aimee knew Ray's infidelity should make her mad, but somehow she only felt empty. She looked at her mother uncertainly.

Her mom began to cry, which made Aimee's heart feel like it was splitting open.

"Well, you cheated," Aimee said, shocked as the words surged from her mouth. "The least you could do is help her out until she gets on her feet."

Aimee watched her mom—wiping away the tears and giving Aimee a small, appreciative smile—as a terrifying silence stretched through the phone.

When Ray spoke again, his voice was strange and high-pitched. "I did the best I could with your mama, Aimee. Believe me. I really tried to make her happy. But what I've learned—that you have not—is that there will never be enough for that woman. Not enough love, not enough money, not enough attention. Now you want to go get lunch sometime? Get some ice cream and talk about something besides her? I'd be happy to do that. I'd *love* that. I care about you, kiddo, and this doesn't have to be the end of you and me. And the same goes for Andy. You make sure he knows that. But don't call here again asking for money or trying to talk to me about your mama. I've given her all I can."

Aimee blinked, finding herself in front of the florist, her heart pounding, and a freezing pool of something awful filling her stomach—exactly the way she'd felt that day on the phone. She shook her head, trying not to think about the fact that she had no recollection of driving for the past ten minutes.

She grabbed her purse and got out of the car, wondering how things might have been different if she'd ever taken Ray up on that offer for lunch or ice cream. The one time she'd casually mentioned wanting to see him, her mother had flown into a fury that wouldn't be quieted until she watched Aimee delete his number from her phone. Andy—twelve years old, his eyes wide and brimming—had witnessed that scene, then run to his room. Aimee knew Ray's number by heart. But it wasn't in her to go behind her mom's back.

In the months afterward, Aimee had been amazed that she could live in such a small town without running into a particular person. But she didn't see Ray once.

Within the year, she heard that he and his new wife had moved away.

◆ ◆ ◆

"What do you mean, something's blocking us in?" Lianna shoved Gillian aside and, once again, spun the doorknob and pushed.

The door barely moved.

She flung both hands back, managed to bang one fist against the cheap wood, and let out half a word, "HEL—" before Gillian was on top of her, crawling up her back like a spider monkey and pulling her backward. Gillian's tiny viselike hand covered Lianna's mouth. "Shhhh!"

Lianna frantically wiggled away. "What the fuck is wrong with you?" she whisper-barked as she hurled herself toward the far wall.

"Can you please stop saying that word?"

Lianna closed her eyes and made herself count to three before she opened them.

"I'm not sure we want to call attention to ourselves," Gillian said quietly. "Maybe," she bit her lower lip, "Drew slid something in front of the door to hide it. So they wouldn't know there was a door there." She raised her eyebrows dramatically. "So they wouldn't know about us."

"So who wouldn't know?" Lianna wiped the back of her hand across her mouth, watching Gillian carefully in case she pounced again.

Gillian's eyes flickered to the ceiling and back. "The bikers."

Lianna pressed fingers to her temples, wondering how she had landed in this wretched bathroom with Psycho-Barbie. "You mean the one biker." She held up a finger and walked toward the sink. "Who"—she glared at Gillian through the mirror—"because he rides a motorcycle and has tattoos, you are certain wants to rape and kill us."

Gillian grimaced, turned, and marched to the far wall. She folded her arms across her chest.

Lianna yanked her purse from her shoulder and glanced first at the sink—grimy and wet—then down at the floor, streaked with brown and gray. "Gross," she hissed before pulling out her wallet and sticking it under her arm.

Gillian sighed, walked back to the sink, and—to Lianna's surprise—held out her hand.

Lianna didn't really want help. But after another glance at the disgusting floor and sink, she handed over her wallet. "I've got over an hour and a half left to drive and a shitload of work to do before tomorrow morning," Lianna muttered, pulling things from her purse, her heart beginning to race at how long it would be before she could accomplish anything. She removed a ring of keys, a work badge, and a phone charger and shoved them all at Gillian. "I don't have fucking time to be stuck in here"—she chunked over some Burt's Bees lip balm—"with you."

"This language." Gillian caught the small yellow tube, studied it a moment, then mumbled something about no color at all. She shook her head and added it to the pile cradled in one arm.

Lianna continued to dig through her purse. She scooped up a handful of pens, loose change, and wadded-up Snickers wrappers, then turned the purse upside down and shook it. Her defeated eyes met Gillian's. "My phone's definitely in the car."

Gillian nodded and handed back Lianna's things.

They stared at each other.

"This is crazy." Lianna scanned the windowless walls, the floor, and the water-stained ceiling. There was no way out except an air vent that didn't look big enough for a cat to get through. She stormed back toward the door, her fist raised.

"Please, Lianna," Gillian said in a soothing mom voice that actually gave Lianna pause. "Let's just—" Gillian patted the air with her hands. "Let's just wait and think about this for a minute."

Lianna dropped her arm. Quietly, she turned the knob and pushed. When the door didn't budge, she placed her purse back on top of the paper towel dispenser and blew out a long, slow breath. There had to be a solution, she told herself, because there was always a solution. She just needed to break down the problem.

Which suddenly seemed very simple.

She turned to face Gillian. "Either the door is just broken, and we should scream so that what's his fucking name will come let us out."

"His name is Drew, and can you please stop—"

Lianna shot her a venomous look. "Don't. Talk." Tapping her index finger against her lips, Lianna paced toward the opposite wall. "Or I will concede there is a possibility that what you said is true. A group of bikers has come into the store, and," she glanced at Gillian, "*Drew* slid something in front of the door to protect us."

"Hasn't anybody taught you it's rude to interrupt?" Gillian planted both hands on her hips.

Lianna continued as if Gillian hadn't spoken. "Or there are no bikers." Her voice dropped. "And Drew has locked us in here for some other reason." Something cold and dark was beginning to press against the walls of her stomach. "How well do you know him?"

"He's only worked here for a couple of months, but he's always been real sweet. One day my four-year-old bit my eight-year-old, and—" Gillian shook her head. "I still can't believe I've managed to raise a biter."

Lianna gasped. "Fuck, do you have kids in the car?"

Gillian's flustered expression melted. She stared at Lianna for several seconds. "No, my children are not in the car." She appeared shocked, as if Lianna had suggested the kids were tied up on top of it. "Do you think I'd be in here with you if my children were in the car?" Her voice began to rise. "That I'd abandon them to some biker gang while I hid in here with you! And can you please stop saying that word!"

Lianna held up her hand. "Calm down," she said, trying to suppress a hysterical laugh because—despite their mind-bending circumstances—all she could think was that Gillian looked like a possessed doll. *Get a grip*, Lianna silently commanded herself. She blew out a slow breath. "Tell me, again, exactly what happened out there."

S till trying to shake the memories of Ray, Aimee walked into the florist shop and was relieved to see that Bonnie had her order of potted ferns and dieffenbachia waiting. Aimee had not consulted with her manager, Jonathan, and so wasn't comfortable buying too much. But the deep-emerald and mossy greens would inject a bit of life into the bank's boardroom—which always made her feel like she'd stepped through a time tunnel into a long-past decade when everything was decorated in some shade of brown. She ran a finger over a taffeta-like dieffenbachia leaf. "These are so pretty, Bonnie."

"They are, aren't they?" Bonnie was never one for modesty. "I know it looks full, but I've left plenty of room for them to grow." She pressed a thick card into Aimee's hands. "Just follow these instructions and they'll thrive for months. Let me just—"

The door to the florist shop burst open so hard that the bells at the top rattled instead of jingling.

Bonnie and Aimee turned as a small woman marched inside. She wore a straw sun hat, its yellow ribbon tied under her chin in a perfect bow, with massive sunglasses, a starched button-down shirt, and chambray capri pants that were stained at the knees.

She stood in the doorway for a moment, then ripped off her glasses, revealing crinkly blue eyes that were not the least bit friendly. Her gardening clogs made squeaky, thumping noises as she stomped through the store. "Bonnie, I ran out of Miracle Gro, and Troy Aikman ran off with my spade again," she called from the back. "I swear once I find out where he's burying them, I'm gonna shoot that dog."

Aimee swallowed, knowing the woman probably meant what she said. People in town were careful to be respectful of Big Floyd. But they'd cross the street to avoid a run-in with his terrifying wife.

Bonnie sped from behind the counter, a nervous smile on her lips. "Let me help you find those." Before she got to the first aisle, Mama W—that's what everyone called her—appeared with a giant jug of Miracle Gro in one hand and a green-handled spade in the other. "I've been coming here for forty-five years, Bonnie. I know where everything is." She stepped beside Aimee and dropped everything on the counter with a clatter. "Hello, Aimee," she said as she dug in her purse and pulled out a matching wallet. "You look pale."

Bonnie began punching keys on the antiquated cash register.

"Hello," Aimee said as politely as she could, trying not to think of the stories her manager Jonathan had told her about Mama W, his aunt—like when he was little and had accidentally thrown a football into her prize rose bushes, and she'd chased him around the outside of the house trying to clobber him with a giant wooden spoon. Or when, in high school, he'd tracked dirt into her marble entryway, and she'd hit him with the straw end of a broom. Or the time—for reasons no one knew or dared ask about—Mama W had wheeled her barge-like Cadillac up to the side entrance of the bank, stormed inside with the motor still running, slapped Big Floyd across the face, then marched back out and driven away. Aimee had been working at a different branch back then but had heard the story from at least five people who claimed to be eyewitnesses.

"Please tell my nephew that you saw me, and I said it is high time that he paid me a visit." Mama W spoke quietly to Aimee as she handed Bonnie a crisp one-hundred-dollar bill. "And please tell Big Floyd that if he's late for supper again, he's going to wish he wasn't."

"Yes, ma'am," Aimee said.

In a flash, Mama W grabbed her things and was gone. She hadn't smiled once.

Bonnie's shoulders relaxed as soon as the door closed. "How's your love life?" she asked with a twinkle in her eye. "Beautiful girl like you must have men falling all over themselves."

Aimee stared at her, shocked, as always, by this question, not to mention the assumption that such a thing could ever happen. Other than a few awkward dates and drunk hookups in college, she'd never had anything close to a boyfriend. She made herself smile. "Oh, you know. No one really special right now."

"Playing the field!" Bonnie let out a hearty laugh. "Good for you. I'm just gonna go grab you a carrying tray. Otherwise those ferns'll be all over your car."

"Thanks."

As Bonnie made her way to the back of the store, Aimee let out a breath. Seeing Big Floyd's wife had bizarrely made her think of her earlier conversation with her mother.

"No, Mom. I haven't talked to Andy this week," Aimee had said as she settled down at her desk, her eyes automatically drifting to the picture of herself and her cousin at one of his high school football games. She'd been a freshman at Rice that year and had come home to watch him play. Andy in that picture— with his toothy, innocent smile, his shiny mahogany hair flopping over one eye, his whole face brimming with pride—always filled her with a huge bubble of love swirling with worry and something else that was hard to name.

"Aimee." Her name, spoken in her mother's sharp, disappointed tone, always felt like a slap. "You know what today is."

"I'll call him tonight," Aimee was surprised at the defensiveness in her voice.

"I'm worried about him." Her mother sniffed. "He gets mad when I try to talk to him."

I wonder why. Aimee blinked, shocked at the snarky words rolling through her head. "I talked to him last week, and he seemed fine," she said instead.

"He needs a haircut."

Aimee sighed. "Mom."

"Well, he does. And he's not fine. He won't even drive anymore. He just rides around on that old green bike when it's a hundred degrees outside."

Aimee dug the heel of her hand into her forehead. This was the first she'd heard about Andy refusing to drive. But there were worse things. "He's as fine as Andy's probably going to be."

Silence.

"He's doing well at the hospital job, I think. He says he likes it and—"

"But what does he even do there?" her mother asked.

Aimee slumped over her desk, desperate not to have this conversation again. The truth was, she wasn't sure what Andy did. It was something in the lab. Something that didn't require a college degree. "He works in the lab. He's been there for three years, and I think he's doing well." This was a lie. Aimee had no idea whether Andy was doing well at his job or not. But every time she considered trying to find out, a bone-melting exhaustion swept over her. All Andy ever said was that it was fine. "What exactly do you want me to do, Mother? Call his boss and ask for a report card like he's nine years old? Ambush him in the middle of his shift?"

Silence.

With horror, Aimee realized her mother was probably considering these suggestions. "Andy is an adult. I can't—"

"Aimee, he's your cousin. I can't believe you didn't drive back to be with him, today of all days."

Aimee always planned something with Andy on August 22nd. But this year, with Lianna coming, the date seemed to have snuck up on her.

Aimee blinked, realizing that Bonnie was speaking and had slid the receipt for the plants toward her.

"You all right, hon?" Bonnie's face puckered in concern. "Those boys at the bank got you working too hard?"

Aimee blinked again. "No ma'am," she said.

"You want to sit down and have a cup of coffee? I can send Bob over to the bank with these." Bonnie motioned toward the plants.

Aimee smiled as brightly as she could. "Thanks, Bonnie. Really, I'm fine."

◆ ◆ ◆

As Gillian told Lianna what had led her into the bathroom, a strange thing began to happen. Facts that had been so clear moments earlier—memories of the awful TV show, Drew's worried face, the man on the bike—seemed to rearrange themselves into a completely new picture. The logic of Lianna's incredulity shot straight through Gillian like an arrow from one of the bows her daddy used to hunt with sometimes. "You should have seen that biker," Gillian heard herself say with conviction she no longer felt. "Covered in tattoos and chains and ... and ..." Gillian realized she wasn't sure she'd actually seen tattoos.

Lianna rolled her eyes. "Give me my stuff," she said, reaching grabby fingers toward Gillian who was used to eight hands—Bobbie's, Carly's, Ashley's, and Trip's—thrusting and snatching at her, usually at the same time.

Gillian handed back Lianna's things, one by one, marveling as she did. Lianna didn't even have a *hairbrush* with her. Gillian thought of her own cavernous Coach hobo bag, now sitting on the passenger seat of the Lincoln next to Ashley's new shoes. Inside her purse—along with the Band-Aids, Neosporin, baggies of Cheerios, Kleenex, and toy trucks that life with Bobbie required—was a full set of travel-sized makeup and two different hairbrushes, one round and one paddle. Sometimes, she threw in her mini flat iron just in case. Watching Lianna—her movements still fitful, so much like Ashley tearing through the house when she couldn't find her favorite hoodie—Gillian felt her heart soften as she wondered how any mother could let a daughter out into the world so unprepared.

"There must be something we can do." Lianna put her purse back on the paper towel dispenser and began turning around in a small circle.

Gillian shivered and rubbed her hands over her arms, frowning at the vent blowing out icy air and trying to think of what people in movies did in situations like this. "Whatever is happening outside, we should probably . . ." She walked over and picked up the trash can. It was plastic and flimsy. Grimacing, she set it back down. "We should probably be ready to protect ourselves." Her nervous eyes met Lianna's. "In case they come in here."

Lianna's face instantly mirrored Gillian's worried expression. "That's smart."

Gillian fiddled with the paper towel dispenser, trying to pull the front cover off. Lianna's purse, still on top of it, toppled over.

Gillian managed to catch one end just as Lianna lunged and snatched the other.

"Sorry," Gillian said, lifting the strap she'd caught toward Lianna. She braced herself for a hateful reprimand.

"It's okay" was all Lianna said.

Gillian nodded, thinking Lianna really would look so pretty if she tried just a touch of lipstick.

Lianna put her purse back on top of the dispenser then turned to the sink and stared at it. After several seconds, she made a face as if she'd just eaten something awful she wasn't allowed to spit out and wrenched the stopper from the drain.

Gillian lifted the heavy porcelain back off the toilet and stepped into the center of the room. Despite the circumstances, she felt a puff of happiness at the muscles bulging in her thin, toned arms.

"Yours is much better than mine," Lianna said, wrapping her fingers around the stopper so that the pointy end poked out.

"I know." Gillian held the rectangle at arm's length and whipped it from side to side.

Lianna scanned the room again. "There's nothing else here. I can't believe there's not even a fucking mop."

Gillian smirked. "Does this floor look like it's ever been mopped to you?"

"Good point."

"I'll hide behind the door." Gillian tiptoed to the corner. "If anyone sets foot in here, I'll whack him with this." She swung the toilet-back up high. "If I knock him into the room, we can run out."

"But if there's a gang of them . . ." Lianna couldn't seem to finish that sentence.

Gillian swallowed. "Then what we do probably isn't gonna matter." She studied the floor. "Maybe there's not a gang."

Lianna raised her eyebrows but didn't say anything.

Gillian cleared her throat. "You stand over there."

Lianna nodded and gripped the stopper.

"Put it behind your back."

Lianna did.

Gillian frowned. "I can see it in the mirror. Move over that way."
Lianna shuffled to the right. "Like this?"
"Yep."
Lianna widened her stance, her attention focused on the door.
Gillian—still holding the toilet-back—squared her shoulders, did two half squats, and settled into a position.
Lianna rolled her head from side to side.
Gillian's chest rose and fell as she sucked in a large yoga breath and pushed it out.
They glared at the door.
They waited.
They waited.
Lianna slapped her free hand onto her forehead just as Gillian slumped, laid the toilet-back on the floor, and muttered, "I can't hold this thing any longer."

◆ ◆ ◆

Balancing the plants in their tray and dangling her car keys from one finger, Aimee hurried through the parking lot. She'd spent more time at Bonnie's than she'd intended and was worried about finishing the rest of her errands before Lianna reached the bank. As Aimee worked the key into the car door, a young woman passed by with a little boy in tow. His fist was wrapped around a Baskin-Robbins ice cream cone.

Suddenly, Aimee could see herself and Andy—she couldn't have been more than eight years old and he three—sitting in the back of her mother's new Crown Victoria, cones of mint chocolate chip ice cream clutched in their hands. Four tiny square napkins covered the front of Aimee's puffy-sleeved shirt and matching purple shorts, which her mom had surprised her with the previous day. Her mom always bought pretty clothes for her, and Aimee had learned how important it was to take good care of them. Her hair was pulled into tight, perfectly symmetrical pig-tails, held in place with elastic bands topped with giant purple flowers. She licked her ice cream methodically, making sure to get each side before it melted in the summer heat.

Andy's cone was a glistening mass of melting cream and slobber.

Her mother's familiar gasp-shriek erupted from the front seat. "Lick harder, Andy!" she called. "It's melting, honey."

Aimee inched farther into her corner.

"Andy. Harder. It's gonna drip, baby."

Aimee closed her eyes and savored the sweet, chocolatey mint.

"Aimee!"

Aimee's eyes flew open and found her mother's panicked face in the rearview mirror.

"Help him," her mother wailed. "It's getting everywhere."

Frowning, Aimee scooted closer to Andy and began dabbing his hands—now covered in melting green cream and saliva—with her napkins. She swiped her tongue around her own cone to keep it from dripping.

Andy wrapped his whole mouth over the ball of ice cream. When he pulled back, the melting blob was worse than before. A long string of spit stretched between his lips and the cone.

"Aimee!" Her mother's head whipped around from the front seat, then back to the road.

"Mama, I've given him all my napkins."

"It's *go-in'* to stain the upholstery!"

Aimee agreed that the gray cloth seat didn't stand a chance. Usually they weren't allowed to eat in the car, but her mother was fanatical about having dinner on the table for Ray by six o'clock and was in a hurry to get home. "Mama, I don't know what you want me to—"

"Lick it."

Aimee was sure she hadn't heard her mother right. Her eyes shot up to the rearview mirror.

"I need you to lick it, Aimee."

She stared at her mother in horror. Then at the slobbery blob of melted cream on top of Andy's cone.

Andy looked out the window.

Aimee felt her stomach turn over. "Mama, no."

"Aimee Eileen Harmon." Her mother's voice was suddenly menacing. "This is no time for you to be selfish. You lick that ice cream. Now."

Aimee watched a spit bubble pop on top of Andy's cone. "Mama—"

"This instant!"

Powerless to defy the command, Aimee closed her eyes. Fighting the gags ripping through the back of her throat, she lapped up the entire outer layer of spit and melted cream.

6.

G illian stared at the toilet-back—now laid out on the floor—
and wondered what in the world she'd gotten herself into.

"Does anyone know you're here?" Lianna asked as she studied
the filthy floor and scowled. She leaned against the wall.

Gillian shook her head. "I told my husband I was taking the
night off."

Suddenly, she missed him terribly.

And found herself thinking of when they'd met in college.

Trip had been six feet five inches of solid muscle back then,
but he'd held her hand like it was made of blown glass. The
first time she saw him, he was sitting on a lawn chair in front
of the Delt house a few blocks from the University of Texas
campus, while pledges fanned him and several other brothers
with palm leaves. She would later learn that Trip had purchased
the leaves and had them shipped from Los Angeles to Austin,
courtesy of his daddy's American Express card. It was Texas OU
weekend, so most people had headed to Dallas for the game.
As Gillian and a friend approached the keg, Trip jumped up so
fast he nearly turned his chair over. "You ladies sit here," he said
grandly, kicking the boy next to him so that he also offered his
seat. Trip had given her his full attention the entire afternoon,
insisted on walking her and her friend back to the Kappa house

after the party, and tried nothing more than a chaste kiss on her doorstep.

Her mind wandered to Trip when they'd first been married—still buoyant, still full of hope—having agreed to come back after graduation and work at his daddy's bank for a few years. Trip's goal was to save enough to launch a fishing tour company that worked the world-class bass lakes sprinkled around their corner of the state. At the time, Gillian hadn't understood why he insisted they not tell anyone, including his parents. But having a secret plan—something just the two of them knew—turned out to be so much fun! They'd cuddle in the single bed of the tiny one-bedroom bungalow his parents had rented for them, and she would marvel at the wonder in his voice as he talked about spotting the shady places on the water where the fish stayed cool, the art of casting, the beauty of a glassy lake on a clear morning. Most evenings after work, she went with him to a nearby pond where he kept a small flat bottom with a trolling motor. Though fishing never held the awe for her that it did for him—she felt bad for the fish, even though he released all except the ones she'd cook for supper—his happiness was contagious. And she'd been making her own plans.

Gillian's breath caught as she remembered—for the first time in years—how happy she'd been in that little house. Happier than she was in the bigger house his parents had bought for them in town when Ashley was born. Happier than she was in the sprawling six-bedroom rancher they lived in now, which his parents had built for them after she'd had Bobbie.

How on earth had they managed to lose themselves so completely? she wondered for the hundredth time since Saturday.

Something pulled Gillian from her thoughts.

"Hel-*lo*? Anyone there?" Lianna was waving an arm.

Gillian blinked. "Pardon?"

"I *said*, what does that mean?" Lianna held up both hands and made air quotes. "Taking the night off."

Gillian glanced down, frowned, and shifted her stance. "It's a long story," she said. "My husband won't expect me for hours. What about you? Who're you here visiting?"

Lianna stared at her.

"Obviously you're not from here, because *obviously* I would know you if you were."

"Obviously." Lianna closed her eyes and shook her head. "There's a colleague expecting me at seven in Bramble Briar." She muttered something that Gillian didn't quite hear but sounded suspiciously like *fuck it*, and slid down the wall until she was seated.

"They won't figure it out for a while, then," Gillian said. Her lower back was beginning to ache. After a moment, she found a space between the sink and the paper towel dispenser. Sighing, she sank to the disgusting floor.

◆ ◆ ◆

Aimee blinked and found herself sitting in her Mustang—her purse on the passenger seat and the plants carefully laid out across the back. She cranked up the air-conditioning but didn't take the car out of park as she tried to steady her breath. She hadn't thought of what happened with the ice cream in years.

A tapping at her window nearly sent her through the roof of the car.

"You forgot your receipt, hon," Bonnie said, pushing the slippery paper through the window that Aimee rapidly lowered. "You sure you don't want to come sit for a few minutes and let Bob take care of these for you?" Bonnie tilted her head toward the plants in the back.

Aimee pushed her face into a smile she did not feel. "Thanks, Bonnie. But really, I don't need any help."

Fifteen minutes later, Aimee was in the liquor store, staring at a sign that said BIG REDS and still trying to get her bearings.

Focus, she thought, summoning all her intuition because Lianna's assistant had given her nothing to go on when they'd spoken that morning.

"I'd like to make sure we have what Lianna needs in the office," Aimee had said. "What should I know?"

She'd been met with silence.

"Meredith?"

"I'm not sure what you mean." Meredith sounded distracted.

"Okay, let's start with her food and drink preferences for the breakfasts and lunches I order in," Aimee said. "Does she have any allergies or special dietary needs?"

There was a pause. "She's picky."

Aimee could hear a beeping melody in the background and wondered if Meredith might be playing some kind of computer game. "Does she drink coffee or tea in the morning?"

"She gets it herself, but I'm pretty sure it's coffee."

"Does she take crea—" Aimee stopped herself. There was no point asking. "What does she eat for lunch?"

"Sometimes she asks me to pick up chicken noodle soup, but only on days when she's in back-to-back meetings." There was another pause filled with beeps. "I see her with sandwiches a lot of the time? And she likes cookies." Meredith's voice hardened. "Her metabolism is ridiculous."

Aimee hadn't had a chance to ask anything else before Meredith explained that it was noon in New York, and it was time for her to go to lunch.

Aimee studied the dark, elegant bottles, finally choosing a Syrah. It was more expensive than anything she would buy for herself, but a tiny yellow sign proclaimed it was a STAFF PICK!!! and winner of a Decanter award. She was guessing but hoped that if Lianna didn't like wine, at least the gesture would be appreciated. Aimee stopped at the refrigerated section and picked up a small round of Brie, a block of Manchego, and two apples, which she carefully checked for bruises. On her way to the register, she grabbed a travel corkscrew, two bottles of water, a small cheese knife, and a box of Carr's Table Water Crackers. The Hampton Inn had refrigerators in the room, but Lianna probably wouldn't have time to go to the store herself.

As Aimee waited in line, the memory of Baskin-Robbins continued to hover at the edges of her mind. Mentally, she swatted it away.

At least, she understood what was happening. The books had said that old memories might rear their heads with unexpected vividness, especially on dates that were meaningful. Which just . . . sucked. Uncomfortably, Aimee's mind floated to the bigger question, the one all the books seemed to ask, *Was she ready to be different?*

The books had sent her whole inner mind into a tailspin. She still remembered the first one she'd stumbled upon. It was back in January when she'd run out to the local bookstore to buy a wall calendar for Big Floyd. She smiled at the memory—of Big Floyd bellowing from his office that his wall calendar was out of date; of Jonathan fumbling with his phone to pull up the Amazon app and calling Big Floyd to ask what kind of pictures he wanted; of herself, rising from her desk thirty seconds later and stepping in front of Big Floyd, who was storming toward Jonathan's office with murder in his eyes. She'd calmed both men down then headed out to get a calendar for Big Floyd herself.

Searching the little bookstore for calendars, Aimee's gaze had floated over a table display, which filled her with a sudden curiosity. Her hands had reached for one of the books while her mind wondered what she was doing. As she read the back cover, a tingling sensation came over her. She felt like she was reading excerpts from her own life. Five minutes later, she stood in the checkout line, a tasteful calendar with pictures of pond life under one arm and—astoundingly—the book gripped in her other hand.

Over the past months, Aimee had returned to the store again and again, stealthily devouring a good chunk of the self-help section and learning about words like *narcissism, triangulation, boundaries*. Before she'd begun reading these books, she'd never considered the idea that she'd had a difficult childhood. Maybe her mother could be hard sometimes, but she'd never beaten Aimee or Andy. Or burned them with cigarettes. Or locked them in a broom closet for two days just for spilling milk on the couch. Or any of the other horrifying things Aimee's mother had suffered at the hands of her own parents.

But there was a logic in the way the books explained how behavioral patterns take shape and burrow into the fabric of day-to-day life. Next to passages that felt like they'd been lifted directly from Aimee's own childhood—labeled as covertly dysfunctional and filling her chest with an aching sadness—were examples of healthily functioning families that seemed as alien to Aimee as living on the North Pole.

And of course, there was everything that had happened with Andy.

"That'll be seventy-six dollars and twenty-nine cents." The liquor store cashier's voice startled Aimee out of her thoughts. She slid the bank's credit card toward him and studied the receipt, forcing herself back into the present.

She wrinkled her forehead, knowing Jonathan would fuss over the amount she'd paid for the wine if he saw it. She'd just have to bundle it with Lianna's hotel charge and bills for the working lunches and breakfasts. Hopefully, he wouldn't pay attention. And if he did, she'd remind him of the one hundred and twenty-five dollars of fishing tackle he'd expensed for one of his and Clayton's *strategy sessions* held at a nearby lake famous for its proliferation of largemouth bass.

As soon as she got settled in her car, her phone lit up.

Her mother's face glowed on the screen.

Aimee pressed the ignore button.

❖ ❖ ❖

Sitting on the awful floor of Buck's bathroom, Gillian was lost in memories again—spinning back in time to that night when she'd wandered into the little room Trip used as an office and found him taking down the maps. After several years working at the bank, he'd said he was finally ready to tell his daddy about the fishing business and head out on his own. Trip had been planning to do it before Ashley was born, but then she'd come early.

Trip had maps of every lake within a fifty-mile radius covering the walls. He'd spent years marking them with color-coded pushpins to note the best fishing spots and how they changed with the seasons.

Now he was ripping them down and shoving the push pins into a coffee cup—even in his anger, careful not to let a single pin escape where Gillian's foot might find it.

"Honey, what're you doing?" Gillian had asked, stunned.

Trip didn't answer. He just continued to pull out the pins.

She stepped between him and the wall and put her hands on his chest.

Finally, he stopped and met her eyes. "The fishing business isn't going to happen."

Instantly, she knew. He'd asked his daddy to invest, and Big Floyd had said no.

"We planned for this," she said calmly, although she had been sure Big Floyd would help. "We knew he might not agree." She fingered the glittering diamond tennis bracelet Trip had given to her in the hospital the night Ashley was born—which she loved—and swallowed. "We can sell my bracelet." She tried not to wince. "We can sell the house and move back to a smaller place in the country. I can go back to—"

Trip's face was a blank wall. "Gillian, leave it."

In the following months, she'd asked him at least a dozen times what had happened, and each time, he was as silent as a dadgum rock.

Sitting on the wretched bathroom floor, a strange, whooshing sensation swirled over Gillian as she realized that was the moment when Trip had begun to change—that's when he'd started talking to her in that strained way that made her feel like a child who couldn't quite keep up; that's when grabbing a cold beer from the refrigerator had become his first stop when he walked in the door instead of kissing her. And she'd been so wrapped up in being a new mother and trying to make the new house look nice, she hadn't paid much attention at all.

Something smacked her on the nose.

Gillian blinked and looked down at a wadded-up ball of toilet paper bouncing on her lap.

Across from her on the floor, Lianna's arm was flapping. "I *said*, why won't your husband come look for you?"

"Did no one teach you not to throw things?"

"Seriously. What do you mean you're," Lianna made air quotes again, "taking the night off?"

For a moment, the thought of just telling Lianna everything filled Gillian with the most exquisite sense of relief. Then her good sense kicked in. She simply could not explain the upheaval her world had undergone to a complete stranger. She bit her lip and decided to give a partial answer. Because the fight with Trip *had* started the whole thing. "My husband and I had a fight."

"About what?"

"He shushed me."

Lianna's eyebrows puckered. "He—what you?"

"He shushed me."

Lianna's expression did not change.

"He told me to hush up." Gillian folded her arms across her chest. "At a party. At my house. Which I'd done all the work for." The scene from the previous Saturday—only two days ago, but it felt like eons—spiraled into Gillian's mind.

People were milling all over the backyard, sweltering in the heat even though the sun had long since disappeared. It was a political fundraiser, and truthfully, Gillian didn't care for many of the people attending. She'd spent most of the night keeping track of the thousand little things that no one really thought about unless something went wrong—waning citronella candles, disappearing servers, drunk guests harassing the handsome young bartenders who were half their age. Not only had her husband left all of this to her, but now the caterers needed help with the big grill and he was nowhere to be found.

She walked into the garage—which she'd spent half the afternoon cleaning—and found Trip and his buddies, all of them with lit cigars. She watched the trails of ash fluttering down onto the newly swept floor and had to dig her nails into the palms of her hands to keep from shrieking at them.

Trip was in the middle of one of his stories, grinning like a little boy. "That's when we come up on the alligator." He spread his hands wide. "And that ol' boy was twelve feet long if he was an inch."

Gillian's gaze traveled to the ceiling then back to her husband. This was at least the fourth time she'd heard Trip tell the story, and that alligator had grown by *at least* five feet. And she hated when Trip talked like he'd been raised in a barn.

Plastering a smile on her face, she waved him over.

"Hey, honey!" Trip trotted next to her and leaned down to kiss her cheek. "I told the boys no smoking in the house."

Gillian allowed the kiss and continued to smile serenely at the other men.

Once Trip's broad chest was shielding her from their view, her face twisted into a scowl. "Get those filthy cigars out of my garage!" she hissed.

His smile faltered.

"The caterers are fixin' to put the steaks on," she continued before he had a chance to say anything, "and they can't figure out how to light the big grill. I need you to show them."

Trip tried to smile again. "Sure, hon—"

Gillian's eyes, still blazing, swiveled from his face to the cigar he held in two fingers and back again. *NOW*, she mouthed before resuming her smile and stepping around him so that she was visible to the other men. Waving her hand like a beauty queen, she turned and sauntered back into the house.

A while later, sitting on a lawn chair with her second glass of wine, Gillian wondered if perhaps she'd gotten onto him a little too hard in the garage.

She noticed Trip waving to her from the caterers' makeshift buffet.

She sighed and heaved herself up. Deciding to forgive him, she gave Trip a real smile and headed over. As she wound her way through the crowd, her eyes landed on the guest of honor, who was standing at Trip's side—a weasely little man with an unfortunate mustache. He was running for Congress, and Gillian couldn't bring herself to like him even a little bit.

She ground her teeth to keep the smile in place, remembering the profile of him she'd stumbled on in *Texas Monthly*—his rabid support of fracking, promises to reduce funding for Head Start, a militant position against abortion under any circumstances. Reading about his agenda had actually made her stomach hurt. Certainly, she didn't approve of abortion. But if Ashley or Carly ever made a mistake. Or God forbid—

Gillian shook the horrific thoughts away and focused on Trip, whose mouth was moving as he watched her approach. She couldn't hear anything over the music from the band on the other side of the yard.

"What?" she asked when she was in earshot.

Trip was smiling, but in that pained, forced way, which had become a habit of his lately and drove her absolutely nuts. He spoke as if she were a child testing his patience. "I said, where are the rib eyes?"

Gillian wondered, for the thousandth time, when this conde-scension—so familiar now—had first crept into his voice. She felt her chest tighten. "Hon, there are plenty of filets."

"But I told you we wanted rib eyes." His eyes moved point-edly to the would-be congressman's empty plate.

Gillian worked to keep her smile from faltering. "Rib eyes weren't an option." She turned to the other man and tried to force hospitality into her voice. "We've got filet mignon and salmon and shrimp. How about you let me fix you a plate, and—"

She was sure smoke was about to spew from her nostrils when that awful little man smirked, pressed his unused plate against his chest, and interrupted. "No, thank you. But bless your little heart for tryin'."

Gillian straightened her shoulders, mildly aware that one hand had flown to her hip. "Now, listen here, Dicky. If you think you're gonna talk to me like that in my own backyard, you have got a whole 'nuther thing com—"

That's when Trip had done it. His eyes flashing, teeth gritted. "Gillian, shhhh." He'd never spoken to her that awfully before.

He grabbed Dicky by the shoulder and the two of them walked away.

"He was pissed because you got a different cut of steak?" Lianna's eyes were blazing as much as Gillian was sure her own had been.

"Apparently, Trip had mentioned rib eyes." Gillian shook her head. "Which I sort of remember. Because *apparently*, Dicky has some weird tic about beef, so he only eats rib eyes. He just won't admit it publicly because he needs the cattle ranchers' money."

"Dicky?" Lianna's eyes seemed to lose focus. They darted from side to side.

"Dicky Worth. He's running for Congress." Gillian sighed. "But I swear, Trip couldn't have mentioned the rib eyes more than once because I don't think we talked about the party *more than once*. Because he just assumes I'll take care of everything." She could feel the heat stirring in her chest. "Which doesn't really matter because Trip knows as much about planning parties as a pig knows about Sunday." Her mouth pinched into a tight line before she spoke again. "And a pig would probably be more help." As soon as the words left her mouth, the tiny voice whispered that she probably wasn't being fair.

Lianna was staring blankly into the middle of the room. "Dicky Worth?" Her voice sounded strained. "The guy with all the billboards?"

"Yep." Gillian nodded. "You probably saw those driving in from Dallas."

Lianna's face seemed to flit through several apoplectic expressions at once. "Wait a minute. You're a fucking Republican?"

G illian watched Lianna leap up and pound on the door. "Let me the fuck out of here!" Lianna screamed. "Hey, cashier guy! Drew! I'm trapped in here with Nancy fucking Reagan! Let me the fuck out!"

Still seated on the floor, Gillian didn't try to stop Lianna or react to the hateful words. At this point, yelling to be let out probably made sense. Gillian had no idea how long they'd been there. And the thought of a biker gang—or, if the bikers did exist, that they automatically meant harm—was feeling more and more unlikely.

Lianna leaned her ear against the door. After a moment, she banged her head softly against it a few times. She turned around and slid back to the floor, her eyes lasered on Gillian in what appeared to be disgusted fury.

"There is no need to look at me like I just told you I was a leper. It's a free country." Even as Gillian said the words, the tiny voice in her head reminded her of the awful things she'd read about Dicky Worth.

"Leprosy would be fucking better."

Gillian decided not to respond.

"Why?" Lianna sputtered after a moment.

"Why what?"

"Why are you a Republican?"

Gillian blinked, feeling like the room had shifted. A strange, dizzying sensation moved through her head as she realized—in her entire life, nobody had ever asked her that question.

"Hel-*lo*?" Lianna was waving her arms.

"What?" Gillian's voice felt like it wasn't working.

Lianna made a sound like a snort. "*Whyyyyy*"—the "I" sound came out long and grating and was clearly meant as a barb—"are you a fucking Republican?"

"There is no need to be ugly," Gillian said automatically, her mind spinning around this simple-yet-unconsidered question. She groped for words. "It's-It's just what we are."

Lianna stared at her.

Gillian felt as if she were being asked to explain why her hair was blonde and not brown, why she was five foot two inches instead of six feet tall. "My family is Republican. We always have been. Trip's is too."

"So?"

"It's our heritage. It's who we are." Although this was what Gillian had always believed to her core, the words suddenly felt flimsy. For the first time in her life, Gillian asked herself the question. Strange thoughts began to spool into her mind. "Do you remember Ronald Reagan?" she asked.

Lianna scowled.

Gillian pressed on, now desperate to understand for herself. "Well, he's the first president I paid attention to. My—"

"How old *are* you?"

"Did no one teach you—" Gillian glanced to the ceiling and back. "I am forty-six," she said, certain that she looked younger. "My daddy adored Ronald Reagan. Growing up, all I heard was what a fine man Ronald Reagan was and how he saved us from recession. How he got the country back on track."

Lianna began rhythmically banging the back of her head against the door. "S&L crisis, Iran-Contra, ignored AIDS, tried to hijack the EPA," she muttered.

Gillian had heard bits and pieces of those things—but that information had seemed separate, never quite penetrating her mind's holistic idea of Reagan. "Then there was George Bush, and, well, he was a Texan, so," Gillian heard herself say.

Lianna's voice began to rise. "A Texan who *pardoned* the Iran-Contra motherfuckers. Who backed out of the Kyoto agreement, making America look like the Neanderthals we are. Who tried to kill the science on global warming and withdrew all support for endangered species."

Gillian had never heard those things about Bush before. The tiny voice suggested that perhaps there was much more she didn't know. She ignored it, searching for the logic she was certain had to be there. "See, in my house it was the First Baptist Church." She raised her hand high above her head. "The Republican Party." She lowered her hand until it was even with her shoulder. "Then everything else." She dropped her hand into her lap. "God. Country. Family. It's who we are. And Trip's family's the same."

Lianna's face twisted into an expression like she'd just smelled spoiled milk. "Fuck, you had to have thought the second George Bush was a disaster."

Once again, the room felt like it was shifting. "I didn't really pay attention," Gillian said in a small voice. "I'd just gotten married. I was trying to help Trip with his fishing business and figure out how to be a wife." She felt herself filling with something vicious. "And, let me tell you, Mama W had very specific ideas about what that meant." Gillian shook her head. "Then I got pregnant and had Ashley."

Lianna closed her eyes. Her face twitched. "Mama—what?"

"Mama Wilkins. My mother-in-law. Anyway, Trip's parents

are the biggest donors to the Republican Party in the county, and they expect Trip and me to—" Gillian stopped herself. Because the little voice was asking if, after everything she knew now, she really cared what her in-laws expected her and Trip to do.

"What about the last crew? You can't deny that was a pure shit show." When Gillian didn't answer, Lianna narrowed her eyes. "It's the taxes, isn't it? You're one of those," she spoke in a squeaky high voice, "'The Democrats want to take all my money!' people, aren't you?"

"No." Although along with declaring that the Democrats would take the country to hell in a handbasket, Gillian had heard Trip's daddy say those exact words.

Lianna was shaking her head. "Did it ever occur to you that if the richest Republicans actually paid the same percentage of income that you do, no one would have to raise your taxes? That if those fuckers could wrap their heads around the fact that they could contribute their fair share and still be rich, there would be enough to go around?"

The tiny voice was chirping that there was a point here, but Gillian suddenly wanted that voice to shut up.

"Do you know the definition of conservative?" Lianna practically spat. "Someone averse to innovation or change. And the definition of liberal is being willing to respect behavior or opinions different from one's own. Look it up if you don't believe me."

Gillian raised her hand to her head, which was beginning to throb. "Can we talk about something else, please?"

"Do you honestly believe that guns aren't a problem?"

Gillian didn't answer for several seconds. "I hate guns," she finally said. "But hunting's a way of life for a lot of folks. It's the only time some kids ever get close to their daddies." Most men she knew—Trip and all her brothers included—had been sitting in deer stands and duck blinds before they'd been old enough to ride a bike. Still, the idea of her own son with a gun made Gillian's stomach lurch.

Lianna snorted again.

Gillian studied Lianna—so obviously smug and sure of herself—and searched for a rationale that was irrefutable. Her mind served up exactly what she wished for. "The biggest reason I support the Party is that I believe in family values," Gillian said, feeling her footing return.

Lianna now looked like she'd drunk spoiled milk. And her neck was turning the color of a strawberry. "Family values?" She scooted farther away, her eyes blazing. "So you believe that giving oil companies the right to drill into every last inch of forest and ocean until there's nothing left promotes family values?"

Gillian felt herself waver. "As a matter of fact, I do not, but—"

"And you don't care if women are forced to have children they don't want and can't afford to take care of?" Lianna's voice rose. "Or does your personal brand of family values extend to actually making sure all those kids eat and have roofs over their heads?" She didn't give Gillian a chance to answer. "Oh, wait, you're terrified they're going to take all your money."

Gillian looked away. "I think that abortion is wrong, but I also think that—"

"And while there are kids going hungry and feeling unwanted, you think it makes sense for our government to spend time and resources on *preventing* people who love each other from getting married? And *making it difficult* for people to transition into their authentic selves?"

"I don't!"

Lianna threw back her head and screamed. "Then how the fuck can you be a Republican?"

◆ ◆ ◆

Aimee saw Big Floyd's Chevy Tahoe as soon as she pulled into the bank's parking lot. "Gone for the day, my ass," she said to herself, pulling plants from the car and remembering how Clayton and Jonathan had been so certain that Big Floyd wouldn't return. As soon as she walked through the front door, her gaze landed on a path of muddy boot prints leading directly to Big Floyd's office. Mr. B kept an ancient upright Hoover in the supply room for exactly this reason. Aimee made a mental note to run it as soon as Big Floyd left.

She hurried into the conference room, one box of plants balanced on her forearm and a paper grocery bag dangling precariously by the single handle that hadn't ripped. She got to the table and let everything go, relieved she'd managed to get back ahead of Lianna. The clock on the wall showed it was ten minutes until seven.

Feeling that buoyed sense of accomplishment she always got when she finished things, Aimee smiled at the fresh ferns spilling from the box. Their rich green fronds already spruced up the room in a lovely but understated way. She'd had time to drop off the wine and groceries for Lianna at the Hampton Inn and to swing by Albertsons to pick up decent coffee and tea from the Starbucks counter. Big Floyd preferred Folgers.

"I should have known I'd find you here," a deep voice growled from across the room.

Aimee jumped—horrified when her feet actually left the ground—and did a minor juggling act with the fern she'd just picked up. She turned and grinned sheepishly.

Big Floyd, dressed in khaki slacks, khaki shirt, and khaki cap—Aimee rarely saw him in other clothes—didn't exactly smile at her because he didn't smile at anyone. Instead, he shook his head in a flustered motion, marched over, and started pulling out the other plants.

"Thank you," Aimee said as she lifted sugar, cream, and honey from the paper bag.

"I suppose those turkeys took off hours ago."

Aimee didn't meet his eyes. "I'm not sure what time Jonathan and Clayton left."

Big Floyd mumbled something about sons-a-bitches.

"Lianna should be here soon." Aimee folded the paper bag.

"What time'd she land?"

"They didn't touch down until three. I talked to her a little before five. She should be here anytime." Aimee turned to him. "Oh, I almost forgot. I saw Mrs. Wilkins at Bonnie's when I was picking up the ferns. She said—" Aimee coughed. "She wanted me to ask you to be on time for dinner."

Big Floyd glanced at his watch. "She'll have supper on the table in five minutes."

Aimee's eyes widened. "You live twenty minutes away!"

Big Floyd gave her a rare grin and wiggled his eyebrows. "I know. I best get my show on the road." He turned toward the door.

"And also?" Aimee couldn't believe she was about to say this, but Mama W's words had been haunting her since she left the florist. "You might keep an eye on Troy Aikman. He's been stealing her gardening spades and"—Aimee coughed again—"she's not happy about it."

Big Floyd stared at Aimee a long moment. "Don't you worry about Troy Aikman." His eyes turned to slits and his smile disappeared. "That woman knows better than to mess with my dog."

He turned and stomped out of the room.

❖ ❖ ❖

"I don't know why I'm a dadgum Republican!" Gillian wailed, knowing this was the truth and feeling as if she were in some kind of mental freefall.

Bizarrely, the fight with Trip bloomed in her mind.

"How dare you shush me!" she'd hissed, standing at the edge of her garage not twenty seconds after she'd smiled warmly and waved to the last bartender, who was getting into his truck. The shushing had taken place nearly two hours before, and it seemed to take Trip a moment to put the pieces together.

"You're still mad about that?" He appeared genuinely perplexed. "I was just making sure you didn't bow up and insult him."

"I wasn't going to insult him!"

"Oh, no?" Trip laughed. "Listen, sunshine, I've been married to you for twenty years. I know the look you get when you're about to fly off the handle."

Gillian folded her arms across her chest and glowered at him.

Trip shook his head. "I know you don't like Dicky."

Gillian's hands flew up. "Of course I don't like Dicky. Who in their right mind likes Dicky?"

Trip snorted. "Since when do you pay any attention to politics?"

"Since I picked up a *Texas Monthly* and read about everything he's trying to do! Why on earth are we supporting this wretched man? What he stands for—"

Trip rubbed his hands over his face so hard Gillian thought he might take his skin right off. "Do you think I don't know that? But he's gonna win, and Mama thinks—"

"I knew your mama was behind this," Gillian practically snarled. "She's always wanted you to go into politics."

"Gillian!" The anguish rippling through Trip's voice stopped her cold. "There's more to it than that."

"What do you mean?" Gillian asked more harshly than she'd intended.

He stared at her.

She took a step toward him. "What do you mean?" she asked, softer this time.

He sighed and paced to the other side of the garage. "Nothing."

She followed. "What?"

He turned and stepped out onto the driveway.

Gillian kicked her sandals off—they'd been pinching her pinkie toes all night—and followed him.

"Trip?" She reached for his hand.

He stopped. Slowly, he turned to face her. "Dad's selling the bank."

Gillian felt her mouth fall open.

Trip nodded. "The deal's pretty much done. There's a lady flying in from New York day after tomorrow."

"When? How?"

"I just found out. He's had Jonathan working on it."

"Your daddy didn't tell you?" Gillian asked, aghast. She'd worried a little when Trip moved his office from the headquarters in Bramble Briar to one of the branches near their house in Sweet Leaf. But she had never dreamed Big Floyd would punish him for it.

"He did tell me, but then he told me I didn't need to concern myself with it."

She threw up her hands. "Honey, he'll take care of us. He'll make sure you keep your job."

Trip blew out a rush of air. "No one on the executive team is keeping their job. Jonathan told me. He wasn't supposed to, but he did."

Gillian bit her lip. *None of this made a lick of sense.* The relationship between Trip and his daddy was complicated, but he would never— "Trip, he'll make sure we're taken care of."

Trip's voice turned hard. "Mama's not so sure." He turned and walked to the edge of the driveway.

Gillian followed him. "He loves you, Trip," she said with a conviction she felt in her bones.

"It's not about love." Trip stepped into the yard and began pacing in a circle. "I never wanted to work at the bank. I've never been good at working at the bank."

Her breath caught at how emphatically he said this.

"But at least I had a decent salary. Enough so that I only—"

She waited for him to finish.

He didn't.

She stepped in front of him and put her hand lightly on his chest. "So you only what?"

He waved his arm at the house. At her Lincoln. "Enough so that I only had to ask for help with the big things." His eyes fell. "The nice things that make you so happy."

Something clicked in Gillian's head then. She eyed her bracelet. One hand fingered her diamond earrings, which he'd given her when Carly was born. Her gaze floated to her Lincoln. Trip managed all their money. After his parents bought them the first house, Gillian just assumed. "You've had to—" Her voice caught. "All these years you've had to *ask*?"

When Trip finally met her eyes, his voice was soft. "Dad always says yes, Gil."

Trip hadn't called her Gil in years. Her head was spinning. Spinning and sending her back in time to that night, when Ashley was a baby and Gillian had wandered into Trip's office and found him taking down the fishing maps.

Standing in the yard, Gillian's fingers curled into his chest as she asked the question he'd refused to answer so long ago. "What happened with the fishing business, Trip?"

Trip's pained, shadowy face was silent.

"What happened?" she asked again. "Why didn't you even try?"

The agony that spread through his eyes at that moment made her heart hurt. "I did try!" He raised his hands to his head and squeezed the roots of his hair as words came tumbling out. "I used the logo you made and that ad you mocked up. I bought space in *Texas Fish and Game*! All those weekends I told you I was scouting? I was taking out customers. It was working!"

Gillian felt dizzy. "Why didn't you tell me?"

He turned to face the driveway. "I wanted to surprise you."

She blinked, trying to digest what he was saying. A thought—unbelievable, but it was the only thing that made sense—sent a wave that rose through her torso like a brush fire. "Your daddy—" Anger made her voice crack. She'd always loved Trip's dad and had always believed he loved them. She shook her head, feeling more foolish than she ever had.

Trip looked back at her. "It's not what you think."

But the inferno rolling through her was so strong her body started to shake. "He told you to quit fishing, didn't he? He made you—"

"Gillian."

"He threatened you, didn't he? It wasn't just that he wasn't gonna invest. He wasn't gonna have his son doing anything except strutting around that bank."

Trip took a step toward her. "Gillian, it's not—"

"And you had no choice with a wife and baby at home."

Suddenly, Trip was grabbing her by the arms. "Gillian, Dad didn't threaten to cut me off." Trip leaned down so that his face was even with hers. "He didn't refuse to invest. I never had the chance to ask."

She stared at him. "You never told him about the fishing business?"

Trip shook his head.

"Why not?"

Trip closed his eyes. "He had a damn heart attack."

"He *what*?" Gillian hadn't thought she could be any more stunned. "When?"

"A couple of weeks after Ashley was born. Remember when Mama stopped coming over for those few days?"

Gillian turned away, her voice careening higher. "Why didn't you tell me?"

Trip raced around in front of her. "Because Dad didn't tell me!"

Gillian felt herself sinking. Then, somehow, she was sitting cross-legged on the speckled, pebbly concrete of the driveway. Some faraway part of her mind wondered if she'd get her blush-colored sundress dirty, but she didn't move.

Trip knelt beside her. "They medevacked him up to Dallas, and he was out in a few days. Ashley was only a month old. You remember how she was."

Gillian nodded, remembering the haze that had been Ashley's first few months of life—a baby incapable of sleep unless she was moving. The only things that calmed her were being walked across the back porch or driven in the car. Gillian and Trip had been zombies back then.

Trip reached for her hand. "I didn't find out until several weeks later. To this day, he does not know that I know. It was—"

Gillian felt a long, slow breath escape from her lungs, which took all the fire inside her with it. "Your mama."

Trip nodded. "I went over to tell her about the fishing business and get her advice about telling him."

"She told you about his heart attack." Gillian stared into the empty yard, her voice a monotone. "She asked you to stay on at the bank."

"Yes."

"But, why?" Gillian turned and searched his eyes with hers. "Why didn't you tell me, honey? I mean, when you found out?"

Trip shook his head and looked away. "I was going to." His voice dropped. "You and I talked about everything back then."

Gillian drew in a shaky breath, realizing how much she missed how they'd been.

"Mama said it'd be selfish of me. It would be better to let you think I didn't want it anymore." He turned back toward her, and Gillian saw such sincerity in his eyes. "You'd passed up that promotion they offered you at the bank."

Gillian felt her stomach leave her body.

"I hadn't really thought about that until Mama pointed it out." Trip smiled sheepishly. "Things would have been so tight for us while I was getting the business up and running. I didn't want you to have to go back to work if you really wanted to be home with Ashley."

The cold loathing that ripped through Gillian next was the closest thing to hatred for another human being she'd ever felt. She raised Trip's hand to her lips and kissed it, while the most vengeful thoughts she'd ever had looped through her brain. Because Trip's dream wasn't the only thing Mama W had torn to pieces.

The feeling of someone beside her pulled Gillian out of her thoughts. She was shocked to realize tears were streaming from her eyes—something that had only happened in her adult life when she gave birth.

She looked up and saw that Lianna had moved next to her on the floor.

Lianna's face was pure horror. "What—what's happening? What's wrong with you?"

Gillian pressed her hands to her face and continued to cry.

"It's okay," Lianna said in an unsoothing voice. "It's okay. It's okay. It's okay."

Gillian began to blink back the tears.

Lianna swallowed. "This isn't because you're upset about being a Republican, is it?"

Gillian shook her head.

Lianna looked a tiny bit disappointed. "I didn't think so. Is it because your husband shushed you?"

"No." A noise that was half hiccup, half laugh leapt from Gillian's throat.

Lianna stared at her.

Gillian sniffed, thinking of Trip. Up until two days ago, she'd always thought of the fishing business as something he'd quit without even giving it a good try.

She thought of all the petty grievances and grudges that single belief had spawned over the course of their marriage.

She thought, with startling clarity, of the fact that she'd hosted a fundraiser to help get Dicky Worth elected to Congress.

"Nothing in my life is what I thought it was!" Gillian's hands covered her face as the tears spilled out again.

8.

Aimee sat up from where she'd been hunched at her computer and arched her back over the chair. The knots in her spine loosened one by one. Putting together Jonathan's expense reports was one of her least favorite tasks—the smoothing out of the receipts, which he relentlessly wadded into tiny balls; squinting to decipher dates and places and cross-referencing them against his calendar; and, finally, documenting what he'd been up to in a way that wouldn't cause Big Floyd to try and take his head off. She stretched her neck from side to side. This month had been a doozy, but waiting for Lianna had been the perfect time to just get it done, and—

Aimee gasped when she saw the clock on her computer. Eight thirty-five p.m.

She snatched her cell and studied the screen, her stomach curdling with the realization that she hadn't missed any calls.

She dialed Lianna's number.

Voice mail.

She dialed the Hampton Inn, feeling sick, but not surprised when the manager—the same man who'd taken the wine and groceries to place in Lianna's room—told her that Lianna had not checked in.

"She could have stopped somewhere to eat," Aimee whispered

to herself. But even as she said the words, she felt certain Lianna would have called.

She looked at the clock.

She dialed Lianna again.

Voice mail.

Aimee blew out a breath, pulled up the merger contact list, and called Lianna's assistant's cell.

"Where are you?" a screaming voice answered. Music thumped in the background against laughing voices.

"Meredith?"

"Uh, yeah! We're starving! Are you here?"

Aimee cleared her throat. "Meredith, hi. This is Aimee Harmon with First State Bank. We spoke earlier today?"

"This isn't Seamless with our pad Thai?"

"No, it's Aimee Harmon. In Texas. I talked to you about preparing for Lianna's meetings with us tomorrow?"

"Are you kidding?" Meredith seemed to be moving away from the party. "I thought this was—it's nearly ten o'clock here!"

"Meredith, I'm sorry, but Lianna should have arrived an hour and a half ago, and I can't reach her. She hasn't checked into her hotel, either."

There was a gulping noise, followed by a sound Aimee could swear was Meredith burping. "So?"

"I just thought—" Aimee squeezed her eyes shut. "Have you talked to her?"

"Yeah. A while ago. She forced me to stay and scan, like, fifty pages, which made me late to my friend's birthday party." More gulping.

Aimee rested her elbows on her desk. "Is there anyone else I could call? A boyfriend or girlfriend?"

Silence.

"Does she have a roommate?"

Meredith laughed unkindly. "Her mother calls sometimes, but that woman's more miserable than Lianna is." She hiccuped. "Look, Lianna doesn't *do* other people. She works." Meredith blew out a huffy breath. "And she expects everyone who works for her to have a similar pathetic existence."

Aimee leaned her head into her hand. "Meredith, I'm really worried."

The gulping noise again. "I don't know what to tell you. She never says where she's going. She—" Meredith's voice cut in and out. "The guy with our food is on the other line, and this is my personal time. I'll tell her to call you when I talk to her tomorrow. Byeeee."

Before Aimee could respond, the line was dead.

She exhaled and dialed her manager's number, knowing that Jonathan's house at this hour—he had three unruly boys ranging in age from four to eleven—would be a disaster. As she suspected, the sounds that burst through the phone when Jonathan finally answered were like a circus in a hailstorm.

"Aimee?" His voice was full of irritation with a splash of worry.

"Jonathan, hi. I'm so sorry to bother you."

A child's voice in the background shrieked, "Never!" Jonathan cleared his throat. "Aimee, what do you need?"

"I talked to Lianna Matthews nearly three hours ago. She was driving and tracking to meet me here at seven. She hasn't shown up, and she hasn't checked into her hotel. I'm worried."

"Well, hell. How should I know where she is? She proba-bly—" Jonathan's voice changed. "Honey? Honey, do you see what he's got? He's gonna—" The phone clattered. When Jonathan returned, he sounded out of breath. "She probably stopped off somewhere. Did you try to call her?"

"Three times. It keeps going to voice mail."

"Did you try her hotel?"

"Yes, and she hasn't checked in."

"I don't know what to tell you, Aimee. Lianna lives in New York City, so I'm sure she can take care of herself. I have no idea how she likes to do things, but I don't think it's our business to—" There was a terrible commotion, followed by a wail.

Jonathan's voice sounded far away. "Aimee, I've got my hands full. Don't worry about Lianna. I'm sure she's fine. I'll see you tomorrow."

◆ ◆ ◆

Gillian gaped at her reflection in the smeared mirror. "Oh, my Lord! I look like a deranged clown!" Two surprisingly symmetrical black streaks shot from her eyes to her cheeks, and parts of her face had become orangey while other parts were much paler than they'd been earlier. Her mouth was one giant red smear.

"Yeah." Lianna was still sitting on the floor. "You do."

Gillian pumped a wad of the toxic soap into her hand, smelled it, then washed it down the drain without touching her face. She leaned over the sink and splashed water onto her cheeks for what felt like a very long time. When she finally stood back up, most of the colors had disappeared.

"There aren't any paper towels. Do you want toilet paper?" Lianna asked, not moving from where she sat.

Gillian pressed her hands to her eyes then blinked a few times. "No, thank you." She pulled up the hem of her tank top and dabbed her face until it was dry.

She turned toward Lianna, who was watching her as if she might implode again at any moment.

Gillian blew out a breath but couldn't stop the memory of that long-ago lunch from tumbling back—the year *before* Trip had given up his fishing business. She closed her eyes and saw her twenty-nine-year-old self, sitting in the club dining room, wearing the third sundress she'd tried on that morning. And still foolishly believing she could find a way to make her mother-in-law like her.

"That's a pretty dress," Mama W had said as she sat down, wearing a frilly yellow pantsuit and sensible shoes. She immediately emptied three sugar packets into the iced tea that waited for her.

Gillian's smile filled her whole face.

"Too bad you couldn't find it in a flattering color." Mama W stirred the glass with a long spoon.

Gillian tried to keep her smile intact as she smoothed her skirt under the table. She'd thought the burgundy polished cotton was so pretty.

"You should never wear jewel tones." Mama W took a sip of tea. "They don't suit you at all."

Gillian smiled harder. "Thank you for inviting me to lunch today."

"When do you plan on giving me grandchildren?" was what Mama W said next.

Gillian could feel the color creeping up her chest. The truth was that she'd always thought she'd have had a baby by the time she was twenty-nine. She cleared her throat and tried to hold onto her smile. "We're really looking forward to having kids. We're talking about it."

Mama W's mouth twitched into a tiny horseshoe, which Gillian had learned was her version of a smile.

"But I'm really enjoying my job at the bank." When Gillian and Trip had first graduated from UT, she'd found herself in a whirlwind of wedding planning. Trip, of course, had been given a job in the executive offices of his daddy's bank as the vice president of community relations, whatever that meant. After they'd gotten married, Gillian had quickly discovered that the only jobs that fit her marketing degree were in Dallas or Houston or Austin. After months of fruitless searching and setting up the bungalow Trip's parents had rented for them, she'd agreed to become an entry-level teller—mainly as a way to be close to Trip and pass the time until they decided to have kids.

Mama W eyed her with a strange expression. "You're enjoying it?"

"Yes, ma'am." Gillian felt a bubble of pride in her chest. To her surprise, she'd been promoted to senior teller after only a year, ahead of three women twice her age. But the job was so easy! Most of the day-to-day was simply doing what customers asked—taking deposits and giving cash to the old-timers who didn't trust ATM machines—which Gillian did flawlessly and in half the time of her peers. When there was a problem, such as a questionable transaction or a disputed overdraft charge, Gillian solved it by meticulously crawling through records and tracing anomalies with the speed and thoroughness of an expert private detective. She had no qualms about calling over to the executive offices and advocating on behalf of a customer who deserved some type of remedy. Most importantly, she disarmed those customers who did not have a claim with her beauty-pageant smile and a factual explanation of why nothing was owed to them.

The horseshoe smile disappeared, but Gillian didn't notice.

She hadn't told anyone about her news except for Trip. "Missy Potter, who's the head customer liaison for the private wealth group up in the executive offices—" Gillian's throat seized. She took a sip of water. "Missy's moving to Shreveport to get married and—"

"I know about Missy Potter."

Gillian continued more tentatively this time. "They're offering me her position. It would be a big promotion, but Sharon, my manager, says that I'd be great, and—"

"I know who Sharon is." Mama W's voice turned icy. "How is Trip doing at work?"

Their salads arrived then, but Mama W's pale blue eyes didn't leave Gillian once. When the waiter left, Mama W raised her eyebrows. "Well?"

Gillian knew Trip wasn't impressing anyone—he came home every day for lunch and left early to scout new fishing spots any chance he got. In the evenings, he'd work on his maps. Gillian helped by putting together a target list of advertising opportunities and mocking up ads. They'd never breathed a word of the plan to anyone.

For a moment, Gillian thought that perhaps she could find an ally in Mama W—*Mamas wanted their boys to be happy, didn't they?* "Sometimes I think his heart really isn't in it," Gillian said carefully. "I think he'd be happier if—"

"Happier?" Mama W practically spat the word.

Gillian closed her eyes, thanking the Lord she hadn't said more.

"Who gives a feather if his heart's in it? It's his head that needs to get in the ball game."

Gillian could only nod.

"If Big Floyd sees you getting promoted when Little Floyd's barely keeping his nose above water? Well." Mama W shook her head and had another drink of tea.

Gillian cringed. Trip hated being called Little Floyd. But his parents and most of the old guys at the bank refused to call him anything else.

The next day, Gillian turned down the job. Trip was surprised when she told him but shrugged in that easygoing way he had and said she should do whatever made her happy. A few months later, she was pregnant with Ashley—something she was thrilled about, but also something she hoped might oil the wheels a little bit for

Trip's exit from the bank. She was sure she'd go back to work once Trip quit to start the fishing business. She realized now that she'd waited so long to have Carly because she had hoped, even though he'd put all his maps away by then, that Trip would change his mind.

Gillian hadn't told Trip about her conversation with his mother until last Saturday night.

"Hel-*lo*?" Lianna's voice brought Gillian back to the grimy bathroom.

"What?" Gillian blinked, her eyes focusing on her make-up-free face in the mirror.

"I *said*, Are you sure you're okay?"

Gillian bit her lip and turned to face Lianna, who was certainly rude and needed a makeover, but seemed genuinely concerned. Suddenly, Gillian didn't have the energy to pretend any longer.

"I came in here because Drew told me there was a biker gang, and I believed him instead of checking for myself." She sniffed. "And I didn't check because I don't know anything about bikers except what I've heard and some terrible things I saw on a TV show." Her eyes began to fill again. "Which means I'm probably prejudiced against bikers even though I don't know a single one." Her voice rose. "Because everything I've been told in this life I've swallowed hook, line, and sinker without question or giving it a second thought."

Lianna was looking at Gillian like she'd spontaneously begun speaking in rhymes.

Gillian wiped the tears away. "And I wasn't truthful before. I'm not taking the night off because Trip shushed me."

Lianna's expression did not change.

"Trip and I may end up destitute." Gillian slumped against the sink. "But I'm taking the night off to decide if I'm ever going to let my mother-in-law see her grandkids again."

Aimee listened to the hold music and wondered how much trouble she could get into for what she was doing. The first representative had seemed baffled by her request. Thank goodness, she'd asked Meredith to send Lianna's travel itinerary when they'd spoken that morning. She still felt guilty she hadn't checked it then to see that Lianna had a decent hotel room.

An exhausted voice cut through the elevator-music version of A-ha's "Take On Me." "Who did you say you were?"

Aimee squeezed her eyes closed but kept her voice firm. "I'm Meredith Birney. You should see in your records that I made the reservation."

There was a sigh. "Okay, Ms. Birney. What is it you're asking?"

"We can't seem to find Ms. Matthews. I spoke with her over three hours ago, and she was supposed to have arrived well before now. She's driving alone." Aimee forced her voice to remain strong. "I'm hoping you could look at the GPS on her car and let me know where she is."

"No, ma'am, I absolutely cannot do that."

Aimee found herself channeling Lianna. "Why not?"

The man laughed. "Have you ever heard of privacy?"

Fifteen minutes later and still feeling like an idiot, Aimee chewed her thumbnail and stared at the contact list on her computer screen. It was nine forty-five, which meant it was ten forty-five in New York.

She closed her eyes and dialed.

The deep, honeyed voice—the one that had made her stomach swim each time he'd called for Jonathan or Big Floyd—answered on the first ring. "Benjamin Sutter speaking."

Aimee drew in a quiet breath. "Hello, Benjamin, this is Aimee Harmon at First State Bank. I apologize for bothering you at this hour." She was amazed at the smoothness of her voice, at the sleek words that came out so effortlessly. But she'd always seemed to have this ability to mold herself into whatever people expected.

Still, she braced herself for a reprimand.

Benjamin's voice was kind and concerned. "Hello, Aimee. Is everything all right?"

"No." She swallowed. "I may be overreacting, but Lianna is very late and—"

"Lianna is never late."

Aimee swallowed again. "I spoke with her over three hours ago, and she was an hour and a half away. We were supposed to meet here at seven. Her phone is going straight to voice mail, and she hasn't checked into her hotel."

"Hold on." Benjamin's voice was firm yet surprisingly gentle.

A few seconds later, he came back. "I just tried her too. Voice mail."

"Is there a family member? Or someone I could call?"

Benjamin chuckled uneasily. "My experience with Lianna is that she prefers spreadsheets to people." His voiced sobered. "This is very troubling."

"Maybe she had a problem with the car?" Aimee pressed her hand to her forehead. She had hoped Benjamin would provide an explanation that put her at ease.

Benjamin's voice was full of certainty. "She would have called you."

"Maybe her phone died?"

"I once saw Lianna bodycheck a man twice her size in the United Club because her battery was at 20 percent and he was about to take the last outlet. She carries at least two chargers anywhere she goes. This is not like her at all." He paused. "I'll call our head of security and see if he has any contacts down there, but it's not likely."

Aimee chewed her thumbnail. "I'll call for some help here too."

"I can't imagine the police will do anything until she's been missing for longer."

"I'm not calling the police. I'm calling Big Floyd."

◆ ◆ ◆

Lianna stared at Gillian, not really wanting to hear about this mother-in-law or Gillian's kids but preferring that to more tears. And Lianna's exhausted mind craved a distraction. The entire time she'd been sitting on the floor watching Gillian alternately cry and stare into space, Lianna had been mentally buzzing through the probabilities of what was happening out in the store, who or what might open the bathroom door at any minute, how long before someone might find them. "What do you mean destitute?" Lianna asked.

Gillian gave her the mom-frown. "Did no one teach you that it's rude to ask people about money?"

"You brought it up."

Gillian returned to where she'd been sitting and sank to the floor. After a long moment, she began to speak. "Trip works at his daddy's bank. We just found out his daddy's selling it, and none of the executives are keeping their jobs."

Lianna blinked as puzzle pieces clicked together in her brain.

"Big Floyd will always make sure we have a roof over our heads and the kids are taken care of." Gillian rested back against the wall. "But it's gonna be hard on Trip to find something else and have to"—Gillian swallowed—"ask. Trip's gonna have to ask his parents for every dadgum little thing." She covered her eyes and started to cry again.

Lianna's mind was whirling. She could see herself, sitting across Benjamin's gleaming walnut desk, swallowing laughter when Benjamin had begun the call. "Hello, Big Floyd! How are you?"

Lianna had mouthed the words, *Big Floyd?*

Benjamin's dark eyes glared back. "Sure, I'll hold on," he said amiably. He covered the mouthpiece with his hand. "It's called relationship building, Lianna. You might consider trying it." After a few more pleasantries, Benjamin put the phone on speaker. "Big Floyd, I'd like to introduce you to Lianna Matthews, one of our top finance SVPs. She'll be leading the diligence down in Texas."

"Wait a minute." Lianna pulled herself up off the grimy floor and duckwalked over to Gillian. "Big Floyd? As in Floyd Wilkins? He's your father-in-law?"

Gillian, hands still covering her face, nodded.

"I'm here to meet with him. I work for National Behemoth Bank. We're the ones buying First State."

Gillian moaned and sniffled.

Lianna tugged on her arm. "Your husband, Trip. Is he Floyd Wilkins the Third?"

Fingers still pressed into her eyes, Gillian nodded.

Lianna let out a snort, shoved Gillian's crumpled form and sat down. "Will you get a grip? You're not going to be destitute."

Gillian dropped her hands and glowered at Lianna through tears. "How would you know?"

Seeing Gillian's dejected face, Lianna felt something warm and fuzzy and entirely unwanted somewhere in her chest. "Trip's going to take home millions when this deal is done."

Gillian's mouth fell open.

"I've seen the shareholder breakdown. There's a significant amount of shares solely in your husband's name." Lianna touched Gillian's pink sneaker with the toe of her shoe. "You're never going to have to worry about money again."

Before Gillian could say anything, there was a loud, shuffling sound outside the door.

They stumbled to their feet.

Gillian rushed over and picked up the toilet-back.

Lianna sped the other way and grabbed the drain stopper.

There was that low humming noise again, followed by more shuffling.

The doorknob twisted.

We didn't lock it back, Gillian mouthed to Lianna, who nodded worriedly.

The door opened.

Drew poked his head in. "You can come out. It's safe now." He turned and walked away.

G illian looked uncertainly at the back of the toilet in her hands, then at the empty space in the bathroom doorway Drew had just vacated. She turned to Lianna, who shrugged and slid the drain stopper into the baggy front pocket of her pants.

They tiptoed into the dingy hall, just in time to see Drew disappear through the swinging door.

Gillian listened.

The hum of an ice machine in the corner was the only sound.

They took a few steps farther, and Gillian noticed what looked like a small forklift parked beside the door. She tilted her head toward it, certain that must have been what had kept them trapped in the bathroom.

Lianna nodded.

Slowly, they stepped through the flapping door and into the back corner of the store. The overhead lights had been turned off, leaving the room in shadows—lit only by eerie bubbles of pale light from the refrigerators that lined the back and far side wall. To their right, Drew stood in the small stall formed by the counter, his hands busy with something they couldn't see.

Gillian and Lianna glanced at each other, then beyond the counter toward the front windows and glass doors, which led to the darkened parking lot.

They looked at each other again.

For the life of her, Gillian couldn't figure out why in the world Drew had locked them up. She looked to Lianna again.

Lianna shrugged.

They shuffled forward until they were standing next to the tower of sunglasses that stood, like a Christmas tree, next to the corner of the counter.

"Drew, honey?" Still holding the toilet back in her hands, Gillian peeked around the column of glasses and tried to sound nonchalant. "Is everything all right?"

"Yes, ma'am," he answered without looking up. He hurried through the small opening in the counter to the empty space in the middle of the store.

Gillian's heart nearly leapt through her throat when he passed in front of her. He was gripping a small device which, for a split second, she thought was a handgun. Her heart thudded back into place when he walked to the end of the farthest row of shelves and pressed the tool to a box of Cheerios—click, click, click—leaving a trail of dark stickers behind. She watched in fascination through the ghostly light as he stooped and marked a tub of Quaker Oats on the middle shelf—click, click, click—then crouched to reach the Crisco on the bottom.

Click, click, click.

He moved from the end display into the edge of the aisle and began working his way down the row of shelves that crisscrossed the remaining area, creating a narrow maze that led to the far wall. Each time, he tagged the items on the top shelf, stooped to the middle row, and finally crouched to reach the things on the bottom. When he finished, he stood, took a stiff step sideways, and began again.

Click, click, click.

Click, click, click.

Click, click, click.

Gillian turned to Lianna, whose face mirrored her own bafflement.

Click, click, click.

Click, click, click.

Click, click, click.

Drew's skin had that same flushed sweatiness the kids got in the middle of the night when they were sick.

Click, click, click.

Click, click, click.

Click, click, click.

Gillian and Lianna each took a step toward the front doors.

Click, click, click.

They took another step.

Drew no longer seemed aware of them.

Click, click, click.

Click, click, click.

Gillian and Lianna turned and walked quickly toward the front doors.

They were only a couple of feet away when Gillian saw the chain—heavy and thick—wrapped between the U-shaped door handles. Her heart sank.

Lianna took another step, then stopped. "Fuck," she whispered.

They searched the windows. The parking lot was empty except for their two cars. Gillian felt a wave of dismay when she saw that the tall floodlights towering above the gas tanks were dark. The orange neon—which normally articulated Buck's Pantry on the marquee sign—was also turned off, leaving only the dim, silvery glow of the rotating circle. Her heart fluttered when she noticed that the COME ON IN, WE'RE OPEN sign faced her from the door—which meant that the closed sign faced the parking lot. Her arms beginning to tremble, she set down the porcelain toilet-back. She turned to Lianna again.

Lianna silently shrugged.

Gillian scanned the store. The only other door was the flapping one in the back left corner they had just come through. She stared at it a moment, then at Lianna, who shook her head.

Gillian argued with her eyes and mouthed, *There has to be a back way out.*

Lianna scowled as she mouthed something back, but the only word Gillian made out was, *Fuck.*

"Hey!" Drew's head popped up from above a row of Doritos and Lay's potato chips. "What are y'all up to?"

Hearing the shakiness of the breath Lianna drew in, Gillian cleared her throat. "Uh, Drew, honey? My kids are sure gonna be missing me. I need to get home and feed them dinner. Can you please open the doors?"

He seemed to consider her words.

Gillian felt a rush of hope.

Drew shook his head. "I'm sorry, but you need to stay here. It's not safe outside."

❖ ❖ ❖

Aimee steeled herself and dialed Big Floyd's cell from her desk phone, not daring to call his landline and risk disturbing Mama W at this hour. Aimee had never bothered him at home before.

The line clicked, and his familiar voice growled, "What?"

She didn't hesitate for a second. "Big Floyd, this is Aimee. I'm so sorry to—"

"What're you still doing at the bank?" he barked. "Are the doors locked? Who's with you?"

Despite everything happening, the concern in his voice gave her chest a warm, comforted feeling and, strangely, brought her ex-step-dad Raymond to mind. "The doors are locked," she lied. "I'm here by myself, and I'm fine. But Lianna Matthews hasn't arrived and—"

"She was due at seven?"

"Yes, and—"

"Have you talked to her since five?"

Aimee always marveled at Big Floyd's flawless memory. "No, and I've tried her three times. I've called the hotel, and she hasn't checked in. I called the rental car company, but they won't give me the location of the car."

"Which car company?"

"Rent-A-Car-Today."

"Hold on." A moment later, Big Floyd's voice rumbled, more faintly than before. "It's Floyd."

Aimee sat up straighter in her chair. "Um, I know I—"

"We got a girl missing."

Aimee held the receiver away from her ear, trying to figure out what she wasn't understanding.

Big Floyd's voice continued. "She landed at DFW at three o'clock. Last contact was around five p.m., and she was ninety miles out."

Aimee realized he must have made another call from his landline.

Big Floyd's voice got louder. "I don't give a good goddamn whether you think she's off somewhere eatin' catfish, and I'm not filling out any blasted online report! We got a lost girl out there!" he boomed. "I got you elected, Sheriff, and I can damn well get you unelected or replaced. You get on that phone to Rent-A-Car-Today and find out where in the hell she is."

Big Floyd's voice was softer but still commanding when he came back to his cell. "Stay put, Aimee. I'm coming."

❖ ❖ ❖

Gillian and Lianna stood in front of the chained doors, their eyes riveted on Drew.

Click, click, click.

Click, click, click.

Click, click, click.

"There has to be a back door," Gillian whispered as softly as she could.

"Why didn't you say that before?" Lianna hissed.

Gillian searched the ceiling for the strength not to pinch her.

They began making their way through the shadowy room toward the flapping side door—which led back to the bathroom—shuffling a few steps each time the price gun clicked.

Click, click, click.

Shuffle, shuffle.

Click, click, click.

Shuffle, shuffle, shuffle. They were in front of the counter, halfway to the flapping door.

"We could probably take him," Lianna whispered.

Gillian turned toward Drew, who was working the price gun with an unsettling intensity. Something in her stomach rolled over as she thought of that day when she'd been walking into the Neiman's in downtown Dallas and the unkempt man who'd been muttering to himself outside the doors. Just as Gillian hurried past him, her purse gripped to her chest, a woman—dressed well and sounding like she meant well—paused on his other side and asked if she could help him get a bed in a shelter for the night. The change had been instant and terrifying. The man's eyes had speared that poor woman as a guttural scream erupted from his throat. Gillian had bolted as he began to yell at the other woman—that she was part of *IT*, that she wouldn't get away with

IT. From inside the store, Gillian and a salesman, who seemed just as terrified as she was, had watched the woman flee and the man rant until a security guard finally appeared and hustled him away.

Click, click, click.

Click, click, click.

"I'm not sure we should, um," Gillian whispered as they tiptoed a few steps farther. "I'm not sure we should escalate things."

Lianna frowned. Gillian watched her pull the edge of the drain from her trousers, study it, then look over at Drew. She shoved it back into her pocket.

Click, click, click.

Shuffle, shuffle.

Click, click, click.

As they moved past the counter, Gillian saw Lianna's eyes settle on the ancient landline phone squatting next to the cash register. Lianna stopped, then took a step sideways toward the opening in the counter stall.

Gillian watched, hoping Lianna was about to dial 9-1-1. After a moment, Gillian realized the clicking had stopped. She turned and—in the light from the refrigerators—saw Drew's narrowed eyes leveled on Lianna from above a rack of Hershey bars. He seemed to know exactly what she was about to do.

Gillian took a step forward, reaching for Lianna's back, then froze when she saw the—

"What are y'all up to?" Suddenly, Drew was right in front of them, his words crackling with something that might be fear. Or anger. He rushed behind the counter, stepping between Lianna and the phone.

Gillian watched Lianna jump back, clearly trying to find words. But nothing was coming out of her mouth.

"Drew, honey?" Gillian said with strength and fluidity she did not feel as she stepped forward and willed her pounding heart to settle down. "I need to buy one of"—she swiped a package from the small rack on the counter, having no idea what it was—"these." She was amazed that neither her hand nor her voice trembled.

Drew stared at her.

Gillian forced a pleasant expression onto her face.

He blinked.

Gillian smiled.

"Okay," he said slowly. He reached for the—Gillian studied it, trying to figure out what it was—*disposable rain poncho*. He took the small plastic package. "That will be a dollar seventy-five," he said in a cheery store-clerk voice.

Lianna's incredulous eyes darted between them.

Gillian dug out the twenty-dollar bill she kept in her yoga pants pocket and watched as Drew carefully made change. She pulled the plastic poncho out of the case and put it on. "This is perfect."

Drew nodded.

Gillian bit her lip. "Can I take it outside and see how it works out there?"

Drew seemed to consider this request. His face darkened as he pointed to the refrigerated doors lining the back wall. "Y'all need to go wait over there. It's safer."

Lianna reached into her pants pocket.

Gillian pressed against Lianna, digging her fingers into Lianna's arm until Lianna turned and began to move toward the dairy section.

"Owww," Lianna hissed, trying to pull her arm away as Gillian pushed her along. "What the fuck are you—"

"Shhhh." Gillian's whisper came out as a direct order. Only when she'd nudged a silently fuming Lianna to the far edge of the refrigerated section—away from the counter and directly across the room from the flapping door—did she rise up on her tiptoes and speak softly into Lianna's ear. "There's a shotgun on the counter."

❖ ❖ ❖

Aimee sat at her desk and waited for Big Floyd. The manual for the new coffee machine lay open in front of her. She'd tried to read it to distract herself, but her mind kept circling and circling around the problem, her body tense and vigilant. The sensations were depressingly familiar. Memories hovered: a cold hospital waiting room; the nauseating sensation that people were depending on her to fix something vital that could not be rectified. She shook her head, reminding herself that this was completely different.

The buzzing of her cell made her jump. "Big Floyd" flashed at her. She was shocked to see that thirty minutes had passed. "Hello?"

"They found her car." The motor of his truck rumbled in the background. "It's at Buck's Pantry in Sweet Leaf."

Aimee gasped. "She was in Sweet Leaf when I talked to her." She looked at the clock. "That was over five hours ago!"

"I'm heading there now," he said. "You okay to get home?"

Aimee's mind was reeling, but there was that warm feeling again, brushing up against her, reminiscent of her stepdad, Ray. "Yes. I can get home okay," she heard herself say.

She turned off her computer, shoved the unread Keurig manual into a drawer, and straightened a few stray papers on her desk, telling herself that she would head home and wait for Big Floyd's call.

She told herself this even as she locked the door of the darkened bank and walked to her Mustang.

It wasn't until she pulled out of the bank's parking lot—in the opposite direction of her trim little house with the yellow rose-bushes flanking the front porch—that she finally accepted what her body had decided the moment she'd hung up with Big Floyd.

A few minutes later, she merged onto the near-empty highway, and her headlights grazed a small green sign: Sweet Leaf 92 Miles. She hadn't lied exactly.

She was going home.

A weightiness settled over her as she realized she should probably call and let her mother know she'd be staying over.

◆ ◆ ◆

A gun? A fucking gun? Lianna's mind was in a tailspin as she sat on the floor in the pale pool of light from the refrigerators. Next to her, Gillian shivered underneath the rain poncho that, unbelievably, she was still wearing.

Click, click, click.

Click, click, click.

Click, click, click.

For what felt like the hundredth time, Lianna's fingers searched her pocket and found the drain, which seemed incredibly small and inadequate. Her eyes scanned the shelves that stretched in front of her—Frosted Flakes, Lucky Charms, Chinet paper plates. She wondered if there was anything more useful on one of the other rows. "We've got to get back to that hallway and see if there's a way out," she said softly, looking over her right shoulder at the flapping door in the corner. "If there isn't, maybe we can barricade ourselves back in the bathroom."

Sitting to Lianna's left, her back against the refrigerator door, Gillian shook her head. "That gun would blow the bathroom door to kingdom come." She swallowed. "And if he's any kind of a shot, it won't matter a hill of beans if we got to the back entrance. We'd never make it any farther."

Lianna shuddered, mildly annoyed that she was beginning to understand Gillian-speak. "What then?"

Click, click, click.

Click, click, click.

Click, click, click.

Gillian exhaled. "We wait for the right moment. We get that gun. And then we hightail it on out of here."

Lianna gaped at her for several seconds. "Ohmigod," she whisper-barked. "You actually know how to use that thing, don't you?"

Gillian's face darkened. A moment later she nodded.

They couldn't see Drew, but they could hear him.

Click, click, click.

Click, click, click.

Click, click, click.

After a long while, Lianna spoke quietly. "Won't your husband wonder why you're not home yet and try to find you?"

"Any other time Trip would have been having a fit by now." The poncho crinkled as Gillian pulled her knees into her chest. "I'm sure it's killing him, but he's trying to give me space. He probably won't even call his daddy," she sighed, "which is a shame."

"Why? What's the old guy going to do?"

"Did no one teach you—" Gillian looked to the ceiling and back. "I take it you haven't spent any time with Big Floyd."

Lianna shook her head.

"Big Floyd wouldn't care one iota if I'd asked for space. If he hadn't heard from me by now, he'd have every man from here to Dallas out looking for me and wouldn't let a one of them sleep until I was found."

Lianna frowned, hating the idea of having to be rescued by a bunch of men.

Gillian grabbed Lianna's arm. "Wait a minute!" she said too loudly. "You're here to meet with Big Floyd, aren't you?"

Lianna raised a shaky finger to her lips, then scowled and shook Gillian off.

Click, click, click.

Click, click, click.

They looked in the direction of the noise, but Drew was invisible behind the shelves.

Click, click, click.

Click, click, click.

Click, click, click.

Gillian's voice was quiet when she spoke. "Are you supposed to see Big Floyd tonight?"

Lianna's eyes continued to search the shadows for Drew. The clicking was coming from somewhere between them and the cash register, but she couldn't see him. "No, I was just going to meet Aimee."

"Aimee Harmon?"

Lianna nodded.

"She is such a sweetheart," Gillian said, apropos of nothing.

Lianna found the relic-like clock with the Coca-Cola logo on the wall behind the register. It was 10:35 p.m.

Suddenly Gillian was grabbing Lianna's arm again. "If Aimee was expecting you at seven and you haven't shown up by now, she's bound to have called Big Floyd. And he'll be looking for you."

Lianna felt a small burst of hope. "You think?"

"A woman driving alone from Dallas? Missing in the middle of the night?" A smile hovered on the edges of Gillian's lips. "Big Floyd will raise holy hell."

Lianna exhaled for what felt like the first time in hours, realizing that she wanted to be rescued and didn't care who fucking did it.

Gillian squeezed Lianna's arm.

Lianna didn't pull away.

Then Drew was looming over them. "We've got to be quiet now," he said. "It's not safe."

❖ ❖ ❖

Aimee listened to the rumbling of the Mustang as it sped down the highway and tried to make herself relax. Her feelings were seesawing in a way that made her insides queasy. One minute, she was filled with worry for Lianna. The next, she felt like an idiot, certain Lianna had stopped to do something important that Aimee wouldn't understand.

More than once, she thought of turning around.

Her hands stayed steady on the wheel.

She put the car on cruise control and noted the time. At this rate—speeding just a little—she'd get to Buck's just before midnight.

Feeling more and more foolish, she searched for some way to make the trip worthwhile and realized she could at least take her mother's car to Milton's early the next morning. He was usually there before six and would gladly give Aimee a ride back to her Mustang. She'd still be able to drive the hour and a half back to Bramble Briar and reach the bank before breakfast was scheduled to be delivered at eight forty-five. The first meeting wasn't supposed to begin until nine. Since Lianna was already so late, they might even push to a later start time.

Aimee knew she needed to call her mother. When Aimee had moved from Sweet Leaf to Bramble Briar the year before, she'd purposely dropped off some clothes at her mom's house and promised to come home at a moment's notice, if needed.

Her fingers found her phone and hovered over the Contacts button.

She tapped Amazon Music instead and put on Arcade Fire's *Funeral* album.

An idea that was at once liberating and awful popped into her head—she could probably sneak in and be out before her mother woke in the morning. With Sam gone, her mother was most likely back on Ambien. A heaviness settled over Aimee like a thick wool blanket as she thought about what a selfish thing that would be to do.

As Win Butler and Régine Chassagne's hypnotic voices filled the car with the "Tunnels" song, Aimee found her thoughts gravitating to Andy. He loved this band.

She paused the music and tapped in Andy's number. She was slightly sick at the relief that washed through her when the call went to voice mail. "Hey, it's me," she said. "Just thinking about you today. Sorry I didn't call earlier. And that I couldn't make it back to see you. Work's been hectic. But I would—" She coughed and forced the words out of her mouth. "I'd love to make plans for dinner sometime soon. Call me back. Love you."

She hadn't seen Andy in almost three months, not since his twenty-fifth birthday. They still talked at least once a week, but their conversations had become strained.

"Jimmy is such an asshole," Andy had grumbled when she called the week before. This was in answer to her opening words, *Hey, how are you?*

"He's just weak. Can't make up his mind. I asked him about . . ." Aimee propped her elbow on her desk and took a bite of the turkey sandwich she'd brought for lunch from home as he rambled on.

". . . not to go over to his ex-girlfriend's house . . ."

As far as Aimee knew, Jimmy was Andy's last remaining friend. She took another bite of her sandwich but didn't taste it.

". . . had not learned a thing. The whole disaster was completely preventable. Right?"

Aimee startled. Her eyes darted to the clock. Andy had been talking for seven straight minutes. "I guess?"

"What do you mean you guess?" Andy sounded disgusted with her now.

Aimee sighed, feeling as if fifty fingers were plunging into her chest and squeezing whatever they could latch onto. "I wasn't there," she said carefully. This was something the books talked about—how to avoid being pulled into dramas that are not of your own making.

"You're just as bad as he is," Andy practically spat. "But that's not the worst of it. You wouldn't believe what that sonofabitch who lives next door did last night . . ."

The irritation that had filled Aimee as she listened to Andy for another half hour that day bubbled up in her chest now as she drove. Immediately, it was replaced with bone-crushing guilt. The only times she hadn't been with Andy on August 22nd were when he was in high school and she was at Rice. But they always made a plan to talk.

Those were the years when her mother was with Josh, who had materialized not long after Raymond's refusal to provide any more money and, mercifully, before Aimee's mom lost the house. Josh was polite but didn't ask any questions about Aimee's or Andy's lives. He never had a single meal with them before Aimee left for college. She had hoped that he and Andy might have found some kind of camaraderie while she was away.

"He spends all his time at his house in Dallas," Andy would always say when Aimee asked how they were getting along.

"Mom's not working, and the bills are being paid," Aimee would reply, clinging to the hope that Josh actually cared about them.

Andy would answer with something light and funny, but all Aimee would hear was the aching undercurrent of a boy without a father.

Aimee rolled down the window of the Mustang, suddenly needing fresher air. As the sweet scent of pine trees filled the car, a familiar ball of tangled, yarn-like feelings began to move within her. Her heart swam with love as she thought of waking Andy from his nap when he was a dimply toddler—his head a flurry of hot silky curls, which he'd rest under her chin until he was awake. And of the Andy in that high school picture on her desk, so hopeful and confident in his football uniform. She swallowed. She thought of their conversation last week, and the darker feelings began to pour in.

She snatched at her phone and turned the music back on, then firmly turned her thoughts toward all the things that needed to be done tomorrow at work. She still needed to figure out how to use the new coffee machine. She needed to vacuum up the dusty pieces of deer lease Big Floyd had tracked into the hallway. She should send follow-up emails to the business heads to make sure they were preparing their monthly forecasts, which were due the following week.

Slowly, her feelings faded away.

◆ ◆ ◆

Still sitting on the floor in front of the refrigerators, Lianna stared up at Drew, who towered over them. She wondered how he'd moved so quickly and how much he had heard.

"We need to be quiet. It's not safe," he said again.

She looked at Gillian, who was staring past Drew toward the end of the aisle. Toward the gun, which they couldn't see.

Gillian's gaze slid away and met Lianna's. She squeezed Lianna's arm again.

Lianna moved her head in the tiniest nod, terrified of what she was about to do and hoping she had understood correctly. She cleared her throat. "Uh, Drew?"

Gillian's hand slipped away.

Drew dropped to one knee and thrust a finger at Lianna. "Quiet." His skin glowed with an unhealthy sheen, his bald head like a newly peeled, hard-boiled egg.

The air rushed out of Lianna's lungs. He was so close. He was so big.

She felt Gillian sidle a few inches away and hoped Gillian could run fast.

Lianna coughed. "Drew, I—"

He clapped a giant hand over her mouth.

All Lianna's thoughts were displaced by the feel of his rough, salty skin pressing against her lips.

She felt Gillian go still.

Then a pounding erupted someplace deep within Lianna—a feeling she'd never had before, but understood, with complete certainty, was some primal warning from her body. She was in danger. *Real fucking danger.*

A motor rumbled outside, and headlights swept through the murky store. All Lianna could see was the top of Drew's hand and his chest because she couldn't bring herself to look at his face. Her eyes darted right and left—her vision filling with boxes of cereal on the long shelf behind him—as she pulled in air through her nose.

A car door slammed.

❖ ❖ ❖

Cylinders of light penetrated the shadows. *Flashlights?* Gillian wondered. She stared straight ahead, terrified for Lianna but certain that help was right outside the door. Flashlights had to mean the sheriff—probably called by Aimee and Big Floyd.

She heard Lianna gasp.

"Quiet," Drew hissed.

Gillian had managed to get one leg underneath her when

Drew first appeared but had been afraid to move after he'd put his hand on Lianna's face. As slowly as she could, Gillian began to pull her other leg closer. If she could just get her feet planted, she could jump up and surely make it to the front windows.

Gillian nearly screamed when Drew grabbed her arm with his free hand. Without wanting to, she looked at him. "You move or make a noise," he said in a soft voice, more terrifying because of its matter-of-factness, "and I will break her neck." Gillian's stomach flipped over as he released her arm and placed that hand around Lianna's throat.

The front doors rattled.

Gillian's mind was whizzing—if she screamed, she and Lianna might be able to fight Drew off until the sheriff got in. She sucked in a deep breath.

Gillian watched Drew's fingers begin to squeeze.

Lianna made an unholy sound, her eyes like saucers above Drew's giant hands.

A dread like Gillian had never felt before filled her, so cold it was as if her body was filling with ice water. A voice—her voice—spoke calmly inside her head. *Help won't get here in time.*

10.

Aimee yawned as the Mustang swept past the green sign: Sweet Leaf 40 Miles. She pressed the accelerator, blatantly speeding now, her worry for Lianna prickling stronger. "It's fine," Aimee said quietly to the empty car. "It's fine. It's fine. It's going to be fine." A breeze of déjà vu rippled through her, but she couldn't figure out why.

"Oh my God," she said louder as she remembered. There had been another time when she had driven furiously through the night, repeating those words over and over.

The memories came hurtling back at her.

She had been in her senior year at Rice, during the week of fall midterms. Her mother had been calling for days.

"He won't come out of his room," her mom would say.

"Maybe he just needs time," was always Aimee's answer. She suspected Andy's self-imposed sequestration was related to losing his starting quarterback position on the football team to a ridiculously talented junior who had transferred from another school. But Aimee was so busy—her responsibilities in the Accounting Department steadily increasing—that she hadn't really talked with him about it.

On the third day, Aimee had begun to worry too.

"Is he eating?" she asked her mother.

"I have no idea! I put food by the door morning, noon, and night. He won't unlock it if I'm anywhere in the hallway. I don't know how he knows if I'm there, but he does." Her mother sniffed. "When I come back later, it's gone. But who knows what he does with it? I should never have let him put that padlock on his door."

Huddled under a desk in one of the lesser-used sections of Rice's Fondren Library so that she wouldn't disturb anyone else, Aimee hadn't pointed out that it was no longer a matter of *letting* Andy do anything. By that time, he was six foot two and out-weighed Aimee and her mother put together. "What does Josh think?" Aimee asked carefully.

"Josh is down in South America, thank the Lord," her mother hissed, as if Josh might somehow be able to overhear them. "And this needs to be resolved before he gets home."

"Okay," Aimee said soothingly as she felt her shoulders cramp. "I'll drive home tomorrow after my lit final." She was still too young and naïve to suspect what, years later, she would under-stand with humiliating clarity—Josh was married.

Aimee's final was for an afternoon class, and she'd sat in traf-fic for almost two hours before she made it out of the city.

Her mother had called when Aimee was still an hour and a half away. "Why aren't you here yet?"

"I didn't finish my test until almost five, and getting out of Houston during rush hour is a nightmare."

"He's playing music," her mother said cryptically.

"What do you mean?" Without really thinking about it, Aimee accelerated.

"I mean he has his iPod blaring, and it's only one song he plays over and over!"

"What song?"

"How in God's name would I know?"

Aimee punched the gas harder. When she arrived home an hour later, Nine Inch Nails's "Hurt" reverberated through the house.

"You took long enough!" her mother screeched as Aimee walked through the door. Her mom pointed to Andy's room. "Do something!"

Aimee, her stomach sinking through her knees, ran up the stairs. "Andy!" she yelled over the music as she pounded on his door. "It's me! Let me in!"

Relief surged through her when she heard the lock clicking and felt the door pull away from her hand.

Then Andy came barreling out, knocking Aimee against the railing so hard she was sure she would tumble over. He raced down the stairs, making a strange whooping sound. His arms were straight up by his ears, completely rigid except for his fingers, which flexed and spread in time with each howl.

He reached the first floor before Aimee regained her balance. In a daze, she watched his tall, beefy body bounding around the living room—whooping louder and louder—while her mother screamed from the corner.

Aimee dashed down the stairs just as Andy disappeared into the dining room and her mom raised the cordless phone to her ear. "Nine. One. One? We need help!" she shrieked. "My nephew's lost his mind!"

Aimee sank onto the bottom stair and leaned her head against the railing as she listened to Andy roar and her mother shout their address.

◆ ◆ ◆

Gillian had no idea how long she'd been sitting there, watching Drew hold Lianna's face and neck in his hands. Gillian had heard at least two men's voices, pacing around the front of the store, shaking the door from time to time. Her heart sank when the voices faded. She felt a moment of hope when she heard rattling from somewhere behind the flapping side door. But after a few seconds, the sound stopped. Eventually, car doors slammed, and headlights swept one last time around the room. The rumble of a truck faded away.

She waited for Drew to release Lianna.

He didn't.

Lianna's chest heaved.

"Drew, honey?" Gillian's voice came out warbled. She cleared her throat. "Drew, they're gone. Let Lianna go now."

Drew didn't respond. He just stared at Lianna's face.

Lianna's panicked eyes looked to Gillian.

Gillian stared back, two very different choices pulling against each other in her head. Biting her lip, she scooted an inch away. She looked to Lianna for agreement, having no idea if she would recognize it or not.

Lianna closed her eyes and tilted her head the tiniest bit down.

Gillian scooted again and paused, watching Drew for any reaction.

He seemed to have lost awareness of her. His head began to sway from side to side as he gazed at Lianna.

Gillian couldn't bring herself to look at Lianna again. She peered behind Drew and studied the space between his back and the shelves. She would never make it through without bumping him. Turning toward the opposite direction, her eyes traced a path around the end of the aisle into the adjacent one. She looked back at Drew.

He was watching Lianna with an otherworldly stare that was like something out of a horror movie.

Gillian scooted.

◆ ◆ ◆

Lianna's neck was cramping. After Gillian's second scoot, Lianna turned her eyes back to Drew's chest, afraid of calling attention to what she hoped Gillian was about to do. After a moment, Lianna forced herself to look up at his face.

His expression sent her stomach reeling. He didn't look like . . . him. He didn't look like *a person*. She'd heard people talk about "vacant eyes" and thought she'd understood what they meant. But she hadn't. Because she'd never seen anything like the face in front of her.

Drew's hands dropped from her mouth and neck to her shoulders. But she felt no relief because he was leaning toward her, his dead eyes growing larger. She could see a pimple about to erupt on the side of his nose.

The pounding in Lianna's chest started up again. She pressed herself as close to the refrigerator door as she could. The cold glass stung through her thin blouse.

Drew's head wound forward just inches from hers.

Lianna turned her face away and managed to raise her hand.

Her whole body recoiled as his tongue swished across her open palm, his face pressing into her hand.

Lianna pushed back. Then all sensation and thought was lost when his teeth clamped down.

◆ ◆ ◆

Aimee swerved the Mustang, just missing something small with glowing red eyes. She gripped the steering wheel and tried to banish the memories of Andy's first breakdown. She passed another sign: Sweet Leaf 10 miles.

The memories pressed back against her. She was driving, following the ambulance, her mother hysterical beside her. "After all I've done for that boy! Takin' him in and raisin' him as if he was my own. You would think—" her mother had said as she broke into another round of sobs.

Aimee barely heard her because there was a host of thoughts taking up all the space in her brain, *Will he get better? Can he still graduate? Can we keep this quiet?*

They sat in the freezing emergency room for almost two hours before a bleary-eyed doctor came out, spewing words that Aimee scribbled on the back of the privacy policy she'd been handed when she checked Andy in—stress, sleep deprivation, depression. The doctor ended by telling them that the first priority was to get Andy to sleep, and they should go home and do the same. Aimee was so tired by that point that she could barely keep her eyes open, and her mother was nearly incoherent. They hadn't argued.

The next morning, Aimee called the nurses' station on Andy's ward, the only phone number she'd been given. "He's still asleep, which is the best thing for him," a tired-sounding voice explained. "Try back again this evening, and we may know which doctor will be treating him."

Aimee had hung up the phone, filled with the feeling that there was something important she should be doing. She just had no idea what. When she shuffled downstairs in search of coffee, she saw with relief that her mom's door was still closed.

Aimee drifted back upstairs with a steaming mug, still feeling at loose ends. She was exhausted but couldn't imagine sleeping. She wandered into Andy's room.

The smells of a week's worth of untouched food hit her first.

But she wouldn't see the pile of full, molding plates and glasses of curdling milk—he didn't appear to have eaten any of it—in the corner until later, when she began to clean.

Her hand fluttered to her mouth as her gaze traveled over the walls of Andy's room, each covered in scribbles of Magic Marker. On shaky legs, she began to read.

TIME IS TIME. NOW IS NOW. THE BED KNOWS. THE MILK KNOWS. I KNOW. THE TIME IS NOW. NOW IS NOW. TIME IS TIME. THE CURTAINS KNOW . . .

Hundreds of lines, scrawled in purple, red, blue, and green—none of them making any sense.

Aimee sank to the floor.

The next day, she and her mother painted Andy's room.

Three days after that, Andy returned from the hospital with prescriptions for Zoloft and Halcion, and an appointment to meet with an outpatient therapist.

They told the high school he had mono.

Aimee spent the morning Andy was to be released with the hospital's financial counselor, finally signing a contract with a promise to send thirty dollars each week until the debt was paid.

She went back to Rice the day before Josh was due home from South America.

A few months later, her mother whispered through the phone that the hospital bills had been *taken care of.* She didn't elaborate, and Aimee didn't ask any questions.

No one spoke of the incident again.

As Drew's teeth mangled her hand, Lianna could hear herself screaming, could feel the skin on her palm ripping. Yet at the same time, a tiny part of her brain stepped away and marveled at the strangeness of what was happening. She was being *bitten.* She was being bitten by *a person.*

There was nothing else in that moment. No other sound. No sight because she couldn't bear to see Drew biting her and had closed her eyes. She wasn't even aware of any other part of her body. Only the desperation to end what was happening—to get her flesh away from his mouth—combined with the terror that she'd leave half her hand behind if she pulled too hard.

The searing sting was so deep that Lianna didn't really feel Drew let go. She was just suddenly aware of a strange old-timey-phone-ringing sound filling her ears and that he was gone. Propelled solely by her body's instinct to flee, she jumped up and raced toward the front doors.

◆ ◆ ◆

Nearly toppling over when Lianna's bone-chilling scream filled the dark room, Gillian continued around the back of the shelves and pounded down the next aisle toward the gun, unable to bear the thought of what Drew might be doing.

The landline phone began to ring.

Gillian ran harder.

She was less than five feet from the counter when Drew leapt out ahead of her from the adjacent aisle. He stood, seemingly frozen, staring at the ringing phone—his body between Gillian and the gun. She skidded to a stop just in time to avoid running into Lianna, who sped past toward the front doors where she began to beat her hands against the glass and scream.

"Be quiet," Drew said, still watching the ringing phone.

Gillian was shocked at how quickly Lianna obeyed.

The phone continued to ring.

Answer it, Drew, Gillian thought with all her might. If he would just pick up the receiver, she'd scream bloody murder and surely whoever was on the other end would send help. She could see Lianna silently staring at Drew, her eyes wide and terrified. Gillian's breath caught when she saw the blood dripping from Lianna's shaking hand.

The phone continued to ring.

Drew stood at the counter, his arms by his sides.

Eventually, the ringing stopped.

11.

Aimee could see the pale glow of the sign for Buck's Pantry from the highway, but the neon letters weren't on. As she exited, a light flashed on a grassy hill next to the parking lot. She slowed and approached from the service road.

A moment later, the light flickered again. She pulled over, turned off the car, and hurried out. The full moon and her phone flashlight lit her way until she reached the sheriff's Bronco, which was parked with the lights off. She turned her head and squinted at the gloomy store across the parking lot, about a football field away.

Two men in uniform huddled next to the hood of the truck. One she recognized as Sheriff Davis. He had been a deputy back when Andy had his first breakdown and had come to their house the night her mother called 9-1-1. He'd had to radio for backup, and he and two other men had wrestled Andy to the floor of their living room. Aimee still remembered the way then-deputy Davis had sat down beside her on the stairs and explained what was going to happen next.

She didn't know the younger man standing in the moonlight with Sheriff Davis now. He was also in uniform and spoke quietly into a phone. He covered the mouthpiece with his hand and turned toward the sheriff. "Maggie says she's tried him at every number she has."

"He's probably up at the cabin, drunk," Sheriff Davis said. "Tell her to keep trying."

The young man—maybe a deputy?—relayed the message and hung up. "We could just go in."

The sheriff's face pinched into a map of angry lines. "We break into that store without Buck's permission and he will sue you, me, the County, and probably the State. That old coot's meaner than a wet panther when he thinks his rights have been violated."

The deputy frowned and nodded.

"I'm already way out on a limb bullying that kid from the rental car place into giving me the location of the car. And I had a call from the security team of that bank up in New York on the way over." Sheriff Davis shook his head. "We got to rein this thing in before—"

Aimee cleared her throat.

The men startled and turned toward her, neither with a particularly welcoming expression.

"Hi, Sheriff Davis," she said, realizing she had no idea what to say next.

He sighed and planted his hands on his hips, but his expression warmed. "Aimee Harmon, what on God's green earth are you doing here?"

Her voice suddenly felt like it wasn't working. "I was the one—" She coughed. "I'm the one Lianna was supposed to meet. I called Big Floyd."

The sheriff's face soured.

"I don't want to be in your way," she added quickly. "I'm just worried. And if I can help at all . . ." The idiot feeling was in full bloom inside her chest. She had no business being here.

The sheriff stared at her for several seconds. His voice was soft when he spoke. "Aimee, there's nothing we know that you don't. I got Big Floyd's call about the missing lady from New York, and—"

"Lianna." Aimee suddenly felt it was important for the two men to remember her name.

The sheriff nodded, his eyes gentle, as if he understood. "About *Lianna*. We got the location from the rental car company. My deputy Ronnie," he indicated the other man with a tilt of his head, "and I got here about an hour—"

"Ten fifty-one, sir," the deputy broke in. "We got here at exactly 10:51 p.m."

The sheriff closed his eyes. "Right. We went all around the building and didn't see anything other than the two cars you see down there and an old green bike out back. We tried every which way to get in without breaking in."

The sheriff's phone buzzed. He continued as he squinted at the screen. "For the last half hour, we've been waiting up here, trying to raise Buck to come let us in and hoping your girl might just show back up." He brought the phone to his ear. "Sheriff Davis." He turned sharply toward the hill on the other side of the parking lot and stared into the darkness. "No. Are your lights on?"

Aimee watched the sheriff's eyes searching the gloom on the other side of the store and followed his gaze. She couldn't see anything.

He scratched his ear. "Do you see us?"

He held up his flashlight and flipped it on and off twice.

A pause. "Ah'ight." The sheriff winced and hung up the phone. "Goddammit," he muttered, then stood for what seemed like a full minute, staring at the ground.

The deputy watched him with raised eyebrows.

The sheriff finally spoke. "Big Floyd's up on that hill over there." He jutted his chin toward the darkness that loomed above the other side of the parking lot.

The deputy's head snapped in that direction. He looked back at the sheriff. "What's he doing?"

The sheriff grimaced. "Recon."

"Aw, hell." The deputy kicked the dirt. "Will he stay there?"

The sheriff shook his head.

"Respectfully, sir, we should just send him right back home." The deputy seemed slightly terrified as he said this. "I know he likes to run things, but he's got no call to be in the middle of this. He barely knows that girl."

The sheriff blew out a long breath through clinched teeth, which made a whistling sound. "That dog ain't gonna hunt, Ronnie, and you know it."

The deputy sighed.

"Besides, he thinks that Navigator down there belongs to his daughter-in-law."

Aimee felt her heart thud. *Gillian?* Lots of people thought Gillian was a snob, but Aimee had always found her to be kind.

"Yep," the sheriff nodded. "And he is fit to be tied."

◆ ◆ ◆

Gillian gave Drew a wide berth and made her way over to Lianna, who had slid down and was sitting with her back to one of the front windows. The light from the refrigerators barely reached that part of the store. Once Gillian was close enough, she could see that Lianna's face was ashen.

"H-How bad?" Lianna whispered, holding her shaking hand up so that the wound faced Gillian, who knelt in front of her. "I can't—" Lianna looked away.

Gillian's stomach was a knotted ball of fishing line, but she forced herself to examine the wound.

A large flap of skin was ripped and bleeding, revealing flesh that was never supposed to see the light of day.

Gillian forced her face to remain passive. "It's not that bad," she said with more conviction than she felt. She peered over her shoulder.

Drew stood in front of the now-silent phone, still as a statue.

She turned back and saw Lianna wince and begin to turn her hand.

Gillian reached for Lianna's wrist and held it in place. With her other hand, she took Lianna's chin in the firm-yet-gentle hold she used with her kids and stared straight into Lianna's eyes. "Don't look yet. Just trust me that it's not that bad."

Only when Lianna nodded did Gillian let go, squinting at the darkened shelves next to her and hoping the first aid section was nearby. It wasn't, but there was toilet paper within reach. She grabbed a package of four rolls, tore the plastic as quietly as she could, and fashioned a makeshift bandage, which she pressed onto Lianna's palm.

"Thanks," Lianna said quietly.

Gillian crawled around to sit beside her, keeping Lianna's hand softly grasped in her own. "You're welcome." She shivered beneath the plastic rain poncho and wondered how bad things were going to get before Big Floyd found them. *Surely the sheriff would have seen their cars?* Her eyes searched the shadows for Drew. He was still standing by the counter, and although she was afraid to look directly at him, she could have sworn he was having some kind of conversation with the tower of sunglasses.

"What are we going to do?" Lianna whispered.

Gillian, still holding Lianna's hand, answered softly but firmly. "We are going to wait for Big Floyd to come get us. Because come hell or high water, he will."

Drew crossed the open space between the counter and the shelves, taking strange, tiny steps and muttering to himself. He seemed to have forgotten they were there. He picked up a bag of something heavy—charcoal?—from the bottom of a nearby aisle and tottered back the way he had come.

Gillian could feel Lianna trembling beside her.

Drew laid the bag of charcoal in front of the counter, stood, and kicked it.

Lianna's body jerked as if he'd kicked her.

He turned his head in a swift motion toward them. "The time is now," he said crisply before turning and beginning another conversation with the sunglasses.

"Ohmigod." Lianna began to shake.

Gillian put her arm around Lianna's shoulder. "And while we wait for Big Floyd, I'm gonna find a way to get that gun."

Still shaking, Lianna nodded but didn't say anything.

Gillian held her as hard as she could. When the shuddering didn't subside, Gillian slipped back in front of Lianna, blocking her view of Drew, who was now chattering loudly at the glasses. "Lianna?" Gillian took Lianna's face in her hands, whispering in the voice she used with the kids when they woke from nightmares. "You're out here to buy Big Floyd's bank, right?"

"Wh-What?" Lianna croaked, her eyes darting several places before they found Gillian's.

"You're out here to buy Big Floyd's bank?" Gillian asked again, her voice low and calm as she checked Lianna's bandage. It was already seeping with blood. She scooted back to grab the toilet paper, sliding her hand down to Lianna's ankle and holding that as she went. "What do you do at the bank?"

"What do I—*what*?" Lianna's eyebrows were nearly pinched together.

"What's your job, hon?" Gillian said, her voice quiet and steady as she unwound the toilet paper. She risked a quick glance over at Drew, who was muttering at another bag of charcoal.

When she turned back, she could see Lianna's eyes beginning

to focus. "I'm the senior vice president of strategic analysis for high-yield revenue targets and emerging business lines."

Good Lord. Gillian swallowed. "So you live in New York?" she asked as she folded a new bandage. She peeked over her shoulder. Drew had just laid another bag of charcoal down in front of the sunglasses, still squarely between her and the gun.

Gillian turned back to see Lianna gaping at him and squeezed her ankle. "You live in New York?"

Lianna's eyes found Gillian's. "Yeah."

"You have family there?" Gillian took Lianna's hand and peeled away the first dressing.

Lianna winced. "No."

Gillian frowned as the bloody bandage came apart in her hand. She wished she'd been able to find some peroxide. "Boyfriend? Girlfriend?" Gillian asked, feeling incredibly progressive. She blew on the wound.

"Not recently."

Gillian blew again. "Where's your mama and daddy?"

"My mother's in Philly."

Gently, Gillian pushed the new compress into Lianna's palm. "And your daddy?"

Lianna let out a slow breath. "He died when I was little."

Bless her heart. No wonder she's so rude. Gillian placed her hand on Lianna's cheek. "Oh, honey."

Lianna swallowed. "He shot himself when I was six."

❖ ❖ ❖

Aimee heard Big Floyd's Chevy Tahoe before she saw it creeping down the road with the lights off.

Sheriff Davis turned to the deputy. "Get Maggie back on the phone. Tell her I need her to go get Buck from the cabin right now and bring him here."

The deputy hung up just as Big Floyd's truck pulled to a stop next to them. "She's on her way."

Big Floyd jumped out of the truck, his phone pressed to his ear. "What in the hell do you mean, taking the night off?" He bellowed. "What in the goddamn hell does that even mean, son?" He continued to berate whoever was on the other end of the line, but Aimee stopped hearing the words because she was too startled by what she was seeing.

Big Floyd wore a trim navy robe. Blue-and-white-striped pajamas poked out from his cuffs, collar, and underneath the hem. His bare heels were visible in leather house slippers. For a moment, all of Aimee's thoughts were replaced by the bewildered notion that never in a million years did she think she would see Big Floyd in his PJs.

The strangest thing was that his outfit did nothing to diminish his commanding presence. The robe was tightly tied and his back ramrod straight as he stood and continued to yell into the phone.

"Boy, I am looking at her car now! It's right next to the car of the girl who's missing, and the store's completely dark! Can you think of a single *good* reason they'd have left them there like that?"

Aimee took a quick peek at the sheriff and deputy, who appeared as dumbfounded as she felt.

Big Floyd glared into the distance for several moments before snarling something Aimee couldn't interpret and hanging up. He turned to the sheriff, and even though he wasn't looking at her, Aimee could feel the heat of Big Floyd's gaze.

"Little Floyd hasn't talked to Gillian since this afternoon." His long arm stretched toward the store. "That's her Navigator down there."

The sheriff cleared his throat. "Floyd, we don't know for sure—"

"BJX62V," Big Floyd barked.

The deputy's head swiveled between the two other men. "What?"

Big Floyd narrowed his eyes at him. "BJX62V."

The sheriff nodded toward the store. "Check the plate, Ronnie."

The deputy turned and raised his binoculars. When he put them down, his face was paler than before. He nodded. "Yes, sir, that's the license plate number."

Big Floyd exploded. "How in the hell is it that you two sons-a-bitches have been out here for the last half hour and you did not know that?"

"Floyd—" The sheriff held up a hand.

"And how *in the hell* is it that you are still standing up here?" Once again, Big Floyd thrust his arm toward the store. "When you should be down there!"

The sheriff took a deep breath just as the deputy answered defensively. "We did go down there, and the place is empty."

"You went inside the store?"

The sheriff opened his mouth, but the deputy spoke first. "The store is locked and empty, sir."

Big Floyd bared his teeth. "You sure about that?"

"Sir." The young deputy was turning the color of a beet. "We've got this under control, and as a civilian, you have no call being out here. Why don't you just go on home and—"

Big Floyd took a step forward. Aimee was sure he was going to punch the deputy.

The sheriff rubbed his hands over his face and stepped between them. "Everybody just settle down." He dropped his hands to his hips and stood up straighter. "Floyd, I've got a dozen messages into Buck—"

"Buck's probably passed out at the cabin!"

"Maggie's on her way up there to get him right now." The

sheriff took a step toward Big Floyd. "She'll have him here in a half hour, and we can go inside to look around."

Big Floyd's mouth was a pinched line.

The sheriff stared at him for several moments. "Okay?"

"Ah'ight," Big Floyd said with a curt nod.

The sheriff turned back to the deputy.

Aimee watched in amazement as from the depths of his robe—she would never be sure where he'd hidden it—Big Floyd withdrew a handgun.

He bent his arm so that the long barrel pointed straight up to the sky.

Without a word, he began marching down the hill.

◆ ◆ ◆

"He shot himself when I was six," Lianna had just said. Her expression implied she couldn't believe she'd said the words out loud.

The ache in Gillian's heart grew bigger. "Oh, Lianna," she said too loudly.

Lianna raised a shaky finger to her lips. "Shhhh."

They both turned toward Drew. He was talking to the sunglasses again. He picked up the bag of charcoal he'd just put down and crossed to one of the other aisles, still taking those strange baby steps. "The time is now," he said to no one in particular as he laid the bag down. His movements were becoming more and more jerky. His statements more emphatic.

"Do you really know how to shoot that gun?" Lianna whispered.

Gillian felt her body go cold as the shadow memories she'd been pushing away since she first saw the shotgun surged forward. "It's been years. I haven't touched one since I was in middle school, but yes, my daddy taught me." She could still remember the sunshine of her father's attention on the day she'd asked if he would teach her how to shoot like her brothers—could still feel the warmth of his body against her back as he knelt behind her in the field, gently positioning her left hand under the fore-end and her right under the grip of the little twenty-gauge. She was ten years old the first time they went target shooting.

"Don't worry," Gillian said to Lianna. "Big Floyd will find us soon."

"No!" They both turned just in time to see Drew slap the circular rack of sunglasses. The tower wobbled and spun but, unbelievably, didn't fall over. The glasses jiggled violently.

They looked at each other.

"Soon enough?" Lianna asked in a hoarse whisper.

Gillian bit her lip.

They turned back toward Drew just in time to see him kick another bag of charcoal.

Lianna swallowed and pointed to the right end of the refrigerated wall on the opposite side of the store. "I could run to that back corner."

Gillian's eyes followed Lianna's finger. If Lianna could draw Drew into that corner—the farthest point from where the two of them sat huddled by the front windows—Gillian might have time to reach the gun.

"Could you get to the gun by the time"— Lianna's voice caught— "by the time he gets to me?"

Gillian looked down at Lianna's hand. The new bandage would be dripping blood any minute. "Are you sure you don't want me to be the decoy?"

"I'm not touching that fucking gun," Lianna said too loudly.

Both their heads snapped toward Drew. He was turning in a small circle. "The time is now!" he shouted.

"Can you get there?" Lianna whispered, slipping off her heels.

Gillian looked back toward the counter. "God willing and the creek don't rise," she muttered under her breath.

"*What?*"

Gillian nodded and squeezed Lianna's arm. "I can get there." As quietly as she could, Gillian ducked her head through the poncho and pulled it off. She planted her feet and lifted herself into a low crouch. "Try to keep an aisle between him and you for as long as you can."

Lianna nodded. She stood and sprinted toward the back of the room.

◆ ◆ ◆

Aimee watched the deputy take in Big Floyd's gun and fumble for his own.

Sheriff Davis stopped short when the deputy pulled out his firearm and followed the deputy's gaze. "Goddammit, Floyd. Stop right there!" the sheriff yelled. He turned back to the deputy—who now had his gun up and aimed. "Jesus, Mary, and Joseph, Ronnie! Put that back before someone gets hurt!"

The deputy did as he was told.

Big Floyd continued walking.

In several loping strides, the sheriff overtook Big Floyd and stepped in front of him. He raised his hands toward Big Floyd's shoulders but didn't touch him. "Floyd, I do not want to take you down, but—"

"You can sure try," Big Floyd said in a cheerful voice that was terrifying. He stepped to the side, around the sheriff, and continued his march toward the parking lot.

The sheriff glared at Big Floyd's back. "Suit yourself! But who's gonna go get Gillian if you and I are rolling around out here like pigs in shit?"

Big Floyd stopped, the gun still pointed at the stars.

"Lower the weapon, sir!" the deputy shouted, reaching for his gun again.

Big Floyd whipped around and thundered something Aimee couldn't understand.

The sheriff held up a hand toward the deputy. "Goddammit, Ronnie, I told you to stand down."

The deputy let his empty hands drop to his sides.

Big Floyd stuck the gun into the belt of his robe.

The three men stared at each other.

"Damn it to hell." The sheriff reached into his pocket and tossed a set of keys to the deputy. "Get my bolt cutter and a crowbar from the back of the truck. We're not gonna wait for Buck." He looked at Big Floyd. "I'm not gonna tell you not to come with us because I know you're gonna do whatever you damn well please." He jabbed a finger through the air. "But you keep your hands off that gun, and you stay behind me and Ronnie."

Big Floyd just stared at him.

"Sheriff!" The deputy was holding binoculars to his eyes. "Something's happening down there."

12.

Gillian bounded a single step forward, then stopped. Drew wasn't running toward Lianna. "Let there be light!" he hollered, racing behind the counter and flipping a switch. The room blazed as the fluorescent bulbs shimmered to life.

Gillian blinked, trying to adjust her eyes.

In the farthest corner of the store, Lianna stood at the very end of the last row of shelves, the terror on her face slowly melting into confusion.

"The time is now!" Drew yelled, arms outstretched as he turned in a circle. He was directly between Gillian and the gun.

She could see Lianna, who stared back helplessly.

Drew baby-stepped to each of the charcoal bags. There were four he'd placed at the ends of the aisles closest to the counter and several piled on top of one another in front of the cash register. He began to turn each one over, never more than three feet from Gillian's path to the gun.

Gillian looked toward Lianna again.

Lianna pulled in a shaky breath. "Hey, Fuckface!" she yelled from the back of the store.

◆ ◆ ◆

Aimee felt her body jump when she saw the lights of the store come on.

"Ronnie, what do you see?" the sheriff called as he jogged back toward the deputy, who was still peering through the binoculars.

"There's a bald man, and he's—" The deputy didn't finish.

"What's he doing, damn it?"

"He's just sort of"—the deputy sounded baffled—"he's just sort of turning in circles, sir."

"The store's locked and empty," Big Floyd growled as he peered through a small monocular that had materialized from somewhere in the depths of the robe. "I see Gillian. There's another woman at the back of the store."

"All the bald man's doing is moving things around," the deputy said defensively. "The ladies seem fine." He lifted the strap from his neck and handed the binoculars to the sheriff.

The sheriff raised them to his eyes. Abruptly, he lowered them and looked at Aimee. He raised them and turned toward the store again.

"Do you still want the bolt cutters, sir?" the deputy asked the sheriff.

The sheriff didn't answer. He handed the binoculars to Aimee, a strange expression on his face.

She peered through them, taking a moment to focus her eyes. The signs pasted on the front windows blocked much of the view inside. There was a bald man with his back to her, hunched over something in front of the counter. A blonde ponytail—Gillian?— was just visible above a sign about coffee. A dark-haired woman seemed to be searching for something on one of the back shelves.

The man stood up straight, still facing away from Aimee.

There was something strangely familiar about him.

His arms shot rigidly up next to his ears.

An unwanted-but-not-yet-understood knowing began to buzz in Aimee's head.

The man jumped up and down, flexing and splaying his hands.

The humming in Aimee's brain got louder and moved to her chest.

The man turned, and Aimee saw his face clearly.

She let the binoculars fall and doubled over just as the sheriff reached for her. "When was the last time you saw Andy?" he asked.

Before Aimee could answer, Big Floyd's voice rang out behind them. "I see a shotgun!"

◆ ◆ ◆

Gillian's mouth fell open as Drew began to jump up and down and holler—his arms by his ears and his hands making strange, jerky motions. She swallowed a gasp as Lianna hurled a roll of paper towels right at him and screamed, "I'm back here, motherfucker!"

The paper towels whizzed right by Drew. He stopped whooping and watched them roll across the floor.

Gillian's heart was pounding so hard, she thought it was going to explode from her chest.

Drew didn't move.

Another roll of paper towels came flying.

Feeling sick, Gillian crouched again, waiting for Drew to move. He seemed completely oblivious to her.

"You sick fucking fuck!" Lianna reared back like a baseball pitcher and launched a can of Aqua Net.

The can bounced off Drew's chest. He watched it clatter to the floor.

He turned, his eyes narrowed at Lianna.

❖ ❖ ❖

Aimee gripped her stomach as her mother's voice reeled through her head, "You can be so selfish sometimes, and for the life of me I cannot figure out why."

Aimee had just broken the news that she was moving to Bramble Briar to work at the bank's headquarters. Guilt and shame had washed over her, but somehow, she'd managed to stand her ground.

"Andy needs you," her mother had said.

"I'm not abandoning him, Mom."

Although that's exactly what she'd done.

Aimee didn't feel her knees give way. But suddenly she was sitting on the hard, weedy ground, and the sheriff was kneeling beside her.

Through a stream of tears, she gazed into his kind but troubled eyes.

"I could have stopped this. I—"

"Sheriff," the deputy called. "It's heating up down there. We've got to move."

❖ ❖ ❖

Gillian watched Drew, both wishing he would move and hoping that he wouldn't. She could see the gun on the counter behind him. Memories of those faraway days learning how to shoot came hurtling toward her as she tried to remember what to do when she reached it.

The evenings target shooting with her daddy were still among her most vivid memories of him. Out in the field behind their house, with the wind ruffling his hair, he'd smile in a way he didn't at home. At night, they'd sit on the floor of the living room with the gun in pieces between their legs as he showed her how to clean and care for it. Those moments were when she learned who her daddy really was. Instead of tight-lipped, exhausted smiles, he actually talked. He talked about when he'd rodeoed back in high school, something neither he nor her mother had ever mentioned before. He talked about growing up on a farm in Arkansas and a pet pig who slept in his room. Story after story, revealing a man she never could have imagined.

Her daddy never seemed more proud than the day he began pulling the clay pigeons—little terra-cotta disks that he hurled into the air with a strange machine that looked sort of like a record player—and Gillian had hit more than she missed.

When she was fourteen, he invited her to come out with him and her brothers for the opening day of dove season.

She'd sat next to him in the truck, her hands trailing up and down the sleeves of the camouflage shirt he'd surprised her with that morning. Every few minutes, she touched the matching hat and adjusted her long braided ponytail.

Her mama had sent them off with ham sandwiches and thermoses—his filled with coffee, hers with chocolate milk.

Gillian had loved every minute of that day, right up until the dogs raised the first bevy. Right up until she'd followed the small gray shape through the sight and pulled the trigger.

Something shattered inside Gillian when the tiny body jerked midflight and began free-falling to the earth. Her father grinned and patted her on the back while silent tears burned her eyes.

He was aghast the following weekend when she refused to go back out.

Gillian hadn't touched a gun since.

The ice water pouring back into her veins, Gillian watched Drew's eyes move from the Aqua Net bouncing on the floor to Lianna in the back of the room.

◆ ◆ ◆

When Drew's eyes locked on hers, the pounding inside Lianna began again.

She gripped a shelf on the back of the farthest aisle, waiting to see which side he would take when he came. Because looking into those dead eyes—he seemed completely unaware of Gillian, crouched less than ten feet from him—there was no fucking doubt that he was coming. Lianna remembered the drain stopper in her pocket. She reached for it, her fingers clamping around the small piece of metal.

Drew pointed a long finger in her direction. "The! Time! Is! Now!"

He leapt into the back refrigerated aisle and raced toward Lianna like a man shot from a cannon.

Lianna lurched the other way—toward the front windows— keeping herself as far from Gillian as she could.

Drew bolted around the corner after her.

When Lianna reached the front, there was nowhere to go except toward Gillian, who was almost to the gun.

Lianna felt a surge of hope as she passed the end of the aisle and saw Gillian skid behind the counter.

Then a boulder seemed to slam into her from the right.

The drain stopper fell to the floor with a tiny clatter.

Everything disappeared as Lianna fought—and failed—to breathe.

◆ ◆ ◆

Aimee was down the hill and halfway through the parking lot before she heard the sheriff and Big Floyd yell for her. When the deputy had called out that the dark-haired lady was throwing things, the men knelt to the ground. Big Floyd began barking orders and drawing lines in the dirt with his finger.

Aimee quietly slipped away.

As she began to run toward the store, she had a better view through the clear glass doors and could see Andy racing toward the back of the room.

The dark-haired woman that had to be Lianna came sprinting toward the windows.

Aimee gasped when she realized Andy was chasing her.

He wheeled into the aisle next to the one Lianna was running along.

Easily he passed her, reaching the open space between the shelves and the counter before she did.

Lianna ran right into him.

Aimee got to the front door just as Andy rammed his shoulder into Lianna's stomach, like a linebacker scooping up an unprotected quarterback. With a sickening thud, she heard Lianna's body crash into the floor.

Aimee heard herself scream. At his absolute worst, Andy had never hurt anyone before. Even when the deputies had wrestled with him that first time he was sick, Andy had stopped struggling almost instantly.

Aimee wrenched at the doors, but they wouldn't open.

She pounded on the glass and yelled Andy's name.

◆ ◆ ◆

Gillian picked up the gun with a nauseating familiarity and opened the break action. Her stomach flinched when she confirmed it was loaded. She turned, just as Drew slammed Lianna to the floor.

Gillian flicked off the safety, shocked as her hands moved over the gun with a knowledge she was surprised she still had. Her left hand spiraled around the fore-end as her right slipped under the grip and took the weight. Her head filled with the image of that poor falling dove bird and one single thought, *Lord Almighty, don't make me shoot that boy.*

Lianna wasn't moving.

Drew stood over her, his hands clenched into fists.

In one swift motion, Gillian raised the gun and pulled the butt into the soft spot at her right armpit. Her insides were like a blender, but her hand remained steady as she peered through the sight and aimed at Drew's back.

Drew straddled Lianna and knelt.

Oh Lord, don't make me shoot that boy, Gillian thought as she followed Drew's back with the sight. She pressed her cheek against the smooth, creamy wood of the stock and exhaled, just like her daddy had taught her. An image of Drew gently placing the iced towel on Carly's arm filled her mind. Gillian planted her feet and braced herself for the kick. *Oh Lord, please don't make me shoot that boy!*

The most desperate shriek she'd ever heard erupted from the front doors.

Through the sight, she saw Drew's body rise.

A woman was yelling, "Andy! Andy!"

Gillian pulled the gun away from her face, her arms automatically pointing it at the ceiling.

She blinked.

Aimee Harmon was banging on the glass door and screaming like she was on fire.

◆ ◆ ◆

"Andy! Let me in!" Aimee howled as soon as Andy looked up.

Her eyes fluttered down to Lianna, who lay like a rag doll a child had carelessly thrown to the ground. Aimee glanced back up at Andy, pressing against the glass and trying with all her energy to draw him to her.

Andy leaned back onto his heels.

"Andy!" Aimee screamed again.

She felt her panic loosen the tiniest bit when he stood and began walking toward her. But as soon as she registered his eyes—flat, unreadable pools that seemed to have no connection to the cousin she loved—her mouth went dry.

He reached into his pocket and pulled out a ring of keys.

Aimee could feel her palms pressed against the glass, beginning to sweat during the interminable moment it took for him to open the padlock. She took a step back.

Andy was still holding the chain when he pushed the door open and stepped outside.

She took another step back, unable to stop staring at his pale face and bald, sweaty head.

Andy stepped closer to her.

Aimee forced herself to stay still.

There was movement behind him.

Aimee could see past him and gasped. Gillian was standing over Lianna and aiming a shotgun right at them.

◆ ◆ ◆

Gillian wanted to call out to Aimee, but her voice wouldn't work. She'd lowered the gun back down and had Drew squarely in the sight as she hurried over to Lianna, who still hadn't moved.

"Don't shoot, Gillian!" Aimee shrieked, stepping between Gillian and Drew. "The sheriff's coming!"

Gillian pointed the gun to the ceiling again.

"You called the sheriff?" Drew's face twisted in rage. Suddenly, he was yanking Aimee down by the hair, pulling her into a near backbend. His other hand, still clenching the chain, swept up into the air.

Aimee screamed.

Gillian's arms lowered the barrel of the gun without her telling them what to do. Drew's chest came smoothly into the sight.

Several things happened then, seemingly all at once.

A dark figure leapt from the shadows as a man's voice that Gillian didn't recognize yelled something.

There was a shot.

Drew, the dark figure, and Aimee crumpled to the ground.

13.

"Nine plus three is twelve! Nine times three is twenty-seven! Nine divided by three is *fucking* three! Stop asking me these stupid, fucking questions!"

The nurse—a large woman with a poof of gray hair who had just asked Lianna what nine plus three was—pressed her neatly painted lips together. "There is no need for profanity, Ms. Matthews." She wrote something on the chart she held in her hand. "And nobody likes a show-off," she added just loud enough for Lianna to hear.

Lianna scowled at the sleeves of her hospital gown, feeling like she was wearing a Kleenex. "I do not have a concussion," she said, ignoring the strange, buoyant feeling of her head.

"The doctor wants a CT scan," the nurse said, staring her down with a steely gaze.

Lianna turned her head away, which sent a wave of dizziness rippling through her. This was the second nurse who'd come in and asked her idiotic questions. She had no idea how long she'd been stuck in this freezing room.

"Is Gillian here?" she asked as the nurse scribbled something else on the clipboard.

The nurse glared at her. "Ms. Wilkins is with her husband." Then she swiveled and exited the room, her shiny-white orthopedic shoes squeaking as she went.

"But how long do I have to—"

The door shut.

Lianna lay back on the pillows and winced. It shouldn't have been a surprise that Gillian had abandoned her in this hick hospital to go home to her fucking mansion and be comforted by her fucking, dipshit husband.

The last image in Lianna's mind was of Gillian running toward the gun. Then, nothing. She woke on a stretcher. In the distance, she'd seen Gillian, wrapped in a blanket and crying hysterically. Gillian was standing, so she couldn't have been hurt badly.

Lianna had a vague memory of trying to convince the EMTs that she didn't need to go to the hospital. It was possible she had called them fuckwits.

And now she was stuck in this freezing room.

She studied the white gauzy bandages covering her right palm—which was throbbing—then pushed that memory away and turned to the putty-colored phone.

There was no one she wanted to call.

Someone knocked on the door.

Lianna tried to ignore the hope surging through her that perhaps Gillian hadn't deserted her after all. "Come in!" she called more eagerly than intended. She raised her fingers to her pulsing temple.

A man in uniform stepped through the door, a large hat held against his chest. "How're you feeling there, Ms. Matthews?"

"I'm recovering," she answered docilely, deciding that perhaps this man could help her gain her freedom if she behaved.

"I'm Sheriff Davis," he said in a gentle voice. "Do you think you might feel well enough to tell us what happened?"

Fucking hell. Gillian couldn't even be bothered to tell the police what they'd been through? Lianna blew out a rush of irritated air. "Gillian hasn't talked to you yet?"

A strange expression passed over the sheriff's face. "She's still with her husband."

Lianna's lips twisted in disgust. "I'm sure she was anxious to get back home to that asshole, but I would have thought you'd at least have gotten her to tell you something."

The sheriff appeared pained.

"Seriously. I'm stuck in here"—Lianna flicked at the flimsy hospital gown—"and I'm the one who's got to bring you guys up to speed?" She glared at the empty space in front of her. "I hate this fucking place."

"Ms. Matthews." The sheriff's bushy eyebrows drew together. "Gillian's husband was shot."

❖ ❖ ❖

Aimee sat in the glacial waiting room of the mental ward feeling as if she were in a horrible but familiar dream. The colorful blue and orange cushions on the chairs and magazines spread on the coffee table—all designed to make people feel normal—simply couldn't outweigh the antiseptic smell or the sensation of disbelief and defeat that swirled through any person unfortunate enough to be sitting in this room. The chairs were new, but the room was much like it had been before. Never in a million years did she think she'd be back here again.

She stared at her phone, knowing she should call her mother. Her fingers wouldn't budge.

Her purse, Lianna's purse, and Lianna's backpack were piled on the seat next to her. In the aftermath of Buck's, Aimee had found herself dying for a bathroom. Tiptoeing into the disgusting one there, she'd discovered Lianna's purse and the keys to her rental car. Thinking Lianna shouldn't have to ride back for it, she'd driven the Altima to the hospital. Now, Aimee wondered how she was going to get back to her Mustang.

I should call Mom, she thought.

She dropped her phone in her purse and smoothed her hand over the exquisite leather of Lianna's Prada backpack. Aimee had been afraid to leave it in the car in the hospital parking lot.

She hoped Lianna was okay. She'd lurked outside Lianna's hospital room for a while, unable to summon the courage to go inside. When the sheriff appeared, Aimee had fled to the mental ward, hoping he hadn't seen her.

Through the double doors next to the reception window, she could see a young man watching something on his iPad.

They would be observing Andy now.

She wasn't really needed. Andy had technically been arrested, so the sheriff and deputy were responsible for the paperwork. But Aimee knew it would be better for Andy if she stayed. Her thoughts drifted to the second time he had gotten sick.

She could still remember the panicked call from Andy's roommate, his junior year at UT Tyler. Aimee had no idea how her mother was paying for Andy's college but assumed Josh was helping. Aimee had just started working at the bank's office in Sweet Leaf and lived in a tiny apartment about five minutes from her mom's house.

Once again, Aimee had driven through the night in a shocked panic. Andy was on the football team. His grades weren't great, but they were passing. He always seemed to have a girlfriend. *How could this be happening again?* By the time Aimee arrived at his apartment, Andy had been taken away in an ambulance. He hadn't done anything more than run around the living room whooping, but that had frightened his roommate enough to call campus security. She'd known before she entered Andy's bedroom what she would find.

The next morning, she phoned her manager at the bank and said that her cousin had to have an emergency appendectomy.

She spent the next three days painting Andy's room and visiting the hospital, where she made friends with the nurses. Thankfully, Andy had health insurance through the school.

Just like the first time Andy was hospitalized, Aimee had found that adding a sane, sympathetic face to that of the patient mattered. *A lot.* She could still see the transformation of those nurses faces—from exhausted fury at dealing with Andy when he was first brought in, to grandmotherly sympathy once they met Aimee. "Be glad you got this doctor and not that one," one whispered conspiratorially the day Andy's treating physician was assigned. "He didn't like the chicken fried steak last night, so I got him some extra Jell-O," one said when Aimee arrived the third morning. "He really liked the eggs, so I got him a second helping at breakfast," she said a day later.

When Andy refused to go back to school, Aimee packed up his things—alone and working through the night—then moved him back to her mom's in Sweet Leaf.

After a few months, Aimee had helped him get the job at the hospital.

The next year, he'd moved out of her mother's house and into his own apartment.

Aimee leaned back in the blue cushioned chair that looked like it would be comfortable but was not, and waited.

The scene at Buck's came hurtling back to her.

She and Andy were standing on the sidewalk, just outside the door.

"You called the sheriff!" She'd never seen Andy so enraged.

He's never hurt anyone—the thought kept circling through Aimee's mind. Even when Andy grabbed her hair. Even when he yanked her backward. Even when she realized she was screaming as she looked up and saw the chain in his fist.

"Drop the chain!" someone had yelled.

Then something—*someone*—came hurtling out of the shadows from the side of the store.

The sound of a shot stung Aimee's ears as Andy was knocked away from her.

Then she was falling.

The next thing she saw was Andy and the dark figure rolling on the ground.

The sheriff, deputy, and Big Floyd were pounding through the parking lot into the semicircle of light.

Then everything seemed to unfold in slow motion: The deputy—his face blanched and pasty—holstering his handgun and staring at the dark figure with something like terror in his eyes. The sheriff, grabbing the deputy by the shoulder and propelling him toward Andy, who had rolled a few feet away and was trying to get up, the chain still gripped in his hand. The deputy's head twitching before he blew out a breath, dove on top of Andy, and wrestled the chain away.

As she scrambled over to Andy and the deputy, Aimee was aware of the sheriff shouting into his walkie-talkie and of Gillian screaming.

Then Aimee heard the low moans of someone who sounded like he was in terrible pain.

She followed the sound to the spot where Andy had fallen and saw a man writhing on the ground. He wore a camouflage jumpsuit and a hat with leafy twigs sticking out from the top. Dark green paint—the kind Ray used to wear when he went duck hunting—was smudged all over the man's face.

Big Floyd was on his knees beside him and managed to catch Gillian as she leapt nearly on top of them. The man's head turned toward Aimee.

Even with the face paint, she recognized him immediately.

Her heart sank as Trip Wilkins arched his back and thrashed from side to side.

◆ ◆ ◆

Gillian—her body still shaking—knocked on the door to Lianna's hospital room. Over her workout clothes, she wore a brown parka that came almost to her knees with the word SHERIFF printed across the back.

"Come in," Lianna called, sounding grumpier than ever.

Gillian stepped inside.

Lianna's expression changed instantly. "Is he—"

Gillian shook her head and busied herself pouring a glass of water that Lianna hadn't asked for.

Lianna gulped the entire drink down.

Gillian refilled Lianna's cup. "How're you feeling, hon?"

"How am *I*?" Lianna choked through the water. She wiped the back of her hand across her mouth and cleared her throat. "How are you?"

Gillian felt the wet heat of tears spill out. The scene from Buck's tumbled back on top of her.

A shot rang out.

But Gillian couldn't remember pulling the trigger. Confused, she studied the gun, steady and cool in her hands. There was no puff of singed-smelling smoke.

Automatically, she flicked on the safety and pointed the gun to the ceiling.

Her ears pricked up at the sound of a low moan, which she'd known immediately was Trip.

In what felt like one motion, she laid the gun on the ground and flew out the door.

Big Floyd was somehow there, kneeling over Trip and tearing at the top of Trip's coveralls.

Then Gillian was on top of them, pressing her hands to Trip's face—which was painted up like he'd just come from a duck blind—running her fingers over his head and chest, certain a flood of crimson would spread through any second.

But she couldn't find any blood.

From what seemed like far away, she could hear the sheriff shouting for an ambulance.

The deputy stepped forward but froze when Big Floyd shot out a hand and snarled at him.

Then Big Floyd's arms were underneath Trip, his head slowly shaking from side to side. He leaned closer to Trip's face. "What kind is it, son?"

Trip drew in a shuddery breath. "Level IV, Dad."

Big Floyd closed his eyes and let out a breath.

Gillian's frantic hands continued to feel around Trip's neck.

Then the sheriff was kneeling next to Big Floyd, and they were mumbling and pushing her away and turning Trip over, and Gillian might have been screaming that they weren't supposed to do that.

She nearly threw up when she saw the ragged tear in the back of Trip's coveralls.

She kept waiting to see the blood.

"Help me get this off," Big Floyd ordered, his hands tearing at Trip's sleeves. "He could've ruptured a lung."

The sheriff took hold of the other side and gingerly began to peel Trip's jumpsuit down.

Gillian braced herself for the blood.

Still, there wasn't any.

For a long while, Gillian simply stared at the silver blob, splattered into the lower left back of the black vest.

Then she understood.

She leaned back on her heels as her voice rose. "When in God's name and for what purpose, Trip, did you buy a bulletproof vest?"

Trip raised his head and tried to look at her. He winced and rested his forehead back on the asphalt. "Because I thought you might let me take Bobbie hunting if we wore them."

"TRIP—"The word came out as a roar.

"Ma'am, you need to calm down."The deputy—his face pale and sweaty—stood well away from Big Floyd and thrust a muscular arm at her.

The sheriff looked back at him, shaking his head. "Ronnie—"

Gillian's eyes shifted from her husband—who was facedown on a sidewalk, shot, and nearly shot by her—to the deputy. "Calm down?"

The sheriff's head swiveled back to her. "Gillian, please."

Big Floyd—wearing pajamas and a robe, she realized for the first time—spoke to her like she was a spooked horse. "Gilly, hon, everything's gonna be okay."

She glanced to the right where Drew was laid out with his hands cuffed behind his back, surprisingly still. Aimee knelt beside him, dabbing his bloody cheek—he must have hit it when he fell—with the hem of her dress. Aimee met Gillian's eyes. *I'm so sorry*, Aimee mouthed before looking away in what Gillian could see was the worst kind of shame.

Gillian gazed back into the store where Lianna was curled on the floor like a baby. She turned back to the men. She stood.

All three men held up their palms.

"Ma'am."The deputy's voice was a quiet warning.

"Easy does it," the sheriff said softly.

"Gillybean—" Big Floyd said.

A rumbling started up inside her unlike anything she'd ever felt.

"God fucking damn it to motherfucking Goddamn hell!" someone screamed. After a moment, Gillian realized it had been her. Her brain was aghast that she had said such awful things, but her body felt like a dam had burst and the sickening terror of the last few hours—not to mention all the worry and confusion she'd been feeling since the party—flew out her mouth and disappeared into the ether. She stuck out a trembling finger and swung it in a wide arc that swept across each man's face.

The deputy took a step back, his eyes wide.

The sheriff licked his lips.

Big Floyd didn't move.

"Don't you fucking dare tell me to fucking calm down!" she howled.

The men were staring at her like she'd just sprouted snakes from her head.

Then the dam inside Gillian really did break because for the second time that night—the fifth time in her entire adult life—the tears came. Suddenly, Big Floyd was wrapping his arms around her so hard she couldn't breathe. His chest shook as he stroked her head and chuckled, "That's my girl."

"Hel-*lo*!" Gillian retreated from the memory and saw Lianna in her hospital gown, jabbing a tissue at her.

"Thank you." Gillian took it and dabbed at her eyes.

"The sheriff said the doctor thinks your husband cracked two ribs. Besides that, he's okay?"

Gillian nodded. "They just got the X-ray back. He's gonna be sore, but other than that he's just fine."

Lianna patted Gillian's hand awkwardly. "I'm glad, Gillian. I'm really glad he's okay."

"Thank you. They just released him."

Lianna stopped patting. "Why aren't you on your fucking way home?"

Gillian answered in her mom voice, "The doctor said you can go too. And I'm not gonna leave you here."

The glee that bloomed on Lianna's face was like something

out of a Disney movie. "You'll take me to my hotel?" She sat up too quickly, then paused to steady herself.

Gillian shook her head. "The doctor won't let you go alone."

Lianna sank back on the bed. The smile vanished. "You're not possibly suggesting—"

"Yes, ma'am," Gillian said, lifting her chin. "The only way you're getting out of here is if you come home with me."

◆ ◆ ◆

Aimee woke with a start.

Her eyes opened to an unfamiliar popcorn ceiling.

As she moved, a twisting cramp seized her neck. Wincing, she closed her eyes again, trying to get her bearings. Then she remembered. The hospital. Andy. Buck's. She lay there—realizing that her body was sprawled over at least one waiting room chair, possibly two—and wished for it all to have been a very bad dream.

She opened her eyes again.

Gillian and Big Floyd were huddled a few feet away, watching her and whispering. Big Floyd had changed into his regular khaki clothes, including his hat.

In a spasm of movements, Aimee got herself upright and ran a hand through her hair. She opened her mouth, but no words wanted to come out.

Gillian's eyebrows were pinched together—obviously in justified anger—her mouth a grim line.

Big Floyd's face was the frowny mask it always was.

Aimee forced herself to stand. Whatever it was that they needed to say, she deserved it. "He's never—" Her voice caught. "I am so very, very sorry. I—"

"Aimee Eileen Harmon!"

Aimee's body jerked at the familiar voice. Still, she was shocked to turn and see her mother—clutching a cashmere wrap

over what appeared to be a silky, ankle-length nightgown—
storming through the room with a venomous look on her face.
"You just had to move away!" she screeched. "After all I've done
for you, you just had to leave your family behind!"

Aimee wished with all her heart that the floor would open up
and swallow her right there. "Mom—"

"You have always been such a selfish child!"

Aimee felt the room going fuzzy and her temples beginning
to throb. "Andy's sick again."

Her mom's fury mercifully evaporated, her eyes growing wide
and terrified. She gripped Aimee's arm. "They wouldn't tell me
what was wrong. Just that he was here. I thought he'd been in
some kind of accident!"

Aimee pulled her mother a few steps away. "No. He's *sick*.
Again. And it was really bad this time."

To Aimee's horror, her mother rolled her eyes. "After all I've
done for that boy, you'd think he could just pull it together and—"

"Mom, he's sick."

Her mother seemed to suddenly realize that Gillian and Big
Floyd were still standing there. She turned to them, her voice
polite and slightly conspiring. "He's not my son." She took a step
toward them. "He's my nephew. I took him in when my sister was
killed, and he can be a real pill."

At that moment a nurse, wearing blue and pink floral scrubs,
stepped through the double doors next to the attendant.

Aimee's heart leapt as she ran to her. "Celia!"

"Oh, honey," Celia said. "I hoped we were never going to see
you and Andy back here again."

Aimee allowed herself to sink into the warmth of Celia's hug
and feel a little less awful. "Is he asleep yet?" she whispered into
Celia's ear.

Celia pulled back and gave Aimee a pained smile. "No, baby.

They're still evaluating him." She scanned the other faces in the room. When she saw Aimee's mother, the smile disappeared. "It's gonna be *hours* before we know anything," she said loudly.

Aimee waited a beat.

The gasp-shriek erupted from her mother's mouth. "Hours?" She shook her head. "Aimee, honey, I can't stay here all night." She turned to Gillian and Big Floyd, seemingly oblivious to the disgust on their faces. "I am *go-in'* through a divorce."

"How 'bout Ronnie here drives you home?" the sheriff said as he and the deputy walked through a door on the opposite side of the room.

Aimee looked to the floor for escape again when her mother flashed a sparkling smile at the deputy and let the cashmere wrap slip a bit off her shoulders. "Why that would be lovely," her mom said breathlessly.

The deputy's face, which seemed to have finally regained some color, blanched.

"I drove myself here, but I had an Ambien earlier," Aimee's mom said as she took his arm like a high school homecoming queen being escorted off the football field. "I'm sure I shouldn't be driving. Aimee?" She turned, releasing his arm. "Honey, it's way too late for you to drive all the way back to Sweet Leaf." She rubbed Aimee's cheek before handing over a set of car keys. "You'll stay with me? Just drive my car when you come." Her face spread into a maternal smile. "And be careful, sweetheart. It's dark out." She turned back to the deputy and reclasped his arm.

Aimee felt an old familiar numbness descend then. It was partly made up of relief at disaster averted—her mom was clearly happy to be driven home by the deputy, and now Aimee would be free to properly apologize to Big Floyd and Gillian. But for the first time in her life, Aimee realized that the numbness was also a wall. A wall holding something back that, if unleased, would surely shred Aimee and her mother both to pieces.

"Best thing for you is to go to your own house and call me tomorrow," Celia said, glaring at the door Aimee's mother and the deputy had just passed through. "Won't do any good to try and see him before he gets some sleep and comes back to himself."

"Thanks, Celia," Aimee said, putting on a smile. "But I'm fine."

◆ ◆ ◆

"Give me that." Gillian reached for Lianna's sleeve—after watching Lianna try and fail to button the cuff with her wounded hand for several minutes.

Lianna scowled but obeyed.

"When you banished me to get dressed, I went to go see how Aimee was doing," Gillian said as she struggled to grasp the tiny mother-of-pearl button.

Lianna's scowl softened. "Is she okay?"

Gillian's mind wandered back over the past half hour. She'd found Aimee asleep in one of the mental ward waiting room chairs and Big Floyd brooding in the corner. Watching Aimee's beautiful, troubled face and hating to wake her, Gillian had thought again of the day Drew brought ice to Carly and of the scene from a few hours before—the way Aimee stepped in between Drew and the raised gun—exactly what Gillian would have done if she'd come upon one of her own kids in that kind of situation.

Then Gillian's mind stretched around everything the sheriff had told her and Big Floyd while they waited for Trip to be taken to X-ray: of the tragic scene the sheriff had come upon during Drew's first breakdown nine years ago; of learning from the doctors that Aimee, still practically a child herself, had handled everything at the hospital; of the hospital staff's murmurings about Aimee's mother's ability to parent.

Finally, Gillian had witnessed Aimee's wretched mother descend on Aimee right there in the waiting room! As she negotiated the stubborn button into Lianna's cuff, Gillian shared all those things with Lianna.

"Ohmigod." Lianna scowled.

"I know," Gillian said. "And the strangest thing is that Aimee, bless her heart, seems to think this whole thing is somehow her fault."

"It's not her fault her cousin's a whack job."

"He's sick."

"Who called the mother?" Lianna asked.

"Apparently, her number was in the file from last time, and *apparently*, the admittance nurse called." Gillian straightened Lianna's sleeve and released her.

Lianna folded her hands under her arms. "Where's Aimee now?"

"She left, but—"

"Why'd you let her do that?" Lianna's scowl returned. "She shouldn't be driving after all this."

Gillian searched the ceiling for strength. "I know. And she should not be going home to that awful woman. Big Floyd went after her." Gillian sniffed. "He'll make her come home with us and—"

"How many bedrooms do you have?"

Once again, Gillian looked to the ceiling. "That is not a polite question."

Lianna smirked.

Gillian sighed. "Six."

Fifteen minutes later, they exited the hospital.

◆ ◆ ◆

As Lianna moved gingerly into the muggy night air, her eyes landed on a strange scene. A tall man dressed from head to toe in khaki stood beside a giant truck. He held two purses just out of reach of a young—and very pretty—blonde woman who stretched her fingers for them helplessly. Lianna squinted. One of the purses looked just like her own. Another man sat in the front seat, his head resting against the window.

"I promise I am fine to drive," the blonde woman said emphatically. She swiped a hand up and tried to grab one of the bags again.

"Get. In. The. Car. I'll drive you to yours," the man rumbled.

The woman's arms fell to her sides.

She chewed on her thumbnail.

"We'll come back for your mama's car tomorrow," he added even more grouchily than before.

Gillian walked over and patted the arm of the tall man who, Lianna realized, had to be Big Floyd. Which meant the woman had to be—Lianna's eyes fell on the Prada backpack draped over the woman's shoulder. "Aimee, you got my computer bag!" Lianna took a quick step forward, then stopped as her head began to swim.

Aimee turned to them and gasped at Lianna's bandaged hand. She took a deep breath. "Lianna?" she asked, handing over the backpack. "I am so, so sorry. I—"

"Hey." Lianna took her bag, surprised to realize that she wasn't mad. "This isn't your fault. You found us."

Aimee nodded and turned away, rubbing the corner of one eye. "I drove your car here." She pointed to the Altima, a few spaces over. "The keys are in your purse." She motioned to Big Floyd. "I'll follow you in Lianna's car so she has it tomorrow."

"Lianna will not be needing her car tonight or tomorrow," Gillian said, nudging Lianna toward the back seat of the truck. "She's not allowed to drive yet."

Lianna wanted to argue but found she didn't have the energy. Her head was pounding.

Big Floyd turned, stomped around to the driver's door, and got in the truck—purses still clutched in his hand.

Aimee watched him, a helpless expression on her face.

Gillian turned to Aimee and gestured toward the rear passenger door. "You know there's no point in trying to argue with him."

Aimee stared at the door. She sighed and got in the truck.

G illian woke, and that corny phrase, *Today is the first day of the rest of your life*, popped into her head. She let her gaze drift over the hulky mahogany bed posts rising above her and the peach silk drapes framing the window. Emerald treetops and a swath of blue sky greeted her from outside. She smiled at her husband sleeping beside her, his head thrown back, arms bent and knees pulled to his chest—the way she imagined he must have tucked himself inside his mama's tummy before he was born.

Trip's mama. Gillian clapped a hand over her mouth as she remembered the unbelievable scene from the night before. She'd been sitting at the foot of Trip's hospital bed, waiting for an orderly to take him for the X-ray. Big Floyd, still in his robe and pajamas, sat in a chair next to them.

Mama W had burst through the door like a hurricane, wearing a khaki raincoat belted over what looked to be yellow and white polka-dot pajamas. Her hair was wound in curlers and tied up in a yellow scarf.

Without breaking stride or taking her eyes off her son, she threw a brown paper grocery bag at Big Floyd. "Here," she barked. In her other hand, she carried a pair of dirty work boots, which she dropped on the floor.

She sat down on the bed beside Trip and clasped his face in

both hands. "Little Floyd, you scared the tar outta me. If you ever do something like this again, I'm gonna shoot you myself."

Big Floyd rose and took the paper bag into the bathroom.

Trip smiled and put his hands over his mother's. "I'm fine, Mama. Just waiting for the X-ray, but they think it's only a cracked rib or two." He nodded at Gillian. "Gil had it much rougher tonight than I did."

Gillian squeezed his foot and smiled.

For the first time, Mama W looked at her daughter-in-law. She turned back to Trip. "She seems just fine to me."

"Mama." Trip frowned and turned away.

The volcano in Gillian's chest stirred.

Mama W glanced over her shoulder at Gillian again. "How could you?" she hissed. "Out in the middle of the night, and my boy getting shot because of it."

"Mama." Trip turned back to his mother, his voice a warning. "Stop."

Gillian felt the volcano began to rumble. She willed herself to stay calm.

"Don't you talk to me like that, Little Floyd." Mama W stood. "I'm not gonna take one ounce of that lip while I'm taking care of you."

"While you what?" Trip suddenly sounded like a confused and concerned child.

Gillian's head snapped to her mother-in-law.

Mama W put one hand on her hip. "This isn't up for discussion." She shook a finger at Trip, then at Gillian, then back at Trip. "You've got six bedrooms, and one of them's gonna be mine until you're well."

From what felt like somewhere outside of herself, Gillian heard a deathly quiet voice. "I don't think so." She realized it was hers.

Trip's eyes widened.

Mama W's narrowed. "I told you, it's not up for discussion." She began to dig in her purse. "And while I'm there, maybe I'll show you how to cook something that Bobbie can actually keep in his stomach for more than an hour."

"*Mama!*" Trip's voice sounded far away.

"Hush up, Trip," Mama W said, pulling out a lipstick and setting her purse on the nightstand. She ripped off the top and swished the color expertly over her mouth, her eyes never leaving her son.

"You're not staying with us." Gillian didn't remember getting up, but now she was standing.

"What in the hell is going on out there?" Big Floyd bellowed from the bathroom.

"Nothin'," Trip, Mama W, and Gillian all said at the same time.

Mama W's eyes met Gillian's as she shoved the cap back on the lipstick and tilted her head. "You're forgetting who paid for that house, sweetheart." She laughed unkindly and dropped the lipstick back into her purse. "And if you want to keep going to your yoga." She flicked her wrist in the air and made a prissy expression. "And your tennis." She flicked her other wrist in the air and jiggled her hips, then stood up straight, her voice like acid. "You will shut that pretty little mouth of yours and learn to keep quiet unless someone asks you a question."

A single thought filled Gillian's mind: *She doesn't know Big Floyd put the stock in Trip's name.* Then, all of a sudden, Gillian was inches from her mother-in-law, her finger jabbing the air right in front of Mama W's nose. "I. Said. No."

Mama W's arm swooped back. "You ungrateful little bitch!"

"MOTHER!"

Gillian caught her mother-in-law's hand before the slap

could land on her cheek. Out of the corner of her eye, she could see Trip trying to sit up and wincing. She glared at Mama W. "You are done meddling in our lives. I know what you did to keep Trip from starting the fishing business."

Mama W seemed to go still as her eyes darted over Gillian's shoulder.

Gillian pushed her mother-in-law's hand down but didn't let go. Her voice rose. "And we both know how you ended any chance I had for a career at the bank."

"Wait, what?" Trip swung his legs over the side of the bed.

Mama W glared at Gillian but didn't say a word.

"And now you've got Trip mixed up in this ridiculous business with Dicky Worth." Gillian shoved her mother-in-law's hand away. "You are nothing but a . . . a . . ." Gillian stood up straighter and raised her chin. "A Goddamned meddler!"

Both Trip's and his mother's mouths fell open.

"And, as God is my witness," Gillian stomped her foot, her voice pure iron, "it stops right fucking now."

Something stirred behind her. Gillian turned and saw Big Floyd, wearing his khaki pants, khaki shirt, and khaki cap. She had no idea how long he'd been standing there.

He walked past her without a word and picked up Mama W's purse. "I'll walk you to your car, hon," he said quietly. "Best that you head home now."

Lying in bed, Gillian rolled over to see the clock on her nightstand—eight thirty a.m.—and listened. The hum of the air conditioner was the only sound she heard. *Which was strange.* Bobbie hadn't slept past six thirty in his entire four years on earth, and Carly only did when she was sick. Gillian tried to remember what time she'd finally gone to bed. It was after five a.m. She'd called Ashley from the hospital and given her the broad strokes of what had happened with a few strategic modifications—Gillian and Lianna had gotten themselves locked in the store, Lianna had slammed her hand in a door, and Trip had cracked his ribs breaking them out. When they'd finally gotten home, no one argued when Gillian declared that they were all taking the day off tomorrow—no school, no work, just home, just family.

Well, almost. She checked the clock again. They'd been sleeping for less than four hours. *Four hours. Oh. The doctor said to check after two.*

Gillian kicked off the covers, hurrying out of the room and down the long hallway that looked over onto the first floor. Small voices wafted up.

"Shhhh, Bobbie, we've got to let Mama and Daddy sleep," Ashley said, sounding like a Southern version of Mary Poppins.

"But why?" That was Carly.

Gillian paused.

"Because," Ashley said lightly, "they're getting old, and they need their rest. Here. Have some more chocolate milk."

Gillian gripped the railing. But she didn't rush down the stairs to explain that she and Daddy were not old, just exhausted. She didn't snatch away what had to be the second if not third glasses of chocolate milk—*Carly and Bobbie would be bouncing off the walls in an hour*—and she didn't throw her arms in the air exclaiming over Ashley's bizarre lack of judgment. Instead, Gillian stood exactly where she was and just appreciated that she had three healthy, beautiful children and they were all safely in her kitchen. After a moment, she tiptoed toward the guest room where she'd put Lianna and knocked quietly on the door.

Nothing.

Gillian turned the knob and peeked in. "Lianna," she called softly from the doorway.

Lianna lay splayed on the bed like a beached starfish. She didn't move.

"Lianna," Gillian said louder as she walked to the foot of the bed. Nothing.

"Lianna." Gillian grabbed a big toe and wiggled it.

Lianna made a warbled grumbling sound but still didn't move.

Gillian rubbed her eyes and tried to remember what questions the physician's assistant had told her to ask. "Do you know your name?"

Nothing.

Gillian grabbed the toe again and wiggled harder. "Do you know your name?" she called out.

"Fuck!" Lianna's eyes were squeezed shut. She did not raise her head. "What?" she barked.

"What is your name?"

Lianna opened her eyes. They circled wildly before landing on Gillian. Lianna groaned.

"What's your name?" Gillian squeezed the big toe.

Lianna jerked her foot away. "Fucking hell, Gillian! Last night was the worst night of my life. Let me fucking sleep!" She pulled a pillow over her face.

Gillian watched Lianna for a minute and decided she probably didn't have brain damage. She turned, crossed the hall, and stood listening outside the room she'd put Aimee in. She thought of the night before—what a sight they must have been. Lianna, Aimee, and Gillian buckled in the back seat of Big Floyd's Tahoe, and Trip up front. When they'd arrived at the house, Gillian, Trip, and a grumbling Lianna slowly exited the car. Aimee, who had been gaping at Lianna's hand for the entire ride, wished them a quiet good night and apologized for at least the tenth time.

Big Floyd had turned to the back seat.

"Sorry." Aimee shook her head. "I'll come up front. I really appreciate you taking me to get my car." She got out of the truck and walked to the front passenger side.

Gillian saw Big Floyd watching Aimee, his face as soft as she'd ever seen it. He rolled down his window halfway. "You're staying with Gillian tonight."

"But—"

With a click, he locked the Tahoe doors.

Aimee stared at him, her mouth gaping.

"No buts," Big Floyd said more sternly. "Inside. Now." He pushed the purses through the window.

Aimee glanced from Big Floyd to the others and back again. The shame shooting off her was heartbreaking.

Big Floyd shook the purses.

"Come on, hon," Gillian said, gently taking the bags. "It's really no trouble at all."

Trip stepped to Aimee's other side. "You know how he is once his mind's made up."

Now, standing in the hallway, Gillian listened at Aimee's door.

All she could hear was the air conditioner and faint giggles from downstairs.

Gillian tiptoed back to her own room and slipped into bed. She closed her eyes and breathed in the familiar smell of her own sheets, feeling the warmth of Trip's body beside her. Snuggling closer to him, careful not to jostle or put pressure on his ribs, she rested her hand on top of one of his and—for perhaps the first time since she'd had Ashley—went back to sleep.

❖ ❖ ❖

Aimee wasn't sure what woke her. She opened her eyes and sat up with a start, then lay back among the soft lavender sheets and pulled the comforter up to her chin. Every part of her body ached with exhaustion, and her mind couldn't stop circling around the horror of seeing Andy's vacant eyes last night—Andy-but-not-Andy. She burrowed further into the pillows, her brain racing around all the things she'd learned he had done. A shudder rippled through her as she wondered about the things she didn't know. She reached to the nightstand, grabbed her phone, and grimaced. Six voice mails, all from her mother. She picked up the slip of paper with the direct line to the mental ward nurses' station.

Someone answered on the first ring.

"Is—" Aimee coughed, willing her croaky voice to sound better. She propped herself up on one elbow. "Is Celia still on duty?"

"No, ma'am," an unenthusiastic voice replied.

"This is Aimee Harmon," she said as pleasantly as she could. "I'm calling to find out about my cousin, Andy. He was brought in last night?"

"Oh, Aimee! Celia told me you'd be calling, hon." The voice had reconstructed itself and was now warm and kind. "I checked on him about ten minutes ago, and he's out like a light. Which is exactly what we want."

Aimee sank back against the pillows, feeling relieved. "What time did they finally get him to sleep?"

She heard papers shuffling. "Um, looks like it took two doses." The woman made a tsking sound. "They didn't get him down until close to seven."

Aimee closed her eyes, wondering about the hours in the hospital before they'd gotten Andy to sleep. What had it been like for him? What had it been like for the staff? She didn't ask.

"My name's Wendy, sweetheart, and I'll be here until seven o'clock this evening. Why don't you try back close to then. Hopefully, he'll still be out, but I can let you know how the day went. The doctor probably won't see him until tomorrow."

"Thank you, Wendy." Aimee desperately wanted to drive over to the hospital and show them pictures of Andy as a bubbly little boy, smiling proudly beside his monster trucks and the obstacle courses he'd made for them. She wanted to show them the picture of him in his football uniform—that hopeful smile. *This is the real Andy*, she needed to explain. He is nothing like the man the police brought in last night, and can you please, please fix him. "I'd appreciate that" was all she said.

As soon as she hung up, Aimee grabbed the other slip of paper from her purse and dialed.

"Sheriff Davis."

She had to clear her throat again. "Hi, Sheriff. It's Aimee Harmon."

"Where are you?" he asked warily.

"I'm at Gillian's, but—"

"Good. Stay there and get some rest. That's all Andy's going to be doing in the hospital for at least a couple of days."

"I know. But I wanted to ask you about—" Aimee's heart began to thump as she searched for words. "Is he being charged?"

The sheriff sighed, but his voice was kind. "I don't have time to explain it all right now, but we have mental health courts in this county. I've got to talk to the DA, but I don't think anybody's gonna argue that Andy won't qualify. He'll have to go in front of a judge. And he's gonna need a lawyer, but—"

"Oh God."

"Don't start fretting. I think the public defender will be able to handle this just fine. No one's trying to put Andy in jail."

"Lianna and Gillian might." Aimee hadn't meant to say those words out loud.

The sheriff sighed again.

"I will speak to Ms. Matthews and Mrs. Wilkins, but I really don't think—" Loud voices broke out in the background. The sheriff's voice muffled, then became clear again. "I'll talk to them. But I just don't see how anyone can think Andy is best served by being in jail when what he needs is psychiatric care. I've got to go, but I promise, once I get my ducks in a row, I will sit down with you and explain what's going to happen. Okay?"

What the sheriff was saying made sense. But Aimee's shoulders and chest were still stiff in the conviction that she needed to do something.

"Aimee, there is absolutely nothing that you can do for Andy right now," the sheriff said, as if he'd read her mind. "And, hon, there is a limit to what you're gonna be able to do for him going forward."

"But he's sick." Aimee's voice cracked as images of Andy as a sleepy toddler filled her mind.

A note of sadness laced the sheriff's voice. "He's a sick adult, Aimee. Andy is no longer a child."

Aimee's breath caught as the sheriff's words struggled to find a foothold in her mind. A passage from one of the books she'd read bubbled up around them: "Grant me the serenity to accept the things I cannot change. Courage to change the things I can. And wisdom to know the difference." It was something alcoholics were encouraged to say to themselves, but the book had emphasized the benefit to family members of both addicts and adults struggling with mental illness.

"Aimee?" The sheriff's voice broke through her thoughts. "You sure you're okay?"

"I'm fine."

"Stay with Gillian and get some rest." He hung up before she could say thank you.

Aimee stared at the ceiling. The sheriff's words and things she'd read in the books continued to pepper her mind, at odds with the worry and obligation she felt for Andy.

She dialed one more number.

Her manager, Jonathan, answered on the fourth ring.

"Jonathan, it's Aimee." She scratched her head, exhaustion pulling at every cell in her body. "I'm going to be late today. I'm not sure if you've talked to Big Floyd, but—" She had no idea how to even begin the story of what had happened.

"Big Floyd told me about last night and . . . and . . ." Jonathan cleared his throat. "I am not allowed to talk to you."

Aimee's heart sank. Of course, Big Floyd would never forgive her family for the previous night at Buck's.

Jonathan's voice dropped to a whisper. "But my printer says it needs more paper. Can you walk me through how to do that?" There was a commotion. "I didn't call her. She called me," she heard Jonathan say defensively.

A faint white noise filled her ear as someone turned the phone to speaker. "Aimee?" Big Floyd rumbled.

Aimee squeezed her eyes shut. "Yes?"

"What in the hell are you doing calling here this morning?"

Any last hope of not being fired slipped away from her. "I thought—" She cleared her throat. "I'm sorry. I'll come down and get my things as soon as I can." She sat up and looked around the room for her clothes. She didn't see them.

"What?" Big Floyd and Jonathan asked at the same time.

"I'm still at Gillian's, so it'll take me a little while to get back. I can come in after five to pick up my things if that would be better?"

"What?" Jonathan asked again, his voice an octave higher.

At the same time, Big Floyd barked, "What things do you think you need?"

Aimee couldn't believe Big Floyd was being this mean. But her cousin had held his daughter-in-law and an important business associate hostage for the better part of the night before. She had to get the football picture of Andy, though. "There's a picture on my desk that I'd like to have and . . ." She tried to think. "A pair of heels in the bottom desk drawer."

There was a pause.

"Are you quitting?" Big Floyd asked, his voice suddenly gentle.

"What?" Jonathan practically shrieked.

Aimee sighed to herself. Of course, they couldn't technically fire her. "Sure. If that makes it easier. I'm sorry, I should have said that first."

"Aw, hell!" That was Jonathan.

"Johnny, shut up," Aimee heard Big Floyd mumble as the phone clicked off speaker. When he spoke, his voice was soft and right in her ear. "Aimee, I told Jonathan that he was not allowed to bother you today because I thought you needed to rest. That boy doesn't know his ass from a hole in the ground without you here. Nobody wants you to quit."

Aimee was sure she hadn't heard him right.

"And can you please get it through that hard head of yours that what happened last night is not your goddamn fault?" With a click, Big Floyd hung up the phone.

◆ ◆ ◆

Lianna was dreaming. Running through a forest, she barely managed to stay ahead of something terrible. But it was coming. It was coming for *her*. She wanted to stop so badly and rest. But it wasn't safe. She knew this with absolute certainty. Then a gray wolf, with the kindest eyes she'd ever seen, was inviting her into his cave. Bizarrely, she found herself following him inside. The cavern was strangely pleasant, and a luxurious, emerald-colored carpet beckoned to her from the corner. Although the wolf didn't speak, Lianna understood that he would watch over her while she slept. She lay down, filled with relief. The wolf came to rest beside her, his silky coat like a wonderful blanket. She nestled closer to him, feeling safer than she'd ever felt in her life.

Lianna became aware that she was in a bed, but the dream was still happening because the wolf was with her. She could feel his fur and the gentle rise and fall of his chest, hear his soft, fluttery snore. He smelled musky. Refusing to wake—this dream was too lovely—Lianna felt herself slipping back toward the cave.

She heard a child giggle.

With a start, Lianna opened her eyes.

Her face was inches from the back of a giant furry head with pointy ears, her arm wrapped around a massive furry body.

She flung herself back against the pillow, croaking, "What the fu—"

A pounding dizziness seized her.

She closed her eyes and was still, willing the sickness to pass.

She opened her eyes again.

The wolf had rolled over and was looking at her. Except he was black and brown, not gray. He inched closer and rested his gigantic snout on her chest.

"Oh! Oh! Ohhhhh!" Lianna realized the warbled moaning sound was coming out of her own mouth, but she couldn't stop.

The wolf yawned.

His teeth were huge.

Panic surged through Lianna, but she didn't dare move. The ohhs became louder and higher pitched.

There was another giggle. Lianna looked toward the sound. A little girl with sparkly blue eyes and wild dark hair sat on her knees at the foot of Lianna's bed. Tiny pale arms poked from the sleeves of her pink nightgown.

"Tony Romo likes you," the little girl said smiling.

Lianna drew in a shuddery breath. "There's a wolf." She raised her arm to point at him and frowned at the sleeve of an unfamiliar pale-green pajama top. It was covered in yellow flowers and stopped several inches above her wrist.

The little girl tilted her head. "Tony Romo's not a wolf, silly."

Lianna's brain felt like it was being crushed in a vise. "I know," she heard herself say. "He's a sportscaster who used to be a quarterback."

There was a click and the bedroom door opened.

Lianna's eyes darted to the empty space, half afraid she was going to see Tony Romo in his Dallas Cowboys uniform materialize out of thin air.

There was a soft pattering noise that grew louder. Then a moon-shaped face was hurtling toward her, followed by a pudgy little body in Dallas Cowboy pajamas.

"ARRGGGGG," the little boy yelled in a low, guttural voice as he landed on Lianna's stomach and buried his face in the wolf's neck.

Lianna braced herself for a wave of pain. It didn't come.

The little girl rose up on her knees, two tiny hands planted on her hips. "Bobbie," she said, "we're not supposed to bother her." She looked back at Lianna. "Tony Romo's a German shepherd."

The round face peeked up from the wolf's neck, the most carefree grin Lianna had ever seen stretching across the boy's face. "ARRGGGGG!" He burrowed back into the wolf's fur.

The wolf yawned.

"Tony Romo usually sleeps in my room."

Lianna jerked back against the pillow. The little girl had crawled up from the foot of the bed and was now lying on her stomach, her chin even with Lianna's elbow. She took Lianna's uninjured hand and began drawing circles along the edge of the palm. "But I sent him in here to sleep with you. My sister said you hurt your hand."

Lianna went rigid as memories of the previous night flew back at her.

The little girl reached for Lianna's other hand, bound in

white gauze and tape. Gently, she kissed the bandage. "You're okay now," she said with a calming certainty.

Lianna peered into the startling blue eyes and felt her body relax again.

"Y'all are gonna be in so much trouble for waking her up," said a low voice from the doorway. Lianna turned, expecting to see Gillian. But it was a teenaged girl wearing a red sweatshirt and pink shorts with hearts all over them. She leaned back and shrieked with the gusto of a native New Yorker hailing a cab, "Mother!"

The little boy rolled away from the dog, the back of his head pressed against Lianna's stomach, his chin pointing up toward the ceiling. He grinned at her upside down.

There was a sound by the door.

Lianna turned to see Gillian—*her lips glistening with fucking lipstick!*—a strange expression on her face. She wore pale pink pajamas that looked suspiciously like the ones Lianna had on, but the flowers on Gillian's were purple. Her hair was swept up in a messy-but-flattering bun.

Gillian stared at them all for a long moment. "Good morning," she said finally, her face relaxing into a smile that seemed a little bit surprised. "I see you've met the family."

❖ ❖ ❖

Aimee opened her eyes for the second time, startled that she'd fallen back asleep. She braced herself for a tornado of whirling thoughts and worries. Instead, she felt the strangest sensation. She had to think for a moment to name it—*peace*. Andy was safe in the hospital, and there was absolutely nothing she could do for him over the next twenty-four hours. She still had her job. And she was here in Gillian's comfortable bed.

Aimee stretched and rubbed her hands along the silky sleeves of the pale blue pajamas with little pink flowers that Gillian had given her the night before. Without rushing, Aimee rose and made the bed, straightening the ruffles of the pillow shams and hoping that she got the arrangement of the—*wow, one, two, three, four, five, six*—throw pillows sort of right.

The sound of children giggling bubbled in the hallway. It faded as feet pounded down the stairs.

Aimee stepped into the en suite bathroom and was grateful to find a pretty wicker basket filled with tiny bottles of every toiletry she could imagine. A bamboo toothbrush, still in its wrapper, poked out from the top of the basket next to a small tube of Crest.

Aimee brushed her teeth, then walked back through the bedroom, opened the door, and stepped into the hall. The door of the room directly across was open, and she could see inside.

Lianna was sitting up in bed with one hand pressed against her head and the other outstretched. "Just fucking give them to me!"

Gillian stood at the foot of the bed, wearing pajamas just like Aimee's except they were pink with purple flowers. A laptop was pressed to her stomach with one hand and an iPhone gripped in the other. She sighed. "My children are in this house," she said, but she didn't sound mad. "What year is it?"

Lianna grimaced, a wisp of something like contrition passing across her face. "It's 2022."

"Where are you?"

Lianna flopped back against the pillows, winced, and closed her eyes. "In hell."

Gillian's eyes flitted to the ceiling and back. "Okay, I think we've established that you are aware of your surroundings." Her voice softened. "Are you sure you don't want to call someone? Not even your mama?"

"No."

"Lianna." Gillian's eyes looked pained. "I think she would want to know."

"I'm sure she would. But involving her would be in no way helpful to *me*." Lianna opened her eyes. "It's my life, Gillian, not hers. I'm not dealing with her right now."

Aimee stepped into the doorway, mesmerized by what Lianna had just said and the matter-of-fact way she'd said it.

Lianna and Gillian turned toward her.

Aimee's eyes landed on Lianna's bandaged hand. The peaceful feeling buckled. "Sorry," Aimee said quickly. "I didn't mean to interrupt. Gillian, I'll head out now if you can just tell me where my clothes are?"

"How's Drew?" Gillian coughed. "I mean, how is Andy?"

The way Gillian was looking at her—with such kindness and concern—almost took Aimee's breath away. A part of her wanted to turn away in shame. But another part was thinking of a passage she'd read in one of the books—"Can you allow yourself to receive help?"

"He's sleeping." Aimee took a deep breath. "They'll have him sleep for a day or two before I can talk to him or a doctor." She tried to maintain eye contact but couldn't. "That's how it works." She forced herself to look back at Gillian. "It's happened before."

Gillian nodded. "We know," she said lightly. "I soaked your dress last night, but I can tell from the fabric, it's gonna need to air dry once I rinse it out."

Aimee studied the floor, the shame pressing down harder. There had been blood on her dress from Andy's face after the deputy tackled him. "Oh—" Her voice caught. "I can wear it home wet."

❖ ❖ ❖

Gillian surveyed her two guests and felt her mind continue to stretch and rearrange itself. This morning had been so strange!

First, she'd slept in and let the kids fend for themselves for break-fast. Then she'd stumbled on Carly, Bobbie, and Tony Romo in Lianna's room—lolling over Lianna like they'd known her all their lives. Lianna's face had been full of terrified wonder, as if she were being overrun by kittens. Gillian had found herself marveling that she didn't have the slightest inclination to scold anyone. If she'd walked in on a similar scene, well, even yesterday, she would have been hollering at the kids and the dog to get off the bed, filled with shame at her family's behavior. She could almost picture that other version of herself, could almost see her flipping out then finding some reason to be angry at Lianna, just for bearing witness.

And now here was Aimee—who always wore a smile on her face despite a home life that was clearly rougher than anyone had imagined—ready to flee in a wet dress before she'd risk putting Gillian out in any way.

Gillian felt all kinds of out of sorts, but one thing she was sure about was that she wasn't sending Aimee back home to wade through all this alone. And she certainly wasn't letting Aimee go to her mama's.

"Come on," Lianna moaned, sounding like Ashley on one of her grumpier days. "I've already missed three meetings that were scheduled before breakfast. I've got two more over lunch and probably hundreds of emails waiting. I need my computer, and I need my phone." The effort of speaking seemed to wind her.

Piecing together bits of an idea that was still hazy, Gillian gazed at Lianna, then at Aimee.

"Really," Aimee said, looking like she wanted to melt through the rug. "Jonathan's going to need me at the bank. I should go."

Gillian bit her bottom lip, knowing full well Big Floyd didn't expect Aimee back at that office today.

Lianna moaned again and pounded the bed with her fists. "Gillian, you don't understand! There are things I have to do!"

"Lianna, hush." Gillian saw the shame glittering in Aimee's eyes and felt her heart break just a little. The pieces of the idea merged into a whole. "Okay, here's what's gonna happen. You," Gillian pointed the phone at Lianna, "are not allowed to look at a phone, a computer, or anything with a screen for at least three days."

Lianna squawked.

"So I need *you*," Gillian turned to face Aimee, "to help her."

Gillian had to keep from smiling as confusion replaced the shame on Aimee's face. "Of course," Aimee said after a moment.

Gillian handed Aimee the phone. "This is dead, but don't let her have it. She's got chargers everywhere."

Aimee nodded.

Gillian passed over the computer. "Take this and please do whatever it is that needs to be done so Lianna will get some," Gillian tipped her chin up gracefully, deciding that she was enjoying being this new version of herself, "*damn* rest." Smiling, she walked out of the room.

15.

Aimee could feel herself slipping into a gentle rhythm as she and Lianna worked through Lianna's emails. "Robert Somerville thinks the deposit forecast for the fourth quarter is too conservative," Aimee said, paraphrasing in one sentence what the man had taken three paragraphs to write. Lianna's laptop was balanced on Aimee's knees as she lay back against the fluffy throw pillows on the divan next to the bed. The lights were off, and the shade halfway drawn, leaving the room in a pale, buttery light.

Lianna, flat on her back with her eyes closed and one hand stroking Tony Romo's neck, responded with surprising force. "He's fucking wrong. And Benjamin already signed off on the numbers."

Tony Romo grunted in what sounded like agreement.

Aimee absently rubbed the cuff of her pajama sleeve—the fabric was the silkiest, most comfortable thing she'd ever had next to her skin. She thought for a moment, then typed as she spoke. "Thanks for sharing your perspective, Robert. Benjamin and I believe the forecast is sound." She tilted her head. "If you would like to discuss this further, please schedule time with me when I am back in the office. Best, Lianna." She studied Lianna for a reaction.

"Don't give him my best," Lianna mumbled after a moment. "But otherwise that's really good."

Aimee felt a warm rush of satisfaction.

There was a knock on the door.

"Come in," they said at the same time.

Gillian appeared with a white wicker tray, which held two steaming cups of coffee and a matching cream and sugar set.

"Thank God." Lianna sat up quickly. She paused and steadied herself.

Gillian waited until Lianna was fully sitting up, then handed her a brightly patterned blue cup. "You want sugar or cream?" she asked.

"No." Lianna took the cup. "Um . . ." She looked up at Gillian uncertainly. "Thank you." She took a deep breath, her nose just above the rim, then smiled like a little girl opening a box of chocolates.

"You're welcome." Gillian handed a similarly patterned mug to Aimee. "Cream or sugar, hon?"

"Cream, please." Aimee took the cup and poured cream from the tiny pitcher. "You warm the cream?"

Gillian nodded. "It keeps the coffee hot longer. You can use the microwave, but only in ten-second pulses or it will curdle."

Aimee made a mental note—Gillian was the most accomplished homemaker she'd ever witnessed—and enjoyed the steamy coffee.

◆ ◆ ◆

Gillian heard giggling from the doorway and caught Bobbie just as he launched himself at the bed. "Oh, no you don't. Miss Lianna's got hot coffee." Gillian pulled him into her and inhaled that undefinable scent that only came from the tops of her children's heads.

Carly pranced in behind him and sat down at Aimee's feet. "Hi, Miss Aimee," she said shyly.

"Hey, Carly." Gillian watched Aimee's beaming face and, once again, determined that she was not letting her leave the house.

"Hi, Miss Lianna," Carly said.

Lianna startled. A tentative smile crept across her face. "Hi."

Slow and heavy footsteps sounded from the hallway.

Gillian turned and saw a large hand reach through the open door then knock on the frame. "Everybody decent?" asked her husband's rich voice.

Gillian found herself smiling. "You can come in."

As soon as Trip appeared in the doorway—wearing yellow and pink plaid shorts and a burnt orange UT sweatshirt—Bobbie wriggled out of Gillian's arms, calling, "Daddyyyyy!" He ran right at Trip.

Gillian tried to grab him, but he was too quick.

Trip's eyes widened as Bobbie slammed into his leg.

"Bobbie, honey, be careful with Daddy," Gillian yelped.

Trip rubbed his boy's head. "Hey, bobcat. How 'bout them Cowboys?" he said, patting Bobbie's pajamas.

Carly leapt up and ran straight to Trip's other leg. "Daddy, will you make us waffles?" she asked as she stepped onto his foot and clasped his knee with both arms.

"Well, sugarpop, I'm not sure this morning's the best—"

"Pleeeeease, Daddy?" Carly swooped around his leg as if it were a maypole.

Trip turned to Gillian uncertainly.

"Carly, baby, let Daddy rest." Gillian could tell by the way Trip was standing that his ribs had to be hurting.

"We'll do it another day," Trip said, smiling back down at Carly.

But not before Gillian saw the disappointment flash across his face.

Once again, she had that strange, dislocated feeling. Suddenly,

Gillian could see herself storming through the kitchen the last time Trip had made waffles, her teeth gritted as she looked at her usually sparkling countertops splattered with batter. She hadn't even sat down to eat with them. Instead, she'd rearranged the dirty dishes in the dishwasher, making as much noise as she could.

She saw her husband now—standing there grinning down at his little ones, his ribs surely throbbing. "Unless you feel like it, honey?" she asked softly.

Trip's eyes lit up. "You sure?"

Gillian gave him her best beauty pageant smile. "Waffles sound wonderful to me."

◆ ◆ ◆

Lianna watched Gillian's husband and kids leave the room in wonder. An only child—who didn't spend much time with other children—Lianna had never experienced a morning like this. Her eyes traveled down to her near-empty mug. The coffee had been rich and flavorful, but she wasn't feeling the energy buzz she usually got. "Can I have more coffee?"

Gillian, who had been staring at the empty doorway, turned to her. "You drank that already?"

Lianna nodded. She could down two Starbucks ventis in half an hour.

Shaking her head, Gillian took the empty cup.

Thirty minutes later, Gillian breezed by the open door. "The waffles are just about ready. I'll fix a tray and bring it to you."

"No." There was no fucking way Lianna was going to stay in bed like an invalid. "I want to get up." She began to rise.

Gillian gave her some kind of weird mom-look but shrugged. "Suit yourself."

"I'll be right down." Aimee's gaze slowly swept from the laptop to Lianna. "I confirmed that the revenue forecast was the same on the new spreadsheet he sent, but it looks like the expenses increased. I just need a few more minutes, and I can tell you what line item."

"Thanks." Lianna could not remember when she'd had help from someone so competent and easygoing. A surge of anger filled her as she thought of her assistant, Meredith, who had shrieked and shaken her head the one and only time Lianna tried to walk her through a P&L.

"Okay. But that's gonna be all the work for a little while," Gillian said from the doorway.

Lianna frowned at her empty coffee cup as she slowly stood. Her stomach felt saturated with hot liquid, but she was still so groggy.

Then fucking Gillian was trying to take her arm. "Quit it!" Lianna barked, shaking Gillian off.

Gillian pressed her lips together and took a dramatic step away.

Lianna walked to the hallway. "I need more coffee," she muttered.

"I'll get it for you," Gillian said, plucking the mug from Lianna's hand.

◆ ◆ ◆

Gillian braced herself as she and Lianna stepped into the kitchen. The assault on her eyes she expected was certainly there. Every cabinet was open—for the life of her, she'd never understand why her husband wasn't capable of closing them. Bags of flour and sugar, a can of baking powder, butter sticks, and a carton of eggs littered the counter.

Today, though, the strangest thing happened. Gillian's eyes automatically traveled to the goop smearing her countertop, but then she noticed a trail of bubbles where Trip had swiped a sponge. There was a spoon covered in batter next to the waffle iron. But she saw that the spoon had been placed on a folded paper towel. The batter bowl was still in the sink, but suds floated on the water that filled it.

Gillian's breath caught as she pictured herself storming around the kitchen the last time Trip had made waffles. She wondered how many details like these she'd missed. How was it that she'd only been paying attention to what he'd done wrong? Instead of everything he'd done right.

"Lianna, we've got blueberry waffles, bacon waffles, and plain ones," Trip said proudly.

Seeing the beautiful breakfast Trip had laid out, his cheerful face and warm smile, it was all Gillian could do not to throw her arms around him right there in the kitchen.

Lianna, who was halfway to the coffeepot, stopped and turned. "You made *bacon* waffles?"

Gillian narrowed her eyes. It would be just like Lianna to be a dadgum vegetarian.

Lianna grinned. "Ohmigod. Bacon. Definitely bacon."

"They are so good," Carly said with the air of an adult. "Here, Miss Lianna." She patted the seat next to her. "Come sit by me."

"Sure, munchkin," Lianna said, her face filling with surprise as if she weren't sure where those words had come from.

Carly beamed.

Lianna smiled back then turned toward the coffeepot.

"I'll get your coffee," Gillian said, shooing Lianna toward the table.

Trip brought over a plate filled with steaming, golden waffles.

Lianna slathered butter across the top one and took a bite. "Ohmigod, these are so fu—" She coughed, wide eyes flitting across the kids.

From the kitchen, Gillian watched her children's attention

rivet on Lianna and felt the plate she was holding slip from her hand. It clattered onto the counter.

Lianna swallowed. "So . . . fu . . . funtastic!" she exclaimed, once again seeming shocked at the words that had come from her mouth.

"Funtastic!" Carly giggled.

"Funtastic!" Bobbie yelled.

Lianna turned to Gillian.

Thank you, Gillian mouthed, not feeling angry or put out at all.

❖ ❖ ❖

As breakfast wound down, Lianna watched Bobbie and Carly slither out of their chairs to play with Bobbie's cars in the corner of the room.

"So," Ashley spoke tentatively, "you live in New York?"

"Yeah." Lianna leaned back from the table, her stomach full and satisfied. Her head still felt so fuzzy, though, and it was beginning to throb—which was the opposite of how she usually felt after so much coffee.

"I love New York," Ashley said with the reverence of someone who lived there. "I was reading about this Chinese restaurant called Hao Noodle? It sounds so good."

"It is so good." Lianna nodded. "There's one in my neighborhood."

Ashley's entire face lit up. "You live in Chelsea?"

Lianna nodded again.

"Honey, we've never been to New York," Gillian said.

Lianna and Ashley turned and scowled at the same time.

Gillian went still, then cleared her throat. "What I mean is, how do you know about a restaurant in New York?" Her face instantly said that she knew these words weren't very good either.

Ashley continued to glare. "It's called the internet, Mother." She huffed and picked up her phone.

Ashley was pretty fucking cool for a kid, Lianna thought, grinning at the exchange. She stared at her empty coffee cup, and her smile faded. Her head continued to pulse with a dull ache. And she still felt so befuddled. Her eyes floated up to Gillian. They narrowed.

"Sweetheart, I think it's nice that you're reading about New York," Gillian was saying as she tried to pat Ashley's arm.

Ashley pulled away.

Lianna looked at her cup again. Then back at Gillian.

"Breakfast was delicious," Gillian said to Trip.

"It was, Daddy," Ashley said, still staring at her phone.

Lianna rose from the table.

"What do you need?" Gillian asked, half rising.

"Nothing," Lianna said in a practiced nonchalant voice. She picked up her empty plate.

"That's sweet. Just leave it on the counter." Gillian sat back down.

Lianna took her plate to the sink then quietly slinked around, searching for the garbage.

She pulled out the bin.

"I KNEW IT!" Lianna turned, filled with indignant fury. She thrust an empty Keurig coffee pod in Gillian's direction. "You gave me fu—"

Gillian's eyes bulged and shot to the younger kids.

Ashley clapped a hand over her mouth.

Carly and Bobbie looked up from the cars.

Lianna swallowed, channeling every bit of willpower she had. "You gave me decaf?"

Gillian bit her lip. "The doctor said caffeine isn't good for a concussion."

"Mother," Ashley said quietly, shaking her head and sipping the one cup of milky coffee Gillian had let her have.

"How could you?" Lianna shrieked before stalking up the back stairs so she didn't say anything else fucking inappropriate in front of the kids.

◆ ◆ ◆

Gillian had just finished explaining what decaf coffee was to Carly when the doorbell rang. Smoothing the front of her pajama top—and glad she'd at least put on some powder and a touch of lipstick—Gillian hurried to the front door.

A tall Black man—whom she'd never seen before—stood on the porch.

A. Strange. Black. Man. On her front porch.

There was one Black family with children at the private school Gillian's kids attended and two Black families who were members of the First Baptist Church. She'd never seen this man with any of them.

Gillian drew in a breath. "May I help you?" Hearing her own cold, clipped words—born of fear, but sounding sinister—sent the air rushing out of her lungs. She thought of all the old "facts" that had rearranged themselves into new pictures over the past two days—Dicky Worth, Trip's fishing business, the lone biker at Buck's. She thought of the scene in the kitchen less than an hour before. The small voice, which didn't seem small anymore, was indignant: *You don't even know this man. And you've done precious little to get to know those families either.*

Gillian blinked.

For the first time, her eyes registered his open face.

She blinked again and noticed his apologetic smile.

"I'm sorry. I've caught you at a terrible time, haven't I?" He shook his head. "Are you Gillian Wilkins?"

"I am," she said, taking in his rumpled suit and knowing in every cell of her body that her unease was entirely of her own making.

"I'm Benjamin Sutter." He extended his hand. "From National Behemoth Bank. Big Floyd gave me your address and suggested I stop by. He said Lianna Matthews is here. She works for me."

Gillian took his hand and willed herself not to roll her eyes. Only Big Floyd would think nothing of sending a complete stranger to her home—obviously an important man for the bank—only hours after they'd returned from the most harrowing night of their lives.

"I haven't been able to contact Lianna, and I just wanted to make sure she's okay." Benjamin took a step back. "I should have waited until I reached you by phone."

Bless his heart, he must have flown all night to get here. "Please come in," Gillian said, putting as much warmth into her words as she could. She moved so he could enter the foyer. "Did you fly here from New York?"

He took a hesitant step inside. "Yes." His eyes darted around. "I shouldn't have just dropped in on you like this."

"Hi-eeeee." Carly appeared at Gillian's side and beamed up at Benjamin.

Benjamin grinned at Carly. He turned back to Gillian, the smile faltering. "I'm sure I'm imposing." He turned back toward the door. "I'll go wait—"

"You're not imposing one bit," Gillian said, shocked at how much she meant those words. She shut the door behind him. "When did you get in?"

"I landed in Dallas around five this morning."

She began walking him toward the den. It was almost noon. "Where are you staying?"

Carly fell into step beside them.

Benjamin shook his head in an upset, confused kind of way. "My assistant is on vacation, so Lianna's assistant, Meredith"—he seemed to make a point of stating the assistant's name, which Gillian appreciated very much—"made a reservation for me at a . . . a . . ." He looked uncomfortably at Carly. "A motel," he said finally.

"Oh, no." Gillian stopped, aghast. "Not one of those places out on Route Nine?"

Benjamin nodded, his eyes wide. "Five minutes after I got into my room, a . . . a . . ." He glanced toward Carly again. "A woman knocked on my door."

Gillian put her hands over Carly's ears. *A prostitute?* she whisper-mouthed, appalled. She had heard this went on down there but had never had a firsthand account.

Carly wriggled away.

Benjamin searched the ceiling. "I assume so. I left immediately."

Gillian's hand came to her mouth. "Where did you go?"

He shrugged. "I called Big Floyd, and he sent me here. It was too early to knock on your door, so I parked at the end of your driveway and got some work done." Benjamin sobered. "I just wanted to see Lianna for a few minutes, but it was rude of me not to call first." He turned back toward the door.

Gillian took his arm and guided him firmly into a comfortable chair. "She's awake, she's fine, and I'll get her. How about I get you some coffee too?"

❖ ❖ ❖

Aimee was still seated on the divan, laptop on her knees, when Lianna stormed into the room, put her hands on her head, and moaned.

Aimee immediately shut the computer and rose. Finding the expense discrepancy had taken longer than she'd anticipated. But the exercise—sorting through rows of Excel and comparing numbers—had soothed her. "It was the meals and entertainment line," she said, giving Lianna a wide berth and immediately wondering at her own idiocy—Lianna was clearly in no mood to talk about the expense forecast.

Lianna stared at her for what felt like forever. "Thanks for figuring that out." She crawled into bed. "Write back and tell that jackass I'm not approving it unless he cuts the out-months so that the full year is flat."

"Got it," Aimee said, moving closer to the door.

Lianna burrowed under the pillows.

Aimee unplugged Lianna's phone from the charger before tiptoeing into the hall. The smell of bacon and something buttery filled her nose.

After depositing the laptop in her own room—and keeping Lianna's phone just in case someone called in response to one of the emails she'd sent—Aimee started down the stairs. The worry that she was about to interrupt a family breakfast made her pause. Words from the self-help books swam through her mind again. "Will you allow yourself to receive help?" Her stomach rumbled.

When she reached the bottom stair, Lianna's phone buzzed.

Meredith Desk flashed across the screen.

"Lianna Matthews's phone," Aimee said in her most professional voice, turning away from the kitchen and into a beautifully appointed den. "This is Aimee."

"Why are you answering her phone?" Meredith did not sound happy.

"Hi, Meredith," Aimee said pleasantly, walking to the window and looking outside. The sun was shining.

"Why are you answering her phone?"

"I . . ." The thought of explaining everything that had happened over the last twenty-four hours was too exhausting. Aimee cleared her throat. "I sent you an email this morning. It's a long story, but Lianna was in the hospital last night. She has a concussion and can't use her phone or her laptop. The doctor—"

"Oh my God," Meredith cackled so loud Aimee pulled the phone away from her ear. "Lianna can't use her phone or her computer? She must be losing her mind."

Aimee ignored the comment. "I helped her clear out her time-sensitive emails and cancelled her meetings for the next few days." Aimee smiled at a bunny wiggling through the azalea bushes just below the window.

Meredith made a smacking noise. "Let me talk to her."

Aimee felt certain that talking to Meredith was the last thing Lianna needed. She made her voice as polite as possible. "Lianna's resting. The doctor said that's really important. Can I help you with something?"

Meredith made a sound like a snort. "Look," she said, "her eight a.m. meeting tomorrow is with a very senior colleague, and he says it can't be rescheduled."

A picture of Lianna's calendar flashed into Aimee's mind. "That would be with Maxwell, from the mortgage business?"

"How do you know?"

Aimee wanted to sigh but didn't. "I told you," she said as graciously as she could, "I sent out the notes to clear her schedule."

"Well, he says that meeting needs to happen."

Aimee remembered Lianna's scowl when they'd talked about the meeting earlier. "Cancel it," she'd snapped. "He sets up a half hour with me once a month, and all he does is talk about his stupid boat. I'll call him in a few days, and we can cover whatever he needs in five minutes."

"I'm sorry, Meredith." Aimee kept her voice cordial but made it a touch more firm. "Lianna was very clear that the meeting could wait. She has a concussion. She's not supposed to be working. Can you explain that to him, please?"

Meredith made the smacking noise again, and Aimee wondered what she was eating.

There was an awkward silence.

Aimee lifted her free hand and let it drop. "Would you like me to call him?"

A nasally, unkind laugh shot through the phone. Again, Aimee grimaced and held it away from her ear.

Suddenly, there was a large gentle hand on Aimee's shoulder, which sent a shot of warmth all the way down her spine. She turned around and gasped as she stared at the most beautiful man she'd ever seen.

"I'm Benjamin," he said softly to Aimee in that deep, rich voice that made her toes wiggle. "We've spoken on the phone. Lianna works for me. May I?" he asked.

Aimee gave him Lianna's phone. Her hand fluttered through her wild hair, which she hadn't even brushed. Then to the collar of the pajamas she was still wearing. She winced.

"Meredith, this is Benjamin," he said in a completely different voice, one filled with authority and impatience. "Tell Maxwell that his meeting with Lianna will be postponed." His eyes were bright and dancing when they met Aimee's. "And while Lianna is recovering, filter all messages and requests through Aimee."

◆ ◆ ◆

Gillian burst through Lianna's bedroom door, a hairbrush in one hand and a pale-yellow silk robe in the other. "Benjamin Sutter is here to see you."

Stretched across the bed, Lianna raised her head. "He's here?"

"He flew in this morning, and Big Floyd sent him over." Gillian laid the robe out at the foot of the bed and approached Lianna with the hairbrush.

"Get the fuck away from me." Lianna wriggled to the opposite side. She stopped and closed her eyes.

A sound brought Gillian's attention to the doorway where Ashley stood watching them, her nose pressed against the frame, only half of her face visible. She said nothing.

Ashley, honey, come in or go out, but do not lurk! The words were ready to leap from Gillian's mouth. Instead, she smiled at her daughter.

Expressionless, Ashley rolled backward around the corner into Carly's room, where Gillian was sure she intended to listen through the wall.

"You never said Benjamin was Black." The instant the words were out of Gillian's mouth, they gave her pause.

Lianna—lying flat on the opposite side of the bed—swiveled her eyes and glared. "Benjamin is the youngest member of the bank's executive leadership committee." She took a deep breath, sat up, and swung her legs over the side. "He is wicked smart." Slowly, she rose and began making her way to the en suite bathroom. "And rich as fuck." She shot another disgusted look at Gillian over her shoulder. "And he's Black. That's so hard to believe?"

Once again, Gillian felt as if the room was shifting around her. "Of course not," she heard herself whisper, feeling the truth of the words in her bones. "It's not hard to believe at all." She placed her hand on the bedpost to steady herself, aghast that so many ideas she didn't even agree with had occupied space in her mind without her even realizing it. She stood there for several moments letting that understanding sink in.

Something small and hard bounced off her nose. Gillian crouched and retrieved the toothpaste cap from the rug.

"Hel-*lo!*" Lianna gurgled from the bathroom doorway, one hand grinding a toothbrush through her mouth, the other flapping at Gillian.

Gillian blinked.

Lianna turned and spat. "I *said*, do you know where my suit-case is?"

"We didn't bring one home last night. It must be in your car at the hospital."

Lianna turned and spat again. "Do you have a sweatshirt I can put on over these?"

"I have a lovely dressing gown that goes with those pajamas." Gillian set the toothpaste cap on the nightstand and picked up the butter-colored robe. "It's long on me, so I think it'll fit you just fine."

Lianna—eyes blazing and her mouth lined with white foam—turned back to face Gillian. "I am not wearing that fuck-ing thing."

Gillian sighed.

"Where are my clothes from yesterday?"

"Filthy and in the dry cleaning bin." *And bloody from your hand*, Gillian thought but did not say. "You're not putting those back on."

Lianna snatched a hand towel and rubbed it over her mouth. Still scowling at Gillian, she tossed the towel behind her toward the vanity counter.

There was a faint knock on the open door to the hallway. Ashley, her face tentative, stepped forward, holding her favorite black hoodie. "You can borrow this, if you want?"

"Thank God," Lianna said, grabbing it and holding it up. "I didn't think black was allowed in this fu—" She coughed. "In this place." An uncertain look passed over her face then her lips twitched into what might have been a tiny smile. "Thank you."

Ashley smiled a smile that Gillian was sure she hadn't seen in years. "You're welcome."

Gillian wondered how anyone could choose that black mon-strosity over the gorgeous robe she held in her hands. But instead of pointing that out, she walked over and kissed her daughter on the cheek. "Thanks, sweetness," she said softly, pausing to breathe in the pineapple scent of Ashley's hair.

Unbelievably, Ashley didn't pull away.

◆ ◆ ◆

Gillian met a distraught Aimee on the front stairs.

"Benjamin Sutter is here!" Aimee whisper-shrieked.

"I know."

"He's in your living room!"

"I know, hon. I put him there."

Eyes desperate, Aimee gripped Gillian's arm. "I have to get dressed."

For the first time, Gillian noticed the crimson blotches creeping up Aimee's neck. "I will bring you some clothes. Your lingerie's in the dryer, which is not what I'd usually do. It should *usually* be air-dried. But I didn't think you'd want to wait. It'll be ready any minute."

Relief spread over Aimee's face. "Thank you," she said before racing up the stairs.

Gillian continued into the den and found Carly perched on the arm of Benjamin's chair.

"Will you come to my tea party?" Carly was asking.

Benjamin smiled. "I'd love to," he said without hesitation.

"ARRGGGGG!" From somewhere—Gillian hadn't even noticed he was in the room—Bobbie hurtled forward and launched himself through the air, directly at Benjamin.

Carly deftly slipped off the chair. "I'll let you know when it's set up," she said before prancing out the doorway.

Gillian's eyes darted to the cup of steaming coffee on the side table near Benjamin's elbow. She gasped and lurched. Bobbie's head was flying right toward it.

Without seeming to exert much effort, Benjamin caught Bobbie's torso in his hands like a football. He sat him down on the armrest opposite the side table, his hands protectively around Bobbie's waist. "Hey there, little man," Benjamin said pleasantly, as if Bobbie had toddled up to him like a normal, sedate child and tapped him on the knee.

Instead of apologizing and banishing Bobbie to the kitchen, Gillian laughed—a hearty, deep laugh that felt like the best kind of medicine in the world. "I am so sorry. His sister gave him a lot of chocolate milk this morning."

"I have nephews." Benjamin turned back to Bobbie, making an exaggerated frown. "You're a Dallas Cowboys fan?" He poked at Bobby's pajamas.

Bobbie nodded and giggled.

Benjamin shook his head. "I don't know, little man. I'm a Washington fan. It might be difficult for you and me to be friends. What do you think?" He waggled his face and leaned toward Bobbie. "Can we set aside our differences and be friends? I'm willing to try if you are."

Bobbie threw back his head and laughed.

"I can't believe you flew all the way down here." Gillian turned to see Lianna standing in the doorway, Ashley's oversized hoodie covering the beautiful pajamas. Tony Romo stood at her heels.

"You're never late." Benjamin stood and set Bobbie back on the floor as effortlessly as if Bobbie weighed no more than a pillow. "And you hadn't answered your phone in five hours. I was afraid you were—" Benjamin registered Tony Romo and took a startled step back.

"He's friendly." Gillian hefted Bobbie—who'd just raced into her knees—up onto her hip. "Give Mama some sugar," she murmured.

Bobbie planted a slobbery kiss on her cheek.

Benjamin nodded but took another step back.

"Okay, let's go get you dressed," Gillian said, rubbing her nose into Bobbie's hair. She started out of the room, then wheeled around. "The doctor was very clear that Lianna is not allowed to look at a phone or computer or anything with a screen," she said to Benjamin. "And she's been up for a while, so we should probably get her back to bed soon."

"I am standing right fucking here!" Lianna's voice was amazingly similar to Ashley's bobcat screech.

Gillian managed to cover one of Bobbie's ears. Instead of admonishing Lianna, she simply gazed up at the ceiling and shook her head.

◆ ◆ ◆

Lianna raised her hand to the wall to steady herself, knowing her profane words were still hanging in the air and wondering how the fuck people communicated when there were always kids around.

"Lianna." Benjamin's voice oozed disappointment.

"You know what?" Lianna sputtered, feeling her eyes blaze as she turned from Gillian to Benjamin.

Gillian pressed Bobbie's other ear to her shoulder.

"What?" asked a small voice. Lianna jumped, realizing Carly had sidled back into the room and was standing right beside her.

Lianna's indignation faltered as she stared into Carly's pixie-like face.

There was an awkward silence.

Then something Lianna's dad used to say floated into her mind. "You know what, Gillian?" Lianna smirked, feeling a surge of triumph. "Go pound sand."

Gillian's eyebrows pinched together. "What on earth does that mean?"

"What do you think?"

"What does it mean?" Carly asked.

Lianna startled, realizing Carly had slipped around to her other side—*fucking hell, that child was a pint-sized ninja.* "Um, well, munchkin—"

Gillian bit her lip.

"It means go away and leave me alone," Benjamin said smoothly. "Which is not a polite thing to say."

Lianna looked into Carly's flawless blue eyes and felt something shift inside her. "Right," she mumbled, patting Carly awkwardly on the head. "It wasn't very nice."

"Okay, let's get everybody dressed." Gillian shifted Bobbie on her hip and began to shuttle Carly out of the room. She glanced over her shoulder at Lianna and Benjamin. "Holler if you need anything."

Lianna walked over to one end of the couch and slumped down. "I could use some real coffee."

Gillian kept walking.

Benjamin sat down at the opposite end of the couch. "Are you okay?"

"I'm fine." Lianna closed her eyes and sank back into the soft leather cushions.

"*Lianna.*"

"I'll tell you what happened once," she said after a moment, her eyes still closed, "but then I'm not discussing it again. Deal?"

"Deal."

❖ ❖ ❖

Gillian followed the sound of her husband's voice into the den.

"I'd been pacing around the house like a dog that's been cooped up too long when my dad called and told me Gil's car was at the store and he thought there was trouble." Trip—his face animated, elbows on his knees—perched on the edge of a leather club chair. "Dad said the sheriff was too"—Trip glanced from side to side and lowered his voice—"chickenshit to check inside before Buck got back."

Across from him, Benjamin and Lianna sat on opposite ends of the matching couch. Tony Romo rested on the floor in front of them.

"So I cut through the field and went in the back way." Trip leaned forward and spread his hands. "I got right up to the corner of the store. And sure 'nuff, there was Gillian's Lincoln." His eyebrows shot up. "That's when the lights come on."

Lianna and Benjamin looked like children hearing a ghost story for the first time.

"I could see Gillian plain as day, getting herself squared away to take a run at somethin'."

"I was trying to get the shotgun," Gillian said from the doorway. She had changed into a short A-line sundress and held a blue and white patterned china carafe of something steaming. "Anybody need more coffee?"

Benjamin, his eyes riveted on Trip, shook his head. Lianna peeled her gaze away just long enough to shoot Gillian a hopeful expression.

"You can have more decaf."

Lianna stuck her tongue out at Gillian before turning back to Trip.

"I couldn't see what Gillian was after, though." Trip looked from Lianna to Benjamin. "But I could tell from the expression on her face that she was hell-bent on whatever it was." He chuckled, and his voice dropped as he tilted his head toward Lianna. "Then this one here started throwin' things."

Benjamin gaped at Lianna.

"I was trying to distract him, so Gillian could get the shotgun."

"Then, Aimee—"Trip continued.

"Where is she?" Lianna asked Gillian, who was still holding the carafe.

"In the shower."

"Then Aimee Harmon," Trip's rich voice brought all eyes back to him, "come barreling out of the parking lot and banging on them doors . . ."

Gillian caught the grammar corrections that were bubbling on her tongue before she spoke. Trip always did this—broke into some sort of backwoods hick language whenever he told a story. His mother would have thrown something at him if she'd heard him talk this way. But now, Gillian saw him differently. She noticed how his eyes sparkled and heard, for the first time in years, the deep warmth of his voice. Lianna and Benjamin seemed enthralled. It occurred to Gillian that Trip used correct grammar in front of the kids, who, she could see through the window, were all outside.

". . . which is when that boy got ahold of Aimee and raised that chain."Trip shook his head from side to side. "So." He leaned back as if the story was finished.

"So? So what?" Benjamin's voice nearly cracked.

Trip shrugged. "I tackled him, and that's when the deputy shot me."

Benjamin jerked forward. "You were shot?" His head swung toward Lianna. "He was shot? You didn't tell me he was shot."

"I had on a vest."Trip spoke as casually as if he were mentioning that he'd worn sunscreen on a sunny day. "Cracked two ribs." He arched his back into a stretch.

"Does it hurt?" Lianna asked.

Benjamin's mouth hung open as he looked from Lianna to Trip and back again.

Trip grinned. "Not nearly as bad as when I got bit by that cottonmouth last year. You want to know hurt, you get yourself tangled up with one of those ol' boys." He held out his mug to Gillian. "Hon, I think I will have a top off."

It took Gillian a moment to make sure her hand didn't shake when she poured his coffee. She kissed the top of his head and held her face in his hair a few seconds longer than was necessary.

Lianna and Benjamin were sputtering at the same time.

"A vest? Like a bulletproof vest?" Benjamin's eyes seemed like they were going to pop out of his head. "You have a bulletproof vest?"

"What's a f—" Lianna looked around. "What's a cottonmouth?"

Trip nodded at Benjamin, then turned to Lianna. "Water moccasin."

Lianna's head moved from side to side, the fear in her eyes growing.

"It's a snake you don't want to mess with, hon."

Lianna drew her knees up onto the couch.

Gillian took in the sight of Trip, safe in their living room. Through the window, she could see Ashley reading a magazine on a lounger, Carly hanging upside down on the jungle gym, and Bobbie pushing cars through the sandbox. Benjamin and Lianna—the most unlikely pair of visitors Gillian could imagine—sat on her couch, and she found herself glad they were there. Her life was good, dadgummit. And it was high time she started paying better attention to what she thought about things.

"Don't worry, Lianna." Gillian squeezed Trip's shoulder and turned to leave. "We almost never get snakes in the house." She winked at Benjamin and sauntered out of the room.

16.

TWO DAYS LATER

Yawning, Lianna descended the back stairs, Tony Romo trotting along beside her. The waves of dizziness only happened now if she bent over. She did this frequently when she was alone so that she could figure out if the concussion was gone or not. She wore the black hoodie, which Ashley had granted her for the week, and black running tights—the temperature was at least a hundred degrees outside, but they kept the house freezing. The most wonderful, savory smell was floating from the kitchen. But that wasn't a surprise. Lianna shook her head, barely able to believe that she, Benjamin, and Aimee had been staying in Gillian's house for the last two days.

"Benjamin, hon, there's an extra bed in Bobbie's room if you'd like to lie down," Gillian had said after she'd fed Benjamin what had to be his fifth bacon waffle the morning he'd arrived.

Benjamin—who Lianna could swear had been staring at Aimee with the most googly eyes—turned to Gillian, his mouth full and his face shocked.

He swallowed and patted his lips with a napkin. "That's very kind of you, Gillian, but I couldn't impose like that."

"This place is like the fu—" Lianna coughed. "Like the Four Seasons," she'd said, smiling uncertainly at Carly.

"Surely you don't want to go back to that place on Route

Nine?" Gillian asked, her voice falling away to a rough whisper when she said Route Nine.

Benjamin's expression wavered.

"We've got plenty of room." Gillian pushed the butter closer to him as Lianna wondered what in the hell Route Nine was. "Big Floyd called and said he'd be over tomorrow," Gillian continued, "so there's really no point in you driving all the way to Bramble Briar."

Four hours later, Benjamin was still sleeping upstairs while Gillian and Trip thawed steaks for dinner.

Now, two days later, Lianna walked into the kitchen and surveyed a strange scene.

Trip and Ashley stood at the far side, their faces concerned as they watched Gillian, who was stirring milk into a giant black skillet on the stove. Her blonde hair was piled on top of her head, and she wore short cut-off shorts and a blue T-shirt.

Out of the corner of her eye, Lianna saw Trip and Ashley look at each other and shake their heads.

"Um, hi," Lianna said softly. Strangely, she was beginning to hate mornings less.

"Good morning, sunshine," Gillian said over her shoulder. "I'm making biscuits and sausage gravy. It'll be ready in a minute. You want some coffee?"

"I'll get it," Lianna said pointedly—she still didn't trust Gillian not to make a decaf switch—before walking over to the Keurig and selecting a pod she was sure contained caffeine.

"Benjamin and Big Floyd are in the dining room," Gillian said. "They had some of the boys at the bank bring over a bunch of papers."

"Why didn't you wake me up?" Lianna was vaguely aware that she'd shrieked this question.

"Because you are still recovering from a concussion," Gillian said in the irritating mom-voice. She turned.

"That doesn't—" Lianna turned and felt her mouth fall open.

"What?" Gillian asked primly, tilting her head.

Lianna doubled over in a fit of laughter, gripping the counter as her head began to swim. She raised herself up, met Gillian's twinkling eyes, and collapsed into another burst of cackles.

Just then Carly ran into the kitchen, wearing a blue T-shirt that hung past her knees. Printed on the front in red and white letters was "Vote Dicky Worth" next to a giant picture of his face.

But someone had doctored the shirt with a red sparkly paint pen. It now read:

DICKY WORTH

A glittery red X slashed across Dicky's greasy smile.

Gillian's shirt was exactly the same.

Lianna's laughter turned into a snort.

Gillian watched Lianna dissolving in laughter and felt her own insides release into a fit of giggles. She'd been pulling out the ingredients for the biscuits when Carly walked into the kitchen wearing one of those awful Dicky Worth shirts. He'd left a whole box of the things with them after the party.

Gillian had been overcome with a desire to haul that box outside and set it on fire.

"Baby, bring Mama the tub with your art stuff," she'd said instead.

Fifteen minutes later, she and Carly had five shirts spread across the kitchen table.

With every stroke of the glittery paint pen, Gillian felt like a knot was coming loose inside her.

I don't have to be a Republican if I no longer want to be a Republican, she thought as she made a thick slash across Dicky's wormy face. *I can change my mind any dadgum time I please.*

"Mama and I played with my paint pens," Carly exclaimed, holding out the front of her shirt to Lianna. "We made you one too."

"That's awesome, munchkin," Lianna said, through hiccups of what looked like pure delight. "I can't wait to wear it."

◆ ◆ ◆

Gillian stood at the entrance to her dining room, which looked like a FedEx copy shop in the aftermath of a tornado. Trip's cousin, Jonathan, had brought boxes of files—Big Floyd liked to hold documents in his hands—all of which seemed to be spread out on her twelve-seat mahogany table.

"Aimee, I can't find the year-over-year P&L!" Jonathan was manically picking up pieces of paper and putting them down again. "I just had it! Did you see where I put it?"

"Aimee." Benjamin appeared to be reading at an unbelievably fast pace. Most of the papers he dropped into a messy pile to his left. He slid two across the table toward her. "I want these for the executive summary. Can you please find the electronic versions and put them in the shared folder?"

Just then Big Floyd stormed through the front door. "Aimee, call the office and make sure Clayton's there," he barked. "I swear I just passed his truck. If that boy snuck out to go fishing again, tell him he's fired."

Lianna, her socked feet on the table and one of Ashley's put-out expressions on her face, threw down the page she was trying to read and pressed her thumb to the bridge of her nose. "Aimee, can we do my emails now?"

Gillian marveled as Aimee gracefully rose and slipped the pages Benjamin had given her into a bright-red folder. She dialed a number on her phone and, with it stuck between her shoulder and ear, walked to the far end of the table. As she murmured to whomever she'd called, she reached into a pile of papers, pulled one out that—to Gillian's eyes—seemed the same as all the others, and handed it to Jonathan, who let out a visible sigh of relief.

"Clayton's at the office. He says his brother borrowed his truck," she said as she passed Big Floyd, who gave her a single nod. She continued back to a far corner, dug in her purse, and walked back to Lianna with a bottle of Tylenol. Aimee stopped and looked up at Gillian. "Tylenol's fine, right?"

Gillian nodded.

Aimee handed two pills to Lianna. "I'll get you some water, and let's do your emails upstairs, where you can lie down."

Gillian gaped as Lianna rose obediently. "You never go to bed when I tell you to," Gillian whispered when Lianna was close enough to hear.

"I like her better." Lianna stopped and leaned against the doorframe. "Is there any bacon left?"

"I will make you another bacon sandwich and bring it up to your room."

Lianna grinned and walked away. "Um, thank you," she called over her shoulder a moment later.

Gillian started back toward the dining room table, intending to ask if anyone else was still hungry. Before she could speak, she noticed Benjamin—specifically, the way his eyes followed Aimee as she gathered up her computer, her phone, and Lianna's phone. A small smile played on his face, which Gillian was sure he didn't know was there. *Hmmm*, she thought, making a mental note to seat Benjamin next to Aimee at dinner.

"Lunch was delicious, Gillian. Thank you," Aimee said for at least the third time as she walked past.

◆ ◆ ◆

An hour later, Aimee left Lianna resting in her room and stepped into her own.

She sat down on the bed, braced herself, and checked her phone.

Ten new texts from her mother and two voice mails.

Aimee dialed the hospital.

"He was up a little while ago," Celia said a few minutes later.

"Does he remember?" Aimee asked, not knowing what answer she wanted to hear.

"He's still real groggy. The doctor's gonna stop by and see him in a little bit."

Aimee knew she wouldn't be able to speak with Andy until he'd seen a doctor. "Is the doctor one of the," Aimee searched for the words, "*good* ones?"

"Well," Celia's voice dropped, "there's two making rounds today. Let's just pray he gets the young one. How you doing, baby?"

"I'm fine."

"Mmm." Celia sounded like she didn't believe Aimee at all.

Aimee pressed her lips together, wondering how she could possibly explain? A part of her ached with sorrow for Andy so badly her insides stung. But another part was . . . happy. *Which was so selfish!* Being at Gillian's was more peaceful than anyplace Aimee had ever stayed, with the exception of being alone at her own little house. Helping Lianna and Benjamin with the due diligence was the most effortless thing Aimee had ever done, yet they seemed so impressed with her.

Guilt began to rise like bile in her throat.

"Really, Celia. I'm okay. Please tell the doctor I'd like to speak as soon as possible. I can come there, or they can call me anytime."

"Of course, baby."

When they hung up, Aimee leaned back against the ruffled pillows and felt her body ease. She still couldn't believe she'd been staying at Gillian's for almost three days.

She'd intended to leave when Sheriff Davis and his deputy brought her car over the first afternoon. But then Lianna had wanted to check her emails again.

After she and Lianna finished, Aimee gathered up her purse and still-damp dress. When she went to say goodbye, Gillian exclaimed that she'd already thawed out a steak for her and asked for help with the salad.

After dinner, Aimee had surveyed the pleasant table, wishing only that she could go back up to that beautiful spare bedroom and sleep. She told herself she had to go to her mother's. Then Benjamin offered to pour her a second glass of wine, and she'd found herself agreeing. As she stood in the entryway a while later, wondering whether the wine had made her too fuzzy to drive, Lianna stuck her head around the corner and asked what time Aimee planned to get up so that they could go through her emails.

Gillian had materialized from the kitchen, explaining that she'd run Aimee's dress through the wash again; Aimee turned toward the side table, shocked to see it was no longer resting next to her purse. Gently but firmly, Gillian guided Aimee back up the stairs.

The next morning, Aimee's eyes had popped open—without the help of any alarm—just before five a.m. Still in Gillian's glorious pajamas, she'd crept outside before her mind was fully awake. Twenty minutes later, she pulled up outside her mother's house. Relief filled her when she recognized Sam's car parked by the curb. Even though the divorce was almost final, Sam, of course, would not abandon her mother.

As quietly as she could, Aimee slid her key into the front door lock and stepped inside. She nearly jumped out of her skin when she found Sam sitting in the living room, wide awake.

Her eyes darted behind him toward her mother's closed bedroom door.

"It's okay, hon," Sam said quietly, laying down the hardcover WWII novel he'd been reading. "She took the Ambien. She won't hear a thing."

He stood, and Aimee hurried over to hug him.

"I'm staying over at the Wilkins's and helping with some work." The bank deal was confidential, and even though Aimee knew Sam wouldn't say a word, she would never betray Big Floyd's confidence. "I just came by to pick up some clothes for tomorrow."

Sam nodded. "How about I fix you a cup of coffee while you pack?"

"That'd be great." Aimee hugged him again and headed up the stairs.

The world tilted slightly, as it always did when she walked into her childhood bedroom. The Laura Ashley fabrics had faded. Otherwise, the room hadn't changed from when she'd lived there years before. She dug around in the closet for a suitcase or bag. All she could find was her high school cheerleading duffel. Then her body sprang into motion. When she was done, she'd packed up all the adult clothes she'd left when she moved to work in the executive offices in Bramble Briar, as well as her yearbooks and photo albums. She stared at the bag, asking herself what this meant.

She was too afraid to answer.

"Do they have any idea what caused it?" Sam asked in a low voice a few minutes later as they huddled over the breakfast room table, hot mugs of coffee in their hands.

Aimee shook her head. "Andy's still sleeping. It'll probably be tomorrow or the next day before I can talk to him." She stared into her milky coffee. "Apparently, he quit working at the hospital three months ago and didn't tell anyone." She took another sip. "There weren't even any problems. He just stopped going to work. I'm not sure when he shaved his head." Andy's bald head haunted her more than anything else.

Sam frowned. "Your mama said she hasn't seen him or talked to him since his birthday."

"I didn't know that." Guilt began snaking up Aimee's spine. Her mother had kept saying that Andy wouldn't talk to her. But Aimee hadn't asked why or for how long. *She should have—*

Sam covered her hand with his and squeezed. "You shouldn't have to know that. What goes on between those two isn't your responsibility."

Aimee met his eyes as his words swam around her head. She looked back down at her coffee. "I guess he started working at Buck's a few weeks later." She shrugged. "That's what Sheriff Davis told me. Buck said he'd been doing a good job."

Sam chuckled. "Well, he couldn't have found a better place to make sure he didn't run into your mama."

Aimee smiled in spite of herself. Her mother had refused to set foot in Buck's since the day Buck stole her parking spot at the Piggly Wiggly.

The Piggly Wiggly had been closed for more than a decade.

When they'd finished their coffee, Sam walked Aimee out onto the front porch.

"Your mama will not have to worry about money." He patted Aimee on the arm. "I'm taking care of that." Sam had told Aimee this before, right after he'd moved out.

"You're not staying?" Aimee was ashamed at the disappointment she heard in her voice.

"No, hon." Sam shook his head. "It's just too . . ." His voice trailed away.

"I know." Aimee hugged him one last time.

Sam held her out in front of him before he let her go. "Just because I'm not staying," he clasped her cheeks in his hands, "does not mean that you have to. You got a whole life ahead of you." He let his arms fall. "It's high time you started living it."

Sam's words were still swirling in Aimee's ears as she pulled into Gillian's driveway. Careful not to make a noise, she closed the car door, her cheerleading bag slung over one shoulder. It was still dark outside, the ancient oaks in Gillian's front yard lit by soft floodlights.

Aimee tiptoed up to the front porch, realizing for the first time that she didn't have a key. She hoped the door hadn't locked behind her.

It had.

"Damn it," she said under her breath. She crept along the wraparound porch to the back deck. She'd never seen Gillian or Trip lock the back door. Worst case, she could curl up on a lawn chair until the others woke.

"Aimee?"

She jumped straight into the air and barely managed to swallow her scream.

"I'm sorry." Benjamin rose from an Adirondack chair a few feet away. He wore a plain white T-shirt and wrinkled suit pants. Like Aimee, he was barefoot.

Aimee's hand fluttered first to her wild hair then to the collar of her pajamas. She took a step back, a single thought racing through her mind—*I didn't brush my teeth!*

Benjamin was softly chuckling. "I didn't mean to scare you."

His gentle laughter and the concern that still lingered in his eyes melted her unease. She smiled, careful to keep her mouth closed.

"What are you doing?" he asked.

Aimee registered her cheerleading bag—Go Eagles!—and felt her neck start to flush. She took another step back. "I, uh, went to my mother's to grab some clothes," she said, trying not to exhale through her mouth.

He nodded, the concern deepening on his face.

Aimee thought of the awful scene with her mother in the emergency room, which Gillian and Big Floyd had witnessed. Of course, they had all been talking about her. Of course, they thought she and her family were freaks. She realized Benjamin had just said something. "I'm sorry. What?"

His smile was so warm. "I said, would you like some coffee?"

"Oh." More coffee sounded wonderful. "Sure." Aimee started toward the door. "You like yours black, right?"

Benjamin placed a hand gently on her arm. "I'll get it." He nodded to the chair next to the one he'd vacated, and Aimee noticed his laptop glowing from the little table between them. He reached over and picked up his cup. "You sit. Cream, no sugar?"

Surprised, Aimee nodded. As soon as he went inside, she dropped the ridiculous cheerleading bag and kicked it under a chair.

A few minutes later, Benjamin returned and handed her a hot mug.

Aimee took a sip of the rich, milky coffee—he'd done it perfectly—and sank back into the chair.

"It's pretty out here," he said.

"Yeah." She sighed. The air was full of the sound of crickets and bullfrogs and the deep, spicy scent of pine trees. "It is."

They sat for a moment.

"How's your cousin?"

Aimee studied Benjamin, expecting to see judgment.

His eyes were gentle and kind.

"Still sleeping." She took another sip of coffee. "That's the first thing they do. Get him to sleep." She looked out into the distance where the faintest glimmers of light were beginning to glow. "It's happened before."

Benjamin was quiet for a moment. "That must be very hard."

She nodded, feeling like the hard part was just beginning again. "I-I don't know if I can fix my family."

Aimee froze. The words—what a selfish betrayal to her mother and Andy—had just popped out without permission. Aimee waited for the wave of guilt.

It didn't come. Instead, her body felt an unfamiliar ease.

Benjamin leaned back and let out another soft, rich laugh. "I have paid a ridiculous sum of money to one of the top therapists in Manhattan on exactly that subject." His eyes widened. "Which is not something I usually share with people."

"What does he say?"

"*She*," Benjamin took a drink of coffee, "says it doesn't work that way. People have to fix themselves."

"Do you believe her?"

"Yes," he said firmly then was quiet for a moment. "That doesn't mean it's easy to have to stand back and watch."

Aimee stared out into the distance where the pond lay but couldn't yet be seen. Shoots of orange were beginning to poke into the sky. She waited for him to say more.

He didn't.

He didn't ask her any more questions, either.

Feeling something she didn't recognize, Aimee leaned back in the comfortable chair.

In silent contentment, they watched the sun rise.

❖ ❖ ❖

"Transferring him?" Later that morning Aimee gripped her phone. "But I haven't even been able to see him!"

"We're an emergency facility, Ms. Harmon," said the doctor, a sour old man who Aimee couldn't find a thing to like about. "We're not set up to keep patients long term. And your cousin is going to need much more time to recover."

"Can I see him today?"

"I'm afraid not. He's still agitated when he's not under sedation."

Aimee had stepped into Gillian's kitchen to take the call from the doctor. Now she hurried up the back stairs. "Where are you sending him?"

"You'll need to decide that."

She stopped in the middle of the hallway. "*Me?*"

Gillian came hurrying out of Carly's room with an armful of dirty clothes. She paused in front of Aimee, her eyebrows pinched.

Aimee forced herself to smile and walk calmly into her room.

"We have a social worker who can tell you about your options. There are some good private facilities if you have the means," the doctor was saying.

Aimee squeezed her eyes shut.

"Otherwise, you'll need to work with Andy's insurance provider to find out which facilities are in network."

She'd spoken to Buck about this very thing the day before. Working only part time, Andy didn't have insurance anymore.

"If you don't provide an alternative, we'll send him to Hope Springs. They have beds available for patients on Medicaid."

"How long," Aimee asked quietly as she closed the door behind her, "before you transfer him?"

"We'd like to move him Monday."

She sat on the bed in a daze. Today was Friday. Her hand traced a circle on the down comforter, wishing she could crawl under the silky covers and go to sleep. She squeezed her hand into a fist as her mind began to spin in search of a solution.

Benjamin was returning to New York later that afternoon, and a whole team of people from National Behemoth Bank were due to arrive in Bramble Briar on Monday to finish the diligence.

As soon as she hung up with the doctor, Aimee called the social worker.

Thirty minutes later, Aimee had made appointments to see four places—all in Dallas—later that afternoon. She could get the office ready over the weekend. Clayton would most certainly sneak out early to fish on a Friday, and Jonathan and Big Floyd were downstairs. No one who mattered would know she wasn't at the bank.

She began to pack her things, ignoring the disappointment shooting through her that she wouldn't be able to say goodbye to Benjamin—which made no sense at all.

◆ ◆ ◆

Gillian had been picking up laundry from the kids' rooms when she heard Aimee's voice rise out in the hallway.

"I need to get back to Bramble Briar and get the office set up for the New York team," Aimee said brightly when Gillian knocked on her door a few minutes later.

"But Benjamin's leaving right after lunch," Gillian said in her most reasonable mom-voice; something was off here, she could feel it. "Can't you at least stay until then?"

Aimee shook her head and gave Gillian a confident smile. "I wish I could, but I need to get the office ready."

Gillian's mind searched for some task she could give Aimee to do. "What about Lianna?"

Aimee stepped into the bathroom and returned with a hairbrush and small makeup bag. She slipped them into her purse. "I caught her checking her emails last night, and she seemed fine."

"How's Dr—" Gillian stopped herself, wondering if she'd ever get the new name straight. "How's Andy, hon?"

Aimee began folding her clothes and putting them in the cheerleader bag. "I spoke with the doctor a few minutes ago, and Andy's still sedated. They think I'll be able to see him on Monday," she said smoothly.

Gillian scanned the room as her mind continued to spin. Her gaze landed on Aimee's laptop, open on the bed.

Aimee stepped in front of Gillian and snapped the computer shut. She tucked it under her arm and slung the cheerleading bag over her other shoulder. She grabbed her purse and turned to Gillian with a glowing smile. "I can't thank you enough for having me."

Gillian nodded, unease continuing to brew in her stomach.

"I don't want to interrupt them downstairs," Aimee said as she stepped through the doorway into the hall. "I'll just slip out the back."

◆ ◆ ◆

"She left?" There was nothing elegant about Benjamin's voice.

"When's she coming back?" Lianna was saying at the same time.

Gillian nodded to Benjamin, unsettled thoughts still buzzing in her head. She'd googled the website she saw on Aimee's computer, which was for a mental health facility in a neighboring town.

"Hel-*lo*?" Lianna—she'd completely mastered Ashley's bobcat screech—shoved Gillian's shoulder.

Gillian searched the ceiling for patience. "I think you will see her at the bank on Monday."

Lianna huffed and folded her arms over her chest.

Benjamin was still shaking his head. "She didn't even say goodbye," he said, seemingly to himself.

"Why?" Lianna asked in an accusing tone. "Why did she leave?"

Gillian opened her mouth then closed it. She had no idea about the meaning of what she'd seen. All she could do was shrug.

All three of them stood silently for a moment.

With a burst of purpose, Gillian walked to the refrigerator and pulled out the platter of chickens she'd roasted and deboned earlier that morning. Ripping off the foil with a flourish, she laid it on the island counter. Bowls of her homemade ranch dressing, potato salad, two kinds of mustard, and mayonnaise quickly followed. Then platters of washed romaine leaves, sliced tomatoes, onions, pickles, and cheeses. A tray of smoked ham and a bowl of croissants and pretzel buns followed. She put out a stack of plates and the silverware basket, then turned the pitcher of iced tea so that the handle was easy to reach. "Lunch is ready whenever y'all get hungry," she said. "I'm just going to . . ." Her voice trailed away as she left the kitchen.

◆ ◆ ◆

Lianna watched Gillian go, then made a beeline for the food. She pinched off a piece of roasted chicken with her fingers. "Ohmigod," she said with her mouth full. "This is so good."

Benjamin frowned at her but smiled when he saw the table again. "I don't know how Gillian does it. I haven't had food like this since I spent summers with my grandmother in Georgia."

Lianna pinched another piece of chicken and shoved it into her mouth. "Is there any scenario in which you would invite two strangers to stay in your home?"

Benjamin thrust an empty plate at her. "No."

"Me either."

"I think they're nicer people than we are."

Lianna paused and considered this. "Apart from some of their fucked-up views of the world, I agree."

"Perspectives can change." Benjamin turned and picked up a linen napkin.

While his back was to her, Lianna snatched a handful of chicken and dropped it on her plate. "Do you really believe that?" she asked, taking a buttery croissant.

"I have to. Otherwise, nothing will ever get better."

Lianna let his words sink in. It was weird to be in someone's kitchen with Benjamin. She took in a slow breath, deciding she needed to tell him what she couldn't stop thinking about, especially since Aimee had disappeared. "I want to hire Aimee to be my assistant."

Benjamin suddenly seemed very interested in the cheese. "What about Meredith?"

"She'll quit."

Benjamin eyed Lianna warily. "Why exactly would she decide to do that?"

"Because I'm going to start making her do actual work."

He raised his eyebrows in a way that Lianna couldn't quite interpret. With serving tongs, he lifted several pieces of chicken breast onto his plate.

"Did you try this yet?" Lianna used the oversized fork from the ham platter to scoop up a mound of Gillian's homemade potato salad. "She makes it with mustard and vinegar instead of mayonnaise, and it is soooo fu—" She coughed and looked around for the kids. "So fucking good," she whispered. Using the same fork, she speared a piece of smoked ham.

"Lianna." Benjamin grimaced at the tiny dots of potato salad now sprinkling the ham platter. He used the end of a clean napkin to dab them away. "Use this." He held out a clean serving fork.

Lianna shook her head and moved on. "I'm done with the ham."

"Even if you solve for Meredith in a way that does not alienate her uncle," Benjamin took a slice of provolone, "it would be highly unusual to relocate an assistant."

"But she would be so good!" Lianna dumped a blob of spicy mustard onto her plate with an irritated whack. Brownish yellow dots splattered the counter.

"Jesus." Scowling, Benjamin wiped away the spots with his napkin. "Of course, she'd be good." Then quietly, almost to himself. "Having Aimee in New York would be fantastic."

"If I handle Meredith," Lianna jabbed the mustardy spoon at him, "will you sign off on Aimee?"

Benjamin leaned away from the spoon, his face a mask that Lianna couldn't read.

After a moment, he nodded.

◆ ◆ ◆

At nine o'clock that evening, Aimee pulled into the small driveway of her home in Bramble Briar. Her cheeks were tight and sticky from dried tears. Her eyes burned. She turned off the ignition but didn't get out of the Mustang.

Images of the places she'd visited had tormented her throughout the three-hour drive home. The first was a tall, grungy building in a neighborhood that might or might not be gentrifying. As she stepped into the dismal hallway, Aimee was overcome with the realization that everything—the floor, the walls, the ceiling—was gray. The staff was friendly and full of smiles, but the cheer felt so out of place. The second facility had looked more promising from the outside. The inside was worse. The third was newer and less grimy. But the patients shuffling down the halls—some with heads tilted awkwardly to the side, others with faces riveted on the ground—and the weariness in the doctors' and nurses' eyes had left her stomach in sick knots. Her mind kept spinning with a single thought: *How can Andy possibly get better in a place like this?*

For what felt like the hundredth time, she tried to make the math work in her head. If she emptied her meager savings account, if she maxed out both her credit cards, if she cut her living expenses down to the bare minimum—at best, she could afford to send Andy to the least awful place for maybe ten days. His hearing might not even be scheduled by then.

And while the sheriff had succeeded in getting Andy processed through mental health court, he told her that Andy would need to stay in a facility for at least a month, if not longer. She shuddered, thinking about Hope Springs—the place that Andy would most likely be sent. She hadn't had time to tour it but was now fairly certain about what she would find.

She laid her head on the steering wheel. Wherever Andy went, she'd simply have to go and find the *good* nurses. She'd get to know them, let them get to know her, and make sure they all understood who the real Andy was.

Aimee raised her head. She had tons of vacation she hadn't used, much of it rolled over from previous years. She could find a cheap place to stay near Hope Springs and visit every day.

Weariness filled her as she opened the car door and stepped into the driveway of her beautiful little house.

She'd turned the spare bedroom into the most glorious dressing room and closet. Even if she converted it back, Andy would be miserable in such a small space.

And they'd kill each other if they had to share that tiny bathroom.

She'd definitely need to get a bigger place before he was released and came to live with her.

17.

TWO WEEKS LATER

It was early evening as Lianna leaned back in an Adirondack chair on Gillian's deck and studied the scene before her. Endless shades of green stretched in all directions—deep emerald leaves of ancient trees, avocado-colored patches of grass, and everything in between. A family of deer—*they were everywhere!*—grazed in the shade. The air was a soft, warm blanket and smelled like a fresh salad. She took a deep breath, feeling more settled and at peace than she had in her whole life.

She watched Carly hanging upside down on the redwood jungle gym and Bobbie—wearing a Dak Prescott jersey, shorts, and the smallest cowboy boots Lianna had ever seen—rolling monster trucks through the sandbox. "Go pound sand, Bobbie," Carly shrieked when Bobbie ran over and threatened to put a cricket in her hair.

Bobbie released the bug into the grass then went back to the sandbox.

"Kids!" Gillian called half-heartedly as she darted from tiki torch to tiki torch with a long lighter. "Be sweet."

"Watch this one, Miss Lianna!" Carly called. She was hanging from a trapeze bar upside down by her knees. In one swoop—which made Lianna's heart jolt—Carly flipped to the ground, landing perfectly on her feet.

"That's a ten, munchkin!" Lianna yelled, holding up both hands, her fingers spread wide. She turned her injured palm and studied it. The bite wound was still ugly and itchy, but at least the stitches had almost dissolved. She looked back out at the yard, thinking she should offer to help Gillian or at least play with the kids.

She sank deeper into the chair. The sound of a million crickets and God-knew-what-else created a heady white-noise effect. Lianna felt like she could stay in that spot forever.

"Five more minutes, then we'll go help," she said to Tony Romo, who was stretched out beside her. Amazingly, Gillian had coached him to leave the deer alone. Lianna continued to run her fingers lazily over his bristly head, smiling when she caught the soft patches under his ears.

There was a noise beside her.

She looked up and saw Trip, holding what she guessed must be fishing poles in one big hand. "You need a drink or anything, hon?" he asked.

Lianna smiled. In all the time she'd been at their house—nearly a week while she was recovering, and this was the second weekend she'd chosen to come to them instead of flying all the way back to New York—Trip had never approached without trying to do something for her. "*Take this chair, hon. It's the most comfortable,*" he'd say, rising when she walked into the sunroom. "*Let me know when your suitcase is ready, and I'll take it down to the car for you.*" She hadn't opened a door or lifted anything bigger than a dinner plate in Trip's presence.

"I'm fine," Lianna said. "Thank you," she hurried to add. "Are those fishing poles?"

Trip smiled as he sat down on the deck next to her, his ankles crossed in front of him—an unexpected pose for such a large man. "They're called fishing *rods*, hon." He pointed to a large metallic ball on the end of one. "And this is the *reel*."

Lianna nodded. She watched in fascination as Trip pulled two wine corks out of the pocket of his shorts and meticulously fastened them on the ends of the hooks.

"Hey, sugarpop! Bobcat! Let's practice our casting!"

The kids squealed in delight and raced toward the picnic table.

Lianna's eyes flashed to Gillian as they clambered up on top of the table. But Gillian just smiled and continued to light torches.

"You want to try?" Trip asked, like a little boy thrilled to show off his toys.

"I think I'll watch first," Lianna said in a voice she hoped was friendly.

As Trip grinned and stood, it occurred to Lianna that she'd never seen that man frown or show any type of judgment toward anyone.

She watched in fascination as he handed the kids the poles— *rods*, she corrected herself.

Trip began to bellow out targets. "Sandbox! Left corner! Go!"

Carly's pixie face became a mask of concentration as both her hands fiddled with the reel. Then her left hand dropped as she raised her right—holding the rod—in a smooth arc from front to back, her tiny body flowing along with the movement in the most delicate way. Her right arm shot forward.

Lianna sat up in her seat as the cork sailed through the air and landed with a thump at the left corner of the sandbox. "Nice job, munchkin!" she heard herself squeal.

Bobbie was less graceful. But his cork followed the same direction as Carly's and landed a few feet shorter, still very much in line with the target.

Trip was smiling like his children had just walked on the moon.

He turned back to Lianna. "Did you see that?"

"I did!"

"You sure you don't want me to set you up with one? I'll have you casting in no time."

Lianna was saved from having to answer by Gillian, who walked by him and patted his stomach. "Let her rest, hon," she said, then stood on her tiptoes to kiss his cheek. "You want a beer?"

Trip wrapped an arm around Gillian's shoulders and squeezed. "Yes ma'am."

Gillian winked at Lianna as she trotted up the steps. "How about a glass of Sancerre?" She lit the giant citronella candle next to Lianna's chair.

Lianna nodded happily. She'd quickly learned that Gillian's taste in wine—just like her taste in fucking everything—was impeccable.

"Here." Gillian picked up a bottle of Avon Skin So Soft body oil from the railing and handed it over. "Don't forget to put this on."

Lianna took it. She'd been both baffled and intrigued when Gillian had insisted that the musky-scented skin softener also repelled mosquitos. But it seemed to be working. She reached for her phone from the arm of the chair and typed a text to Meredith.

> **Lianna: I didn't receive confirmation of my travel itinerary for my trip home or that you set up the meetings we talked about for next week**

Dots instantly appeared. The only good thing about Meredith was that she stayed frantically connected to her phone.

> **Meredith: IT IS SATURDAY**

> **Lianna: I gave you the assignments Tues. Pls text confirmation before tmrw that all is done**

◆ ◆ ◆

Gillian sank into the chair beside Lianna, a sweating stainless-steel bucket filled with ice and an opened bottle between them.

"This is so good." Lianna smiled as she tasted the wine. "Mmmm."

Trip now had one arm around Bobbie, gently positioning his hands on top of his son's. "If you take your thumb off sooner, it'll go farther," he explained in what Gillian realized was the most patient voice she'd ever heard. He guided Bobbie's arm in the arcing motion a few times before stepping away.

Bobbie threw a nearly perfect cast. He turned to Trip, and Gillian watched identical grins spread across their faces.

"Trip is so good with them," Lianna was saying.

"I know." Gillian winced at how many moments like this she'd missed because all she could seem to focus on was what Trip was doing wrong.

"Is he going to press charges against the deputy for"—Lianna coughed—"you know, shooting him?"

Gillian shook her head. "The deputy was fired. And Trip's okay." She took another drink of wine to steady herself. Thinking of the shooting still made her stomach swim. "It's sad. Sheriff Davis said that boy'd wanted to be a policeman more than anything."

"He wasn't a boy," Lianna said without a trace of sympathy.

Gillian sighed. "I guess maybe his reasons for wanting it so badly weren't gonna make him good at it."

They sat in silence for a few minutes.

"Do you think Trip will do the fishing business once the deal's done and you've got millions?" Lianna asked.

"Did no one teach you that it's rude to talk about money?" Gillian's voice was exasperated, but she smiled. The previous weekend, after the kids were in bed, she and Lianna had finished a pitcher of red sangria. Surprising herself, Gillian had told Lianna everything: Trip's plans for his fishing business; her plans at the bank when they were first married; her mother-in-law's spectacular squashing of both. She topped off Lianna's glass of Sancerre. "I think he might."

"That would be cool." Lianna took a sip. "Thank you."

"You're welcome." Gillian refilled her own glass. "I think it would be nice if he did too." She leaned back in her chair.

"What about you?"

"What about me?" Gillian turned to see Lianna studying her.

"What are you going to do?" In a shocking turn of events, Lianna had begun to smile quite frequently, and her smile was absolutely beautiful. Her grin turned mischievous. "Now that Trip's got twenty mil."

Gillian shook her head in mock consternation. But the truth was that she couldn't seem to stop thinking about that question—couldn't quite imagine resuming her life as it had been before Buck's. She bit her lip and looked back out toward Trip, groping for words to describe the feelings that had begun sweeping through her that morning after they'd come back from the hospital. "I have decided that I need to change how I think about some things."

"Yeah, you do," Lianna said with a laugh. After a moment, her face softened. "What do you mean, exactly?"

Again, Gillian stretched her mind to find the words. "People told me things were a certain way, and I accepted it all without question. Hook, line, and sinker, I swallowed every idea that was handed to me whole. Then, because I expected things to be that way, that's all I saw."

Lianna's brows pinched together.

"It's like I only noticed facts that created the picture I was told to see. I didn't pay attention to anything else—to anything that didn't fit that pattern."

Lianna's expression did not change.

"So I have decided to make sure I take a hard look at what I really think and make up my own mind."

Lianna pulled out the front of her shirt—another doctored T-shirt that said vote no to Dicky. She and Carly played with the paint pens regularly. "Like being a Republican?"

Gillian nodded. She had been reading about Dicky Worth's opponent, amazed at the misinformation that Dicky had presented as hard facts. Because as it turned out, the woman was not proposing double-digit tax increases. Or the complete abolition of the NRA. Or abortion-related health education to ten-year-olds. Gillian hadn't told anyone, but she'd already made a generous donation to the woman's campaign. "And some other things," Gillian said quietly, thinking of the lunch she'd had with Savannah, whose twins were in Carly's class at school. Savannah had been poised and gracious when Gillian said she and Trip would gladly sponsor Savannah's family in joining the club. But it was clear that Gillian's delay in offering had stung. Savannah took a few days to think about it. The day before—to Gillian's great relief—Savannah had called and accepted.

Something soft bumped Gillian's nose.

She looked down and watched the linen napkin she'd handed to Lianna flutter into her own lap. "Hel-*lo*?" Lianna was snapping her fingers. "Just like that. You're going to change your whole outlook?"

"Why not?" Gillian lifted her chin. "It's my mind. And there is absolutely no reason I can't change it about *absolutely* anything."

Lianna snatched her napkin back and seemed to search for a point to argue. After a moment, she shook her head. "That is just so wildly illogical. So fucking"—she grimaced—"*you*." The scowl didn't last long. "Better late than never, I guess." She tipped her glass toward Gillian's.

Gillian toasted back, then quietly watched the deer.

An inkling about something else she wanted to do had begun to bloom somewhere deep inside her. But she wasn't quite ready to tell anyone about it yet.

◆ ◆ ◆

Aimee sat in the sunny room, her mind buzzing as she tried, yet again, to figure out how this whole thing had happened. The morning after she'd visited the mental health facilities in Dallas, she'd been sitting on her couch in her pajamas, scouring the websites of private places she hadn't toured and hoping to find one that might offer some kind of financial assistance.

Her phone rang.

It was Celia. "Somebody paid for Andy to go to Serenity Pines," she whispered as soon as Aimee answered.

Aimee nearly dropped her coffee cup. She had just looked at Serenity Pines online, knowing it was a long shot, but feeling a bubble of hope for the first time since the doctor told her Andy would be transferred. Nestled among the deep woods, Serenity Pines treated both mental health illness and addiction. Their website explained a focus on holistic healing—supplementing medication and traditional therapy with things like nutritional programs, yoga, and nature walks. The place seemed more like a meditation retreat center than a mental hospital. "That's impossible," she heard herself saying even though the bubble in her stomach was expanding into a balloon.

"I'm sure of it, Aimee. Somebody paid for Andy to go to Serenity Pines!"

"Who?"

"I don't know. I'm not even supposed to be calling you. But Carol down in the administrative office is slow as molasses, and I was worried you'd spend all day looking for a place before she got around to letting you know."

It has to be Sam, Aimee thought a while later, after she'd dreamed up an excuse to call Carol, who'd confirmed the amazing news. When Aimee tried to call him, Sam's phone went straight to voice mail, which meant he was probably on one of his fishing trips out of cell range.

And now, here she was. Sitting in this spacious great room—which sort of felt like being in an upscale lodge—waiting to talk to Andy's new doctor for the first time. She made a mental note to try Sam again when her meeting was over. She'd left him two messages, but not hearing back wasn't unusual. His fishing trips sometimes lasted a week or more. After spending so much time at her mom's house, he probably needed the peace and quiet.

"He'll see you now," a pleasant young woman called to Aimee from a doorway.

Thirty minutes later, Aimee sat in a cushy armchair across from Andy's doctor, her mind saturated from everything he had just explained. "This wasn't caused by lack of sleep," she said finally.

"I believe Drew is struggling with bipolar disorder, possibly schizoaffective disorder as well." Dr. Greene was younger than she'd expected, with sandy blond hair and the kindest blue eyes. "Lack of sleep caused the psychotic behavior, but it's not the root cause of what happened. The culprit is mania, and that's what we've got to treat."

"How long will he need to take the Seroquel?"

Dr. Greene's expression turned slightly pained. "He'll likely be on some form of medication for the rest of his life."

Aimee swallowed. "How come they didn't tell us this before?"

"I can't really speak to that." Dr. Greene sighed. "It's unfortunate, but these things can easily get missed. And if he didn't continue with his therapy . . ."

Bile-like guilt began to rise in Aimee's throat. She hadn't thought much about it when, a few weeks after Andy's first breakdown, her mother told her that he was well and didn't need *that therapist* or *those awful drugs* anymore. Aimee had returned home from Rice for Christmas, and Andy had seemed like his normal self, if perhaps slightly subdued. Because his second episode happened in a different town altogether, Andy never even saw the outpatient therapist that had been recommended. When he refused to go back to school, Aimee just took him home to Sweet Leaf. She thought back over the last year. "I knew he wasn't—I knew his life wasn't—" She stared out the window.

"These diseases are tricky." Dr. Greene's voice was so compassionate. "The people experiencing them don't understand what's happening. How can you expect yourself to?"

Aimee looked at him but didn't say anything.

"Drew and I have spoken a lot since he arrived last week. He—"

"Andy." Aimee couldn't believe she'd interrupted Dr. Greene so rudely, but this was the third time he'd gotten Andy's name wrong. "His name is Andrew, but he goes by Andy."

Dr. Greene regarded her a moment. "He told me he prefers Drew."

Aimee felt the floor tilt as a long-ago memory peeked out at her. Andy must have been about twelve. "I'm going to call myself Drew this year," he'd said the night before school started. Her mother's dismissive laughter had been instant and unkind. "That's ridiculous, sweetheart. You'll confuse everybody. You're Andy, and you're going to stay that way."

Aimee turned back toward the window, but everything appeared blurry.

"He says," Dr. Greene continued gently, "that you're the person who's always been there for him."

Aimee let out a shaky exhale and tried to keep the tears down. "My mother can be . . . um . . ."

The doctor chuckled in a way that put Aimee at ease. "Drew's told me quite a bit about your mom. But let's not get into her right now. You and Drew are both adults. Whether she continues to be part of either of your lives is entirely your choice."

Once again, Aimee was struck by the thought that she could simply stop dealing with her mother. The idea felt dangerous, disloyal, and filled her with an exquisite feeling of relief.

"There are a lot of things Drew wants to work on. One is living more independently. He told me he never wanted to work at the hospital."

Deep down, Aimee had always known this. But after he'd dropped out of college, she was so anxious for him to figure out something to do. She'd found the online ad for the hospital job and harassed him about it until he applied. "What does he want?"

"He doesn't know," Dr. Greene said without a trace of judgment. "And that's one of the things we're going to tackle. I don't get the sense that what Drew *wanted* as a child or a young adult was something that was ever given much importance."

Aimee stared at the doctor, feeling the floor tilt a little bit more.

"It probably wasn't for you either," he said softly. "You just coped with those circumstances in a different way."

"What happens now?"

"I'd like Drew to stay for a while, and he agrees. I think he could really benefit from being here."

Aimee swallowed, wondering how much Sam could afford.

"The court will have something to say about that as well. But it's been made clear funds are available for as long as Drew wants to stay."

Aimee squeezed her jaws together to keep her mouth from falling open. Sam was always so frugal.

"Okay." She leaned forward. "What do you need me to do?"

Dr. Greene smiled but didn't say anything for what felt like a long time. "This is where my perspective differs from that of some of my colleagues." He looked down at the floor. "Many would ask you to become involved in Andy's treatment." His gaze drifted back to her. "Family counseling with you, Andy, and your mother. Perhaps make a plan for Andy to come live with you when he leaves."

Aimee felt her stomach knotting. She hadn't done anything about finding a new house yet. She'd need to get on that as soon as she left. "Right."

"That's not what I'm recommending."

Aimee's mind was so busy whizzing with how she'd get out of her lease that she almost didn't hear him. "Sorry. What?"

"I think that when Andy's ready to go home, he should go to his home. Not yours, and certainly not your mom's."

Aimee blinked, a part of her brain insisting that this couldn't be right. That, obviously, Andy needed someone to take care of him. The rest of her felt like she'd just been rescued from something. "But he's sick. And it's not his fault."

Dr. Greene looked at her steadily. "It's not your fault either." His words seemed to hang in the air.

"But somebody's got to take care of him."

"Bipolar disorder and schizoaffective disorder are illnesses. Incredibly unfair ones." The doctor steepled his hands together. "Drew has to learn to take care of himself—choosing to take his medication consistently, choosing to actively participate in his therapy, choosing to accept the help of support structures that are independent from you. He needs you to love him and support him, sure." Dr. Greene paused. "You need to understand that you can't fix him, Aimee."

"I have to!" The words were out before she even thought of them. Then, more softly, "He's my family."

When Dr. Greene finally spoke, his eyes were kind but his voice firm. "Drew is twenty-five years old, and the only person who can fix him is himself." His voice softened. "This disease is tragic. What happened at that store was tragic. What Drew's had to experience has been tragic. And he and I are going to do our best to create the tools and structures in his life so that nothing like this happens again."

Aimee went very still. Something inside her felt like it was waking up from a long and deep sleep.

"The only thing you have power over, Aimee, is whether you let Drew's illness make your life tragic too."

◆ ◆ ◆

Gillian opened the front door, knowing her smile didn't quite reach her eyes.

"Hey, Gillybean." Big Floyd pulled her into one of his crushing bear hugs.

He released her, then turned and stared at his wife. Mama W stood next to him on the porch holding a crystal vase full of her Belinda's Dream roses. She handed the vase to Gillian. "These are for you," she said crisply.

Big Floyd made a growling sound.

Mama W grimaced and looked down at the porch. "Thank you for having me."

"You're welcome." Gillian took the vase. She had never known Mama W to part with any of her precious roses. "These are lovely."

As soon as they were inside, Mama W hurried into the living room where Carly and Bobbie played with monster trucks in one corner and Trip sat on the floor a few feet away, pieces of a deconstructed fishing rod and reel scattered around him. She kissed the top of Trip's head, then plopped down on the floor next to Bobbie and Carly. "I haven't seen you two in a month of Sundays!" she exclaimed, throwing her arms around first one and then the other. She *was* good with the kids, Gillian thought as she put the roses on a side table.

"How're you feeling, son?" Big Floyd stood over Trip and held out his hand.

"Real good," Trip said, accepting the help and only wincing a little when he stood.

Gillian, who was behind Big Floyd, met Trip's eyes and smiled. A few days before, she'd found Trip in the den smoothing out his old fishing maps.

She'd ordered a bunch of colored pushpins from Amazon immediately.

Trip coughed. "There's, uh." He turned toward Gillian uncertainly.

She smiled harder and nodded.

"Something I'd like to show you if you have a minute." He tilted his head toward the den.

"Ah'ight," Big Floyd said.

Watching the two of them, Mama W started to rise. She paused and looked at Gillian, whose eyes dared her to follow them. Mama W's head swiveled to Big Floyd, who glowered at her.

She sighed and settled back on the floor with the kids.

Once Trip and his dad were in the den, Gillian returned to the kitchen to finish dinner. As she snapped the ends off the green beans, fresh from her garden, her thoughts swirled around the idea that had been filling her mind for days. Slowly, her brain drifted over each of the events that had propelled it into being.

That first afternoon after the ordeal at Buck's, Sheriff Davis had brought Aimee's car to Gillian's and asked Gillian and Lianna if they could speak privately. She'd watched the color drain from Aimee's face as they left her in the kitchen and stepped into the den.

Lianna had been apoplectic when the sheriff suggested mental health court—waving her still-bandaged hand, then pausing to steady herself. But all Gillian could think about was the day Drew had put the ice pack on Carly's arm. It had taken her and the sheriff a half hour to convince Lianna to agree.

A couple of days later, she'd watched Aimee become nearly unhinged by a phone call, then pack up her things and race out the back door.

Gillian had called the sheriff thirty seconds after Aimee's Mustang left the driveway. "Is somebody trying to send Drew to jail?" she demanded when the sheriff said, "Hello."

The sheriff sighed, sounding as weary as Moses must have felt when he first stumbled upon the banks of the Red Sea. "No. He's gonna be charged through mental health court, like we agreed. But the hospital is transferring him to another facility."

With startling clarity, Gillian had thought of the website she'd seen on Aimee's laptop.

An hour and a half later, not quite believing what she was doing and hoping she had remembered to put out all the fixings for lunch, Gillian parked in front of a red brick building with white shutters and a trim front lawn. Hope Springs was printed in script across a small, understated sign. *This doesn't seem so bad*, she'd thought.

The lobby, with its potted plants and dated furniture, wasn't exactly nice. But it wasn't awful either.

Then they took her on the tour.

The rough smell of disinfectant hit Gillian's nose as soon as she stepped through the security doors, and she was overcome with an anxiety that she might never be allowed to leave. The stark hallway was freezing. Following the friendly-but-exhausted-looking woman who was giving her the tour, Gillian lifted her chin and smiled at the people she passed. The staff smiled back in a way that made her think of the teachers at Bobbie's preschool. *Bless their hearts for choosing to be here*, she thought. Still, seeing that kind of cheer in a place like this made her feel queasy.

The woman led her to a small dorm-like room. There were two twin beds, two chests of drawers, and a tiny bathroom that wasn't bigger than a broom closet. A small window, high up toward the ceiling, was the only light. Gillian had assessed the bed, certain Drew's feet would hang right off the end.

But it was the common room that did her in. The chairs were a faded green color that had probably once been bright but now made her think of stewed peas. The carpet was a dull gray. Across the room, a woman with wild hair and wearing a pink running suit caught Gillian's eye.

Gillian smiled.

The woman thrust out a quivering finger and gurgled something Gillian couldn't understand.

One of the hulking men in white uniforms who stood on either side of the door shifted his stance and put his hands on his hips.

The woman turned back to the TV.

Gillian searched for someplace else to put her eyes. They landed on a man in a bathrobe, just as he took a jigsaw puzzle piece out of his mouth, a long string of spit trailing down to the table in front of him.

She swallowed hard and focused on the woman giving her the tour, who was looking at Gillian in a slightly pained way. "We do the best we can," she'd said quietly.

As soon as Gillian got into her Lincoln, she called Big Floyd.

"What's wrong?" he barked when he picked up.

"Everybody's fine," she said quickly. "But—" It occurred to her that she and her father-in-law had never in a blue moon made plans alone. She swallowed. "Would you mind meeting me at Starbucks for a cup of coffee?"

"Now?"

Gillian checked the clock. "I need an hour and a half to get there."

"Course," he'd said, then hung up the phone.

"I can set the table, Mother." Ashley was suddenly beside Gillian, bringing her out of her musings. Gillian noticed her daughter's outfit—a black T-shirt with an orange skull on it that Gillian absolutely hated and an unflattering pair of jean shorts. "Thanks, sweetness," Gillian said as she reached over and smoothed Ashley's hair.

◆ ◆ ◆

Sitting in her car in the parking lot of Serenity Pines, Aimee drew in a shaking breath and dialed. She wasn't sure why she needed to do this now, but she did.

"Finally," her mother answered, sounding both wounded and put out. "I cannot believe you would do this to me in the middle of such a crisis. It's been two weeks, and all I've gotten from you have been texts."

I'm sorry, the automatic words sat on Aimee's tongue. "Andy's been moved to a place called Serenity Pines in Muddyville," she said instead.

"Hold on and let me get a pen." As Aimee heard drawers open and close, her mother continued, "I cannot believe that boy would choose this time to pull a stunt like this. I am *go-in'* through a divorce, and—"

"He didn't choose, Mom." Aimee's voice came out harsher than she intended. "He's sick. He has been for a while."

"That's one opinion," her mother said. The shuffling stopped. "I can't find a pen. I'll just get the address when I see you. Oh! Sam took my car into Milton's for me after the sheriff brought it back, so you don't have to worry about that." Her voice dropped.

"He's been staying over while I recuperated from this mess."

Aimee knew this was the part where she was supposed to ask questions about what was happening with her mother and Sam. She was silent.

"Although he took off to go fishing, which wasn't very considerate, but he's coming back today." Cabinet doors opened and closed.

"Mom."

"I made a lasagna, your favorite. It's in the freezer. Let me know when I can expect you because I'll need to take it out a few hours ahead."

Aimee gripped the phone, wondering if she could actually do this. "Mom."

The sound of running water. "What, sweetheart?"

"I'm not coming." Aimee squeezed her eyes shut.

Silverware clinked. "What was that?"

"I . . . I . . ." Suddenly, a line from one of the books flashed across Aimee's mind. "I can't be responsible for your happiness, Mom. I can't be responsible for you."

Dishes clattered on the counter. "What in the world are you going on about?"

Aimee breathed. "I need to take a break for a while." Her heart was pounding. "From us. I need to take a break from you."

Silence.

Silence.

A loud sniffle. "Why are you doing this to me?" A sob. "I don't know how I managed to raise such a selfish child. Andy's in the hospital, and I'm *go-in'* through a divorce, and you choose to do this now? I just don't understand how—"

"I love you, Mom. But I can't do this anymore."

With a surprisingly steady finger and a shaking heart, Aimee hung up the phone.

18.

TWO YEARS LATER, NEW YORK

"I love your new place," Gillian said, leaning back on Lianna's black leather couch—which was not a choice Gillian would have made, but she was working on being more accepting about things.

"Thanks. Oh, the munchkin wants to visit me for her fall break." Lianna, wrapped in a bath towel, her hair in rollers the size of soup cans, paused in the doorway.

Gillian smiled and sighed. "Am I supposed to know this or not?"

"Not yet. She said she's," Lianna made air quotes, "waiting for the right moment to tell you."

"When did she ask?"

"She called me last week."

Gillian's smiled deepened. At ten years old, Carly remained her dreamiest and most enigmatic child. Gillian was as likely to find her sprawled in the wildflower garden with Tony Romo, immersed in some game of her own imagining, as she was to discover her sipping iced tea on the porch, ankles crossed as she enjoyed a leisurely phone call—on the landline—with her grandmother. Carly was fond of the term *social calendar* and curated her own with meticulous precision.

"You don't mind?" Gillian asked. "It won't interfere with work?" For the past fourteen months, Lianna's full-time job had been managing Trip's and Big Floyd's personal financial portfolios. Recently, two of Big Floyd's former business colleagues had approached her about managing theirs as well. She'd told Gillian she was still assessing the workload involved and deciding whether she wanted to expand or not.

"Nope." Lianna breezed past the doorway again.

Gillian made a mental note to suggest to Carly that she might like to visit Lianna and save her the trouble of *finding the right moment*. Gillian's phone buzzed. "Trip just texted," she called. "He and Ashley ran late getting to the second appointment. They're gonna meet us at the restaurant."

Lianna reappeared in the doorway wearing jeans and a bra. "Which campus did she like better? NYU or Columbia?" Gillian's heart leapt when she saw the kabuki brush in Lianna's hand. She'd introduced Lianna to mineral makeup the year before.

"She loves them both. Trip's beside himself."

"He'll survive." Lianna turned and went back to the bathroom. "How's his fishing business?"

"Doing well enough. His daddy and Troy Aikman are his best customers." Gillian slipped off her ankle-strap wedges, which were giving her blisters. She always forgot how much her feet hurt after walking all day in New York. "Trip loves every minute of it. Bobbie goes out with him sometimes too." She stretched. "Of course, Bobbie makes him release every fish they catch."

"Good kid. And he still refuses to go hunting?"

Gillian had never been prouder of her boy than the day Trip tried to get him to watch *Buckmasters* on TV. As soon as the first shot went off, Bobbie had let loose a tantrum like a thunderstorm. He wouldn't be quieted until Trip changed the channel to NASCAR. "Trip's getting over it. The idea of Ashley living in New York is what's making him nuttier than a five-pound fruitcake."

"She'll be fine." Lianna's head popped back. "I meant to ask." Her voice turned serious. "What happened with the boyfriend?"

"She broke up with him."

"Good." Lianna spun and went back to the bathroom. "He sounded like such an inconsiderate dipshit."

"Thank you," Gillian called.

Lianna appeared again, pulling a roller out of her hair. "For what?" she asked in the innocent voice Gillian had learned always meant Lianna was guilty.

Gillian gave Lianna her you-and-I-both-know-what's-going-on-here mom expression. "For getting her to break up with him. I'm pretty sure he was cheating on her with one of the boys from the football team."

Lianna laughed and shrugged her shoulders. "I didn't," she said, her voice even higher this time.

Gillian stared at her.

Lianna's voice returned to normal. "Okay, fine. I did." She whipped around and went back into the bathroom. "How did you know it was me?"

"Because when I asked Ashley why she broke up with him, the first words out of her mouth were that he was an inconsiderate dipshit."

Lianna returned, all but one roller gone. "I'm starving. Will you make snacks?"

"And ruin dinner?" Gillian looked at her phone. "Our reservation's in an hour."

"It'll be another hour before we get our appetizers. That place takes forever." Lianna's eyebrows wiggled. "I've got wine."

"The polite thing to do would have been to offer me that when I got here." Gillian rose. She went to the cabinet next to the refrigerator and took out two crystal wineglasses from the set she'd given Lianna at Christmas.

A moment later, Lianna, wearing a black turtleneck and—Gillian was thrilled to see—a faint pink gloss on her lips, returned and hopped onto a barstool. "How did the fundraiser go?"

"It was good!" Gillian's eyebrows rose as she studied the wine bottle. "What a lovely white Bordeaux." She smiled at Lianna. "We raised almost seventy thousand."

Lianna propped her elbow on the bar and rested her chin on her fist. "I think this thing you're doing is so cool. I'm glad we didn't . . ." Her voice faded.

"I know." Gillian's mind wandered back to the day she went to visit Drew at Serenity Pines. She'd woken one morning about a month after he'd been there, overcome by the feeling that she needed to see him. And following this strange inclination, she'd called. Hearing her intentions, the doctor, who she immediately liked, agreed.

She'd found Drew—Dr. Greene had explained that was the name he preferred, and Gillian was glad because that's how she thought of him—sitting outside on a cushioned lawn chair in front of a stunning expanse of pine trees. He looked at her briefly, then back out at the woods. Studying his pale face, she was struck by the idea that he had somehow shrunk.

"I'm Gillian Wilkins," she said, sounding more formal than she intended. She cleared her throat and pointed to the chair next to him. "May I sit?"

"Yes, ma'am," he said, without turning his head.

"Doctor Greene told you I was coming?" She sat down on the foot end of the chair, so they faced each other.

Drew nodded but didn't say anything.

Gillian swallowed. "How're you feeling?"

He scratched his head. "The drugs suck."

"I've heard that." Gillian had been googling ferociously, filled with a desire to learn as much as she could about the disease.

"They have to play around with the doses before they get it right?"

Drew nodded. Still, he didn't meet her eyes.

She swallowed again. All the words she'd practiced in her head had disappeared.

"I'm sorry," Drew said after a minute, his eyes still locked on the trees. "I'm sorry for what I did to you that night."

Gillian's breath slowed. "Thank you."

He was quiet again.

She groped for what she had planned to say. "We-We're okay" was all she could think of.

After a long moment, Drew turned toward her. In his eyes, she saw the same shame that had hovered in Aimee's in the days following the ordeal. His was magnified tenfold.

She reached to pat his knee, then thought better of it. "That's why I came. I wanted you to know. Lianna, the other woman who was there? She and I are both just fine."

Drew's eyes flitted over her face, the top of her hair, then back out to the trees. "I only remember little pieces."

Gillian could see him struggling not to cry.

He coughed and blinked. "But they told me." He looked at her again. "Sheriff Davis told me what I did."

Gillian wanted so badly to hug him. "We're just fine now, hon. I promise."

"I hurt that other lady," he said, his voice a hoarse whisper. "I remember that."

"You scared her." Gillian felt a splash of disloyalty toward Lianna. But she couldn't stand to see this boy in so much pain. "Mostly you just scared us."

"I hurt her. And I hurt Aimee too." He didn't look away until Gillian nodded.

"Everybody's okay now." She reached over and squeezed his

knee. "You know as well as I do that Aimee is just fine. And I wanted you to know that Lianna and I are too."

Drew flinched but didn't pull away. The tears rolled down his cheeks.

Unable to help herself, Gillian scrambled off her chair and hugged him.

"Thanks, Mrs. Wilkins," she heard him whisper into her ear.

Then he pulled away, rose, and walked back inside.

In that moment, Gillian understood exactly what she wanted to do.

"I still can't believe I have my own nonprofit!" She pulled a wedge of Brie from Lianna's refrigerator and unwrapped it.

Lianna nodded and stared at the cheese longingly. "I can't believe you got it up and running so fast."

Gillian smiled, her mind marveling as it always did when she thought of her new project, which had been so amazingly simple to create. Working with Sheriff Davis—and now with sheriffs in three other counties—Gillian's organization funded treatment at Serenity Pines for people with optimistic prognoses but who didn't have the means to afford private facilities. They worked closely with Drew's doctor, Dr. Greene, who volunteered time to identify the patients and direct the program. "It was so easy once we got started." She began opening cabinets. "Where's that MacKenzie-Childs tray I got you for your birthday?"

"In the oven."

Gillian spun. "It's not heat resistant! I told you that!"

Lianna rolled her eyes. "If I ever use the oven, I will take it out."

Shaking her head, Gillian pulled out the colorful platter and spread a perfect fan of water crackers around one side.

"How many people have you put through your program now?" Lianna asked.

"Ten, counting Drew."

Lianna stuck her finger into the pointy end of the Brie. "How are the other candidates?"

Gillian pushed the cheese knife—another Christmas present—toward her. "They're all doing well. Dr. Greene sees them each once a week. And we helped the ones who've finished inpatient to find apartments and paid six months of rent. Did I tell you that? We're expanding to support the acclimation process. It turns out that my friend Savannah was a social worker back when she lived in Philadelphia."

"Savannah?"

"You met her at the house last Christmas. She chaired the New Year's gala at the club. Her twins are in class with Carly."

Lianna nodded. "Oh, yeah. I liked her."

"Savannah's too busy with her boys to work full time, but she's volunteering to help our patients get situated and find jobs when they leave Serenity."

"And Big Floyd's really helping?"

Gillian nodded, thinking of their first conversation about it, at one of their now weekly coffee dates and moments after she'd taken him to visit Hope Springs, the mental health facility she'd seen so many months ago. Sipping his venti Pike Place, Big Floyd, who'd been silent since the tour began, seemed as conflicted as Abraham lookin' at his boy Isaac upon the sacrificial altar. "You spend your life trying to protect what you've built for yourself and those you love," he'd said finally, "terrified somebody's going to come along and take it all away." He studied his coffee. "Maybe the best way to protect what's yours is to help other folks out."

Something soft bumped Gillian's nose. She looked down at one of the linen napkins she'd put in the housewarming basket when Lianna got the new condo.

"Hel-*lo*." Lianna snapped her fingers. "I *said*, I'm glad the others are doing well."

Gillian blinked and smiled. "Dr. Greene says I need to prepare myself because we'll have some clients who relapse." She lifted her chin. "But we'll see about that. Oh!" She clapped her hands together. "I almost forgot. Can I meet Carson Wentz?"

Lianna's face brightened. "He's resting, but I'll check." She hopped off the barstool and disappeared into the bedroom.

When she returned, her arms were full of a giant silvery-gray cat.

Gillian felt her mouth fall into an unladylike gape. "How much does he weigh?"

Lianna glared at her. "Don't be rude."

Gillian sighed and tilted her head. She reached toward the pink nose and let him smell her hand. "Your doorman just found him in the alley?"

Lianna nodded.

Gillian scratched under his chin.

His purring seemed to fill the room, and Gillian was instantly smitten. "You're giving him wet food along with the dry?" She stepped closer. "Making sure he gets lots of water? That's so important for indoor cats because they are *so* susceptible to—"

"Pound sand, Gillian!" Lianna could still do Ashley's bobcat screech brilliantly. "I read two books, and I am taking great fucking care of him!" She turned away, pulled Carson Wentz onto her shoulder, and rubbed her face against his back. "Don't listen to her, beautiful boy," she said in a high-pitched, squeaky voice Gillian would have sworn with her hand to the Lord that Lianna was incapable of.

"Does Aimee have any news for me?" Gillian asked as she followed Lianna back to the bar.

Lianna's huffy expression softened. "I'm supposed to let her tell you at dinner."

Gillian raised an eyebrow.

Lianna nodded. The cat began to squirm, so she lowered him to the ground. "She and Benjamin set a date."

Gillian threw her head back and raised her arms to the ceiling. "Hallelujah!"

"I think she wants you to help plan the wedding, but I'm not sure she'll actually ask." Lianna leaned forward and reached a finger toward the Brie.

Gillian swatted her wrist and pointed at the cheese knife.

"Ow." Lianna took the knife, cut a piece of cheese, and stuck the whole thing into her mouth. "Can you just, you know," Lianna made a pinched face as she talked and chewed, "be *you* and start doing it?"

"Obviously, I made a planning folder when she told me they were engaged." Gillian took a sip of wine. "Because, *obviously*, I am a huge part of the reason they found each other in the first place."

Lianna laughed. "Obviously."

◆ ◆ ◆

Aimee leaned her head against the town car's back window and watched the buildings swoop by, their lights twinkling against an inky night sky.

"Those numbers do not make sense." Benjamin, on his phone beside her, took her hand in his.

Warmth swirled through her wrist and up her arm. She sighed and felt her shoulders soften even more.

She couldn't wait to see Gillian. Only after Gillian had told her about the nonprofit did Aimee understand Gillian had been the one who got Drew to Serenity Pines.

Aimee's mind fluttered back to that long-ago afternoon, sitting in her car after her visit with Dr. Greene. She'd just hung up with her mother when Sam called her back.

"No, hon," Sam had said, his voice light with wonder. "I'd love to have been able to help Andy, but this divorce from your mama's got me pretty much tapped out."

Aimee had gripped the phone as the familiar, cold trickle of shame hovered just outside her. Big Floyd was the only person she knew who had that kind of money. She looked out at the beautiful grounds, two crushing feelings playing tug-of-war inside her: There was no way she and Andy could accept such charity. But she couldn't fathom taking him away from this place.

"Aimee." Sam's voice cut through her scuffling thoughts. "It is high time you and Andy had some good fortune." He blew out a long breath. "You kids have had the short end of the stick for as long as I've known you. And if you can't let yourself just accept and appreciate this gift," he snorted, "then you are a damn fool."

The next morning, she'd arrived at the bank early. Big Floyd was usually there an hour before anyone else. She found him making a cup of coffee with the new Keurig machine, which he and Aimee seemed to be the only ones who understood how to use. He'd even started using the compostable gourmet pods.

Big Floyd growled something that sounded like good morning.

Without a word, Aimee walked up to him and threw her arms around his waist. Her head barely came up to his chest. She felt him jump. Then a big, paw-like hand patted her back.

"Thank you," she whispered before hurrying away so that he wouldn't see her tears. They'd never spoken of it again.

Aimee and Andy—she caught herself—*Drew* didn't talk frequently. He'd left Serenity Pines after three months but chose to live nearby. As Aimee's salary in New York was beyond anything she could have imagined, she'd been able to help him get an apartment. He'd begun an apprenticeship as a mechanic at a local garage and, after a few months, was supporting himself. When they did speak, stories of his job filled the minutes—of locating parts for obscure or discontinued cars, of detecting the source of mysterious vehicular ailments. For the first time that Aimee could remember, he actually sounded happy.

Their distance was something she and her own therapist, Caitlin, talked about frequently.

"You trigger each other," Caitlin had explained recently. "When you and Drew interact, you automatically fall into the patterns that were established when you were growing up." She seemed to give Aimee a moment to digest what she'd said. "Which can be problematic if you're trying to create a *new* framework. It's not uncommon."

"But I feel . . ."

Caitlin stared at her, waiting.

Aimee sighed. "Guilty."

Caitlin raised an eyebrow. "Guilty because you don't talk to him much or guilty because you're okay with that?"

Aimee studied the floor.

"Neither of you got what you needed, at least emotionally speaking, when you were children. From what you've told me, your mother harbors a lot of unhealed wounds." Caitlin seemed to tread carefully over the next words. "I know you're still grappling with this, but you grew up having to cope with some very unhealthy and confusing patterns. On the outside, your mother was the adult, taking care of you—legitimately trying to give you and Andy better childhoods than she had."

Aimee continued to stare at the floor.

"But under the surface your mother was asking, rather desperately, that you take care of her. That you fix the hurt she still carried from her past." Caitlin's voice was gentle. "An impossible task for anyone, let alone a child."

Aimee's eyes didn't move. She hadn't had any contact with her mom since the day she called her from Serenity Pines.

"When you failed, which is what happens when you take on an impossible task, you were told that you were being," Caitlin made air quotes with her fingers, "selfish and hurtful."

Aimee could feel a headache coming on.

"Children do not harm adults." Caitlin's voice was becoming fiery. "Even if she acts out and causes all kinds of problems, a six-year-old does not harm a twenty-five-year-old. And there are no circumstances in which she should be made to believe that she does."

Slowly, Aimee raised her head.

"The dynamics with your mom created wildly impossible patterns for you and Drew. As a child, he looked to you for things he should have gotten from her and that you were not capable of giving him, no matter how much you tried. As an adult, he looked to you to fill the gaps that developed because of that type of childhood." Caitlin didn't continue until Aimee met her eyes. "And you accepted that responsibility and all the shame that came along every time you failed to live up to it."

The throbbing had spread all the way down through Aimee's shoulders. "Yeah, but there were so many things I should have—"

"You were a child too. You weren't equipped to do anything differently than you did." Caitlin leaned forward. "But you're an adult now, and you have choices that you didn't have then. You can choose to continue with the old patterns. Or choose to let them go and allow yourself to have something new."

It was uncanny how often Caitlin quoted things Aimee still remembered from all those books.

"Something new means accepting that the only one who can sort out Drew's life is Drew. And that you," Caitlin pointed a strong finger at Aimee, "cannot fix other people. You wouldn't have moved to New York if you weren't ready to accept that."

Aimee let these words wash over her, feeling them wrestle with all the layers of obligation that had been with her as long as she could remember. She realized her face was wet.

Caitlin handed her a tissue. "Your mother loved you. Your mother hurt you. I know it's hard to reconcile, but both statements are true."

Aimee wiped her eyes.

"If you can find a way for both facts to coexist," Caitlin was looking at Aimee with such compassion, "I think you'll be able to make some peace with it." She paused before continuing with a small smile. "Just because you finally figured out that you weren't the villain doesn't mean your mom has to be."

As the town car made a turn, Aimee's mind drifted to a different day, which felt like it had happened in another lifetime. Drew had been at Serenity Pines for three weeks. Lianna and her team had just concluded their due diligence and were packing up to leave.

Lianna had waved Aimee into the empty boardroom at the bank, then shut the door. "Meredith just quit!" she said, bobbing up and down on her toes.

"Why?" Aimee couldn't imagine how anyone would give up such an amazing job.

"She says she needs more," scowling, Lianna made air quotes, "me time. Whatever the fuck that means."

"I'm glad for you," Aimee said, knowing Lianna would be better off with someone who actually wanted the job.

"Well?" Lianna looked at her expectantly.

Aimee wondered what question she'd missed.

"Will you come to New York and be my new assistant?"

Aimee watched the lights go by and felt her heart surge at

how much she loved Manhattan. She marveled that she had agonized for nearly a week before agreeing to take the job. After Lianna had left working for Benjamin and National Behemoth Bank, Aimee had worked for her successor. A few months later, a position supporting another executive became available, which had been useful because by that time things with Benjamin had changed.

Sitting in the car, she glanced over at him, still scolding whoever was on the phone. His eyes twinkled when they met hers, and he squeezed her hand.

She turned back to the window. How she wished she could go back to her high school self after Ray left. To the terrified young woman driving home from college in the middle of the night. Even to herself two years ago and say: *Don't worry. Believe things can get better, and they will. Believe you can have what you want, and that you're not wrong for wanting it. Hold on and get through the hard parts. Because you're going to be amazed at how wonderful your life will be.*

THE END

ACKNOWLEDGMENTS

When I started writing novels, the writing part was awesome. The getting published part—not so much. I found myself face-to-face with so many barriers that seemed insurmountable. Impossible. Foolish to even try. But time and time again, there was a person (or several) who helped me over, around, sometimes through. It really does take a village. And my village rocks. Many, many thanks to:

- My editor, Arielle Eckstut, an astute writing coach, teacher, and expert in all the ways to bring a book out into the world. If you're a first-time author (or trying to be), buy her book.
- My trailblazing publisher, Brooke Warner—who imagined there was more space for stories in the world than we'd been led to believe, then created a company to make that happen.
- Samantha Strom, my chief behind-the-scenes magician and hand-holder at SparkPress, who made my life easier each step of the way.
- My other wonderful editors: Samuela Eckstut, Starr Waddell and Pam Nordberg, who fixed my commas, spelling and a host of other mishaps but let me keep my sentence fragments—all while providing insightful comments that made the story better. Any imperfections are my choice, not their miss.
- Julie Metz, Lindsey Clerworth, and the SparkPress creative team: designing my cover was such a collaborative and supportive experience and the end result is just—WOW.

- My BookSparks publicist Grace Fell—a lovely partner to help with the super-scary world of PR.
- Maggie Ruff at BookSparks, the master artist who created my fantastic website.
- Krissa Lagos at SparkPress for her wonderfully keen eye.
- Amy S. Peele and Laurie Gelman for being so generous with their time and praise.
- My sister, Robin, who it turns out has a secret identity as both a seasoned editor and resourceful publicist. You are awesome. And my brother, Michael—you are truly an inspiration. There is no one I would have wanted or trusted to be by my side (and have my back) more than the two of you.
- My neighbor, Robin (yes—I have many amazing Robins in my life), who started reading the moment I gave her the manuscript and called me fifteen minutes later to tell me she loved it. You are the sharpest and most generous reader I've worked with and a great friend.
- My sister-in-law, Jessica, a wonderful friend, wildlife care-taker/photographer extraordinaire, and the first person to ask me how on earth I managed to write a novel—that conversation was such a boost for me at a time when I really needed it.
- My mother-in-law, Catherine, who pulled me aside when I announced at a family dinner that I had nothing to show for my writing (because I didn't) and told me I was just at the beginning of this journey.
- My wonderful beta readers—Robin D, Jessica D, Robin R, Robin S, Catherine, Jessica B, Kim D, Kim K, Katie, Avia, Paige, Heidi, Stacey, Habiba, Sonum, and Sophie—every encouraging word was a lifeline, and your suggestions made the story stronger.

- The best poker buddies and friends anyone could hope for—who listened openly when I told them I was writing novels and then instinctively knew not to ask me how it was going for the next four years.
- Matt and Connor—because being with you is so much fun.

AUTHOR BIO

Khristin Wierman was born and raised in a small East Texas town—which means she came into this world a Dallas Cowboys fan and ardently believes "y'all" is a legitimate pronoun. Some things she really likes are playing golf with her husband and stepson, poker, yoga, chocolate, the Golden State Warriors, and the daily adventure of life with an adorably imperfect cat named Rocco. She lives in San Francisco, California.

Learn more at khristinwierman.com

SELECTED TITLES FROM SPARKPRESS

SparkPress is an independent boutique publisher delivering high-quality, entertaining, and engaging content that enhances readers' lives, with a special focus on female-driven work.
www.gosparkpress.com

Goodbye, Lark Lovejoy: A Novel, Kris Clink, $16.95, 978-1-68463-073-8. A spontaneous offer on her house prompts grief-stricken Lark to retreat to her hometown, smack in the middle of the Texas Hill Country Wine Trail—but it will take more than a change of address to heal her broken family.

Sissie Klein in Perfectly Normal: A Novel, Kris Clink, $16.95, 978-1-68463-099-8. Come back to the Texas Hill Country for the second installment in the Enchanted Rock series, where Sissie Klein meets her destiny—on the other side of tragedy.

Absolution: A Novel, Regina Buttner, $16.95, 978-1-68463-061-5. A guilt-ridden young wife and mother struggles to keep a long-ago sexual assault and pregnancy a secret from her ambitious husband whose career aspirations depend upon her silence and unswerving loyalty to him.

Charming Falls Apart: A Novel, Angela Terry, $16.95, 978-1-68463-049-3. After losing her job and fiancé the day before her thirty-fifth birthday, people-pleaser and rule-follower Allison James decides she needs someone to give her some new life rules—*and fast.* But when she embarks on a self-help mission, she realizes that her old life wasn't as perfect as she thought—and that she needs to start writing her own rules.

Child Bride: A Novel, Jennifer Smith Turner, $16.95, 978-1-68463-038-7. The coming-of-age journey of a young girl from the South who joins the African American great migration to the North—and finds her way through challenges and unforeseen obstacles to womanhood.

Firewall: A Novel, Eugenia Lovett West. $16.95, 978-1-68463-010-3. When Emma Streat's rich, socialite godmother is threatened with blackmail, Emma becomes immersed in the dark world of cybercrime—and mounting dangers take her to exclusive places in Europe and contacts with the elite in financial and art collecting circles. Through passion and heartbreak, Emma must fight to save herself and bring a vicious criminal to justice.